LITTLE
DESTINY

LITTLE
DESTINY

Robert Jones

Published by:

 OMNIBOOK Co.

OMNIBOOK CO.
99 Wall Street, Suite 118
New York, NY 10005
USA
+1-866-216-9965
www.omnibookcompany.com

For e-book purchase: Kindle on Amazon, Barnes and Noble
Book purchase: Amazon.com, Barnes & Noble, and
www.omnibookcompany.com

Omnibook titles may be purchased in bulk for educational,
business, fund-raising, or sales promotional use. For more
information please e-mail info@omnibookcompany.com

CONTENTS

Author's Note

"Little Destiny" was a book that had come out of a Tales of the Green high I had. I spent an equivalent of fourteen months writing that series, which, while still not finished, I was immensely proud of myself for completing four books during that time. It was on the fifth book I started to have a block. I think it was my mind saying, "Slow down buddy, pace yourself." I didn't want to stop, but the ideas were being prevented from that great scourge of all writing, that of writers' block. Reluctantly, I took my hands off the keyboard and relaxed.

I decided the next day to watch some Netflix's. I found "Orange is the New Black," a show that had previously alluded to me, so I decided to take a change. As an off note, I would highly recommend this series. As I watched, one character really got my attention, that of Maria Ruiz, played by the beautiful and talented Jessica Pimentel. I enjoyed each time she was on screen. Though her character didn't have a happy ending, the performance was extremely entertaining and heart breaking, and I always rooted for her. What really cemented her as my favorite character was that she was introduced as the one who was pregnant while in jail, and my heart wept for her the day she returned from the hospital. You could see the pain, the want, the need to be with her child. That stuck with me and made me want to even more have her that happy ending, which, as stated before, she never got. I could tell that if she could, she would have hidden in a corner and given birth to her daughter in the prison, and not let anyone take her away from her child. A brief idea of a story came from that, but, as I didn't see a long story from it, I let the matter drop.

A few days went by, and I continued to watch, but the brief idea I had itched at me, and slowly gave way to another evolved form of the original. What would happen if a child was found in a prison? Again, not an overly long story, but then I asked myself, "What if a baby just appeared there for unknown reasons." Now that was interesting. That stuck. It was like Tales of the Green all over again. A new high, a new drug I wanted to taste.

The full idea of "Little Destiny" came in when I read "The Call of Cthulhu" by HP Lovecraft, an author I both dislike but also admire at the same time. The way Cthulhu interacted in the dreams of humans and his indescribable visage gave me the final peace of the puzzle, and "Little Destiny" was born.

As for the creation of Amos, well, he was much simpler. Amos was based on a man I was friends within my youth. You may question why he is Muslim and the hero of the book, and that is your right, but all I can say is, it fitted with the story.

You may think many things. I have a religious agenda, I'm antizionist, I'm prozionist, I'm anti and pro religious. Think what you will. I know how I see the story of Little Destiny, and for me, it is perfect the way it is. I just hope you enjoy it, and criticize it the way you do, with your true feelings, and not just following a trend. Enjoy!

1

SARAH WATCHED THE MONITORS. A woman of thirty, a slim frame, and little in the way of access, those she had even more hidden by the brown correctional uniform she wore, she had the first interesting thing of the night. Almost all the nights were the same at Grisham Correctional. Watching the female inmates sleep, go to the bathroom, read by a flashlight, or on rare occasions, try and sneak into bunks of their lovers. It was always the same, nothing ever changed here, the same patterns, the same darkness that felt like it was closing in until the sunrise. Tonight, however, there was a change.

Located on the outskirts of Belaphone, in Leon County, the prison was home to over two hundred female inmates. Low security, the inmates were allowed to move freely, and security was minimal, but still vigilant. They had a few problems with tobacco and homemade booze getting in, but that was all. However, tonight, in many ways, was different.

The monitors, which Sarah stared at for hours on end, showed the five dorms that housed the general population. A dorm was primarily black and the fullest. B dorm, Latina, and the second fullest. C Dorm was white, and the least full. D and E dorms held the elderly, transvestites, and the Asians. The last three were the least trouble. They

3

also showed the kitchen, the bathrooms, the Chapel, the lower levels, dining hall, the library, the rec center, and the PX.

It was the Chapel camera that was acting up and that caught Sarah's attention. Lines of static kept coming across it. She tried everything from refocusing to hitting the screen. Nothing.

"What the fuck?" she muttered under her breath. Behind her, Jeff Holden, a man of forty-five, three hundred pounds, and receding hairline, looked up from a mix of paperwork and nodding off.

"What?" he asked in a tired, croaky voice.

"Camera eight is all wacky," said Sarah.

"The Chapel? Fuck it. Nobody should be there anyways. Just leave a maintenance report."

"It could be an easy fix," argued Sarah, annoyed by Jeff's disinterest. Unless there was a fight, Jeff rarely got up from his chair, and there was never a fight at night. Sometimes, Sarah swore Jeff even went to the bathroom in that chair, never once seeing him move from it until his shift was over.

"So," he said, "If you're so gung-ho about it, go."

Sarah stood, annoyed as ever and said, "Fuck you."

She left before Jeff could not say anything and walked down the hall. She swore Jeff existed only to remind her that the world was still one of man, and man, she swore, was the laziest of the genders, and yet made more money than she ever did.

Taking her flashlight out, Sarah walked down the dark halls, taking two lefts, and then a right, leading to the Chapel.

Fishing out the keys, she unlocked the door. It was a large, the Chapel, designed like a school auditorium. There were ten rows of forty chairs and a large stage at the front with a small stand on it. Cheap as hell, and this is where the inmate went to worship and ask forgives, weather from Jesus, Allah, or a Wiccan spirit. Fuck this was depressing. No wonder that blonde girl off herself a few years ago. It was just all so depressing and fake.

Sarah scanned the walls with her light, looking for the camera until she heard a cooing sound. At first, Sarah thought she was hearing things until it happened again.

Pulling out a bottle of mace, Sarah walked slowly forward through the isle. Nobody should be here, not at midnight. If they were, their eyes were about to get peppered. She wished she still had a taser, but the guards had them taken away after one of the inmates took one in a rare escape attempt. Unfortunately, it was during the day shift, so Sarah didn't get to see it. Still, something was going to happen tonight. She could feel it in her bones, something was going to change this boring prison in this boring town in this boring county.

Then the wailing started. It was loud, like….like a baby's cry. Sarah couldn't believe her ears. Only three girls were pregnant here in Grisham Correctional, and none were due.

Sarah kept creeping forward, until a second wail confirmed what she suspected. She moved forward, towards the stand that served as a pulpit. Bending slightly to keep a low profile, she got to the other side, and she saw what was making the sound. It was a baby. The baby was on the stage, behind the stand. Her jaw dropped when she saw it, unable to believe what was before her eyes, and yet clear as God's green earth this bawling child on the floor.

It was a small infant, wrapped in a pink blanket, wearing a pink hat. It was wailing now, as its small infant hands went up and defended itself against the light of the flashlight.

"Oh my God," said Sarah, a primordial instinct to defend surging up. Falling to her knees, dropping the mace and light, she reached out, and picked up the child, cradling it, making soft sounds, and saying, "It's ok, I got you. Where did you come from, little one?"

After a minute of care, the baby, a little girl, as soon to be found out, snuggled and calmed itself against Sarah's breast, looking up with her big eyes at the guard holding her.

She got on the radio and said, "Jeff, get down here. We have a baby."

For a moment, nothing, then, "Say again, Sarah."

"A fucking baby is in the Chapel!"

For a long time, there was nothing, then, "Fuck, ok, is this a joke?"

"No God damn it," yelled Sarah, the baby wailing again, adding to the evidence, "Get your fat ass down here and help me figure shit out."

Jeff was quiet for a long time, and Sarah could just imagine Jeff's doughnut covered brain in his skull firing off the long-neglected neurons up there, long surrendering to the fact that his owner was no longer capable of deep thought suddenly coming back to life. Then he said, "I'll call the Warden, then head down there. Give me ten minutes."

Sarah lifted herself up and said into the mic, "Who is the nurse on call tonight?"

"Kim," said Jeff.

"Right, meet me on the way to the clinic."

"No," snapped Jeff, "Stay there. Trust me ok?"

"Jeff we got a baby....."

"And we have a prison full of lonely, sad, and dangerous women between you and that clinic. Hang on, just ten minutes, ok?"

"Ok."

Nine and a half minutes later, Jeff came in the doors, another guard, this one a younger, bald, black man named Terry, with him.

"Escort," huffed Jeff, not used to the physical exercise that he had just put on himself, "to protect the baby. All other guards are on high alert. Kim has been alerted."

Sarah was impressed, maybe Jeff wasn't such a useless tub of lard after all.

They took off down the hall, Terry taking front, Jeff, his rolls of fat bouncing around, right behind him and Sarah. They were armed with baton's right now, not wanting to risk mase with the child with them, knowing it could harm her greatly. Susan kept the baby quiet as they walked past the dorms. They didn't have to worry too much. These women were mostly all asleep and knew they couldn't leave the dorm until morning unless they needed to use the facilities.

They got to the clinic, where a nurse was sitting in a corner, vaping, and reading a magazine. She was a tall, oriental woman. Jet black hair, a pretty face, and a body they would make even Jessica Alba or Scarlett Jo Hanson jealous, the woman stood, and, seeing the baby, gasped, a tail of vapor leaving her mouth.

"Who gave birth?" asked Kim.

"Nobody," said Sarah, handing her the baby.

Kim flicked a look of confusion to the guard, but, being a caretaker, took the child in her arms, talking the child gently, and saying, "Hi," in that way everyone does upon meeting a newborn. Taking her to an examination table, Kim removed the child's diaper, and checked her temperature, weighted her, and measured her, all the while, crooning, and keeping the child calm, the baby only doing the occasional kick or fist reach, her eyes wandering around the many strange things in her new surroundings.

"Female," said Kim, "I think she is at least seven days old."

"Seven days?" asked Jeff, who just walked in after calling the warden again and the state's doctor. The doctor, as he said, was a half-hour out, but the warden, who lived fifteen minutes away, but had a habit of speeding, would be there far sooner. "You sure?"

"Positive."

"We only have three women pregnant here in Grisham's Correctional," verified Sarah, "One that's due for early release, one that's not due for six months, and a third, high risk up in Marquette General. None have given birth."

"We checked," confirmed Terry, "None have."

Kim shrugged, "Well, I can say one fact about this kid. She may have been abandoned, but she wasn't neglected. Someone was taking care of this kid. This blanket, you find them in hospitals, or places like that. And she is clean, not hungry, hydrated. She is healthy."

"Kidnapped?" asked Sarah, fear clenching her stomach.

"So what?" asked Jeff, "An inmate sneaks out, goes to a hospital over a hundred miles away, grabs a newborn, keeps her for seven days, then gets bored and leaves her in the Chapel?"

"That is pretty unlikely," admitted Sarah.

The radio squawked.

"This is Terry, go ahead."

"Warden's hear."

"Shit," said Jeff.

"One my way," said Terry, walking off, Sarah and Jeff staying behind. "Time to get our asses raped," said Jeff.

Sarah shrugged, happy that she had far less ass as to chew on then Jeff did.

2

Amos Diouf heard the alarm go off in his room at four am, and he opened his eyes. He made himself a promise to try and make all the prayers demanded by Allah, praise be upon him. It wasn't easy for him. Back in the day, Amos' father, an immigrant from Senegal, had made him pray every day since the day he was able to understand what prayer was. Now he lived alone, far away from other Muslims, the demands of his faith felt taxing, and he swore they got worse every day until he made his monthly trip to the Mosque he attended in Milwaukee.

It wasn't easy being a Muslim in a small town full of Christians and Atheists. Worse, it was hard to be a black Muslim. There were no Mosques in Belaphone, Michigan, only two churches. The closest was a six-hour drive to Wisconsin. There he and his father, who lived over there full time found an Imam, understanding of his troubles, and the difficulties he had traveling around, willing to skype with him when he had issues of faith. Once a month, or mostly, he even managed to drive down to Milwaukee for services at the mosque, and often felt renewed by the words of the prophet, most of the time, not all, but most of the time.

However, the alarm wrapping inside of his head was not welcomed, and he felt like switching off his cellphone. Instead, he got his ass out of bed, and shook his head, clearing it, stood, then stopped the beeping of his cellphone. He did his prayers, facing Mecca, and then went to the bathroom.

After a nice shower, shaving his upper lip but leaving his greying beard untouched, unwrapping his du-rag, he headed to his kitchen, where he began to cook. His mother used to prepare dishes from the homeland, however, for breakfast, Amos got a taste for American food. He had eggs, potatoes, and toasted corn muffin, and melted butter on it. He also made coffee. God, he loved coffee. That sweet pick-me-up gave him the strength to get through the day. His father never approved of him cooking but living alone for the past fourteen years had forced Amos to adapt and he now loved the craft.

Amos thought about his dad and smiled, his father, Abdual was a strong man in his life, and the two were still close. Closer now ever since Amos's mother died. A memory that involved her invaded Amos' thoughts as he worked. Amos had once asked his father why Abdual named him Amos and not a more traditional Senegalese name. Abdual responded with, "New country, new traditions. And I thought it sounded cool. Was going to name you Logan, but your mother put her foot down."

Amos chuckled at the memory as he finished cooking, imaging his mother threatening his father if he ever named Amos Logan. Amos always suspected it was because his dad loved the Xmen movies, but he never had confirmation.

Walking outside after he laid his food out, he grabbed his morning paper, went back to his table, and sat to eat. It was Wednesday, the second to last day of work for him this week, and he was looking forward to the weekend, as he was going to go see his dad. Working for Child Welfare was hard, and often got under his skin, but it did help a lot of kids, even those who didn't want to admit it. He had seen his share of horror stories, but also miracles happened here at Belaphone House. Kids there find a home more than they did in Detroit.

Amos grew up in Detroit. Being young and dumb, as his father would call it, he thought he had the world on his shoulders. It was at the age of sixteen when his world would change. That was when he started wearing his pair cap after school. The kids thought it was awesome. Then the towers fell. When the reality, not the world he had accepted, changed in waves, and it hit Amos hard as hell. His hat was seen as an item worn by the enemy, not as a cool thing that once helped Amos stand out. It isolated him up until and passed when he graduated and found a job. There, he found a calling with social services, but the sigma never left him in Detroit, and eventually, he escaped to Belaphone, and was able to hide half of himself to help the children that needed him. He sometimes hated it was his Muslim half and not his black half, but he continued his work and made a future for himself in his work.

As his reflections came to an end, his phone started vibrating, while he was cleaning the dishes. Looking down at it on the counter, and quickly drying his hands, Amos answered the phone in his deep tones, not knowing this was the start of a long chain of events that would shape the rest of his life.

"Hello, Cathy."

Cathy was his boss, and if she was calling before Amos had to get to work, something was up.

"Amos," she said in a clip and authoritative tones, "I need you to go out to Grisham Correctional."

Amos almost grinned. He had three moms there he was working with to arrange proper placement with their families. Two had grandparents and one had a decent father figure, who was nervous as all hell at raising a kid on his own for a while. Amos assured his father that he will be fine and that his partner would soon be free and help him. Slightly odd though, none were due anytime soon. Maybe a premature birth?

"Who gave birth?"

"Nobody, the baby was just found there at the prison."

Amos felt confused, "Uh, say that again. I don't think I heard that right."

"Yes, baby girl, seven days old."

"Well, I guess the fire department was closed."

"You don't understand," said Cathy, "She was inside the prison, alone."

Now Amos had a curious lump in his stomach.

"Someone left a baby inside the prison? Where did they find her?"

"In the Chapel."

This was a new one. He had two abandoned baby cases under his belt. One was a kid left at the fire department out in Hardhome, the county seat of Leon County, and the other was a baby left on the Boston Road. But inside a woman's prison, that was a new one.

"Where is the child now?"

"Police have her at the station. Katerina is going to pick her up and bring her to Belaphone home. I need you to go to Grisham. Get the information and paperwork from the Warden and see if you can schedule some interviews with the women in there. Small chance that one could be our mystery mom."

Amos nodded, though Cathy couldn't see.

"On my way."

Hanging up, and quickly changing to a nice button-up shirt, dark pants, belt, and dark loafers, Amos got into his Ford pickup and drove to Grisham Correctional.

And half an hour later, he was in front of the old, decaying building housing hundreds of female prisoners. The low-slung building of brown brick and glass surrounded by a high fence with barbed wiring. It had once been a private school, but the land and building were purchased by the state, and later the Feds, who converted it into a female prison. The place reminded him of something he read in the Qur'an, though he couldn't remember what it was, some city of darkness mentioned in the book. The place felt too, well, feeble for the task of rehabilitation. The state and the Feds was more than willing to lock up criminals but keeping the building up to code was not a priority. Make America great. For too many, it was getting rid of the Mexicans, the Gays, the Arabs, and the Blacks. How about starting with infrastructure and repairs to homes and buildings instead? But it was a Federal prison, and it was sadly one of the biggest employers here in Belaphone and Leon County. Hell, it employed sixty of the six hundred people who lived here, along with people from Hardhome and Fair Creek, and the other villages, towns, and townships that made up Leon County.

Amos got to the gate, and, after a brief time holding up his ID to the camera, and speaking into a mic, was let in. Two cars from the sheriff's office were in front, as well as the car of the county prosecutor, Dewite Mitchel. Getting out of his car, Amos was met by an old, bald correction officer, Charlie was his name, and was escorted inside after consulting a visitation list. Amos went through a second gate, then went through a pair of doors, led by the correctional officer with a key card.

At a metal detector in an entrance hall, two more corrections officers ordered Amos to remove all metal and anything from Amos' pockets, took off his belt, and removed his jacket. He did, and Amos walked through the metal detector, without setting it off. Returning his items, and putting them back in their proper place, he went to a sign-in desk, had his license taken for the duration of his stay, and walked through the door, leading to the main prison complex.

On that side, a big man, thick armed, chest, and legged, wearing a fake Italian suit walked up to Amos, and held out his hand and they shook.

"Warden Sisko," said Amos, giving him a small smile.

"Hey Amos," said the Warden, "Let's walk."

They headed down the hall, two beefy officers behind them.

"What can you tell me about the girl?" asked Amos

"As of all we know, someone hid her behind the podium in the Chapel," said Sisko, "How it happened and who left her is another mystery."

"And none of the women gave birth?" Amos tried to confirm.

"No," confirmed Sisko, "At least, that is the story we are getting. We have over two hundred female inmates here, Mr. Diouf, and before as well as during their stay with us we do routine pregnancy tests. Almost three-fourths of my staff is male, and often, the only males these women see. It's to ensure the inmate's health as well as the safety and honesty of my men and women here."

Amos nodded.

"What about the video?"

"Nothing," said the Warden, "Oh it gets grainy for a while, bad enough where you can't see what's happening, but only for about thirty seconds. When it happened, one of my officers, Sarah Zimmer, went to go check the camera where the baby was found. While grainy, you can clearly see her enter the chapel, investigate a noise, and find a baby behind the podium."

"When was this?" asked Amos.

"A little after three am."

"And before that?"

"Nothing. The Chapel is locked after six pm. Some of the inmates like to sneak in there for some hanky panky with each other. But even when open, few go in there, save for Sunday, and none are giving birth, or in there long enough to give birth during the day."

Amos thought through everything. This was an interesting mystery. That's when two more people came around the corner. One was a man in a pinstripe suit, grey slacks, and Jew fro. The other was a tough looking man with dark hair, sharp features and wearing a deputy uniform. They were Dewite Michael and Sheriff Deshain for Leon county, two of the biggest politicians in the county. Dewite was the county prosecutor, having sent several of the women in Grisham's Correctional there himself, and Deshain, who gave an air of being for the people, was really a slimy snake. They were both stationed in Hardhome, the county seat, and Amos figured they were working on ways to look like the big heroes in this political nightmare.

"No reporters," Dewite was snapping off as he and the sheriff walked, "Not until we get more info. Put some pressure on the Mayor to ensure this. Who you got investigating?"

"Deputy Butler," said Deshain, "He is my best investigator."

"Will he stay away from the press?"

"He doesn't like the press...."

14

Dewite then noticed Sisko and Amos, stopped and said, "Amos, what are you doing here?"

"Getting info for the baby that was found."

Deshain rolled his eyes, "Don't know why we waste money on that place."

"Helps the kids to have a shelter for a while when you lock up their mothers."

Deshain glared. Dewite shrugged, "They do the crime, they do the time, and their family suffers."

Amos rolled his eyes. Dewite looked at Sisko and said, "I don't want this story on Facebook or any social media, you hear me? Period."

"I know," said Sisko, "Wasn't planning on it."

"Leon county doesn't need the press, and we still need the federal dollars from Belaphone, so let's not screw this up."

"I informed the Feds down in Lansing."

"You did what?" snapped Deshain, "Without my say so?"

"I had to," snapped Sisko, "All prison related incidents have to be sent to the federal level."

"God damn it."

"They won't let it leak, but it's done."

"Fine," sighed Dewite, "Come on Sheriff, let's get back to Hardhome."

They left. Amos muttered under his breath, "Bastards." He continued down the hall with Sisko, imaging his mother slapping his hand and saying in her thick, Senegalese accent, 'Don't you ever swear again, Amos.' He shook and had a small smile with that image. He missed his mom, now dead for ten years.

"Well, I'll still need to test the inmates," said Amos, getting back on topic, "We've got to know who is mother."

"The cops are on that," said the Warden, "They were here all last night. Both local and county, taking DNA swabs from everyone."

"Very good," said Amos, "Well, I'm going to need the medical reports at least, and when it's over, a copy of those DNA reports."

"That be Nurse Kim," said the Warden, "I'll call for her. As for the DNA, it depends on how long it will take the lab in Marquette."

They entered the warden's office. It was handsome. The walls were the white-painted concrete of the rest of the facility, but placards, pictures, an oaken desk, and leather chairs gave the room some charm that the rest of the facility lacked.

On the desk, the Warden picked up the phone, pressed a button, and said, "Nurse Kim, can you bring up the records for the child. That be all."

After a brief affirmative exchange, the Warden hung up, and then pressed another button, and said, "Graven, bring some coffee and pastries for our guest please."

Again, an affirmative exchange, and hang up, and the Warden and Amos sat down across from each other. As they waited, Amos asked, "Any suspicions that this might be a kidnapping?"

"That is the million-dollar question," said the Warden, "The Feds and the county are breathing down my necks right now, trying to figure out if the kid was brought in by one of the inmates. But I don't see how it could have been done. This is a minimum-security prison, and most of the inmates are nonviolent offenders. Mostly thievery, drugs, that sort of thing. Some of the older inmates have harder records, but they have spent years trying to get into facilities like this one and don't want to fuck it up, but I don't see how any of them could have gotten out and got a baby in here. My men checked around the perimeter, and there are no holes in or around the fence that would explain this. It isn't electrified, so someone could theoretically climb over it, but it's barbed up top, so they be more cut up than a pig at a butcher shop, and none of the inmates have any sort of wounds that configure with that line of thinking. As for getting the child in the middle of the night, that would be impossible. The front and rear exits are locked tight at night, and ten guards monitor all the dorms, plus the alarm system would wake the dead. Also, with the prison only having one exit and entrance to get you off the prison's grounds,

I just don't see how anyone could have gotten her in here without being caught."

"Does Marquette Hospital report any missing children, or Aspirus in Keweenaw, or any of the other hospitals in the UP?"

"No," the Warden sighed, leaning back in his chair. There was a knock at the door and a young guard brought in a tray of two mugs of hot coffee, a metal pot, some powder creamer, Splenda, and a half dozen doughnuts. He put the tray on the desk and walked out.

"The perks of the system," said the Warden with a smile, "You can get anything here, as long as it is cheap and powdered. But to answer your earlier question, no, no reports yet. It's possible she came from a different town or county, even the LP or Wisconsin, but I don't see that panning out."

Amos took a drink of the weak coffee in the chip mug, added the Splenda, and powder cream. It didn't improve the flavor much.

A minute later, there was another knock at the door and Nurse Kim walked in saying, "This was just finished and approved by Doctor Wats."

"Thank you, Nurse Kim," said the Warden, "and thanks for staying late. Go and get some sleep."

She left, and Warden handed Amos a copy of the file. It was basic, as blood tests, DNA tests, and other such tests would take time, so this was only preliminary. This was only a copy, and another file had been transferred to a Doctor McMath up in Marquette, where also the blood test would be sent.

"Any idea when the child can be sent to foster care?" inquired the Warden.

"Don't know," said Amos, "In these cases, we try to find blood relatives first. Belaphone isn't a big town, but Leon County has almost twenty thousand people, not to mention the over three hundred thousand people in the UP, so we have our work cut out. If none can be found then we transfer her up to Marquette in a few days, and they try to get her into a good home. If that doesn't work, they will have to put her into a long-term facility. Luckily, most of the time, infants get pick up quickly."

"Not always," said the Warden, sipping at his coffee.

"True," said Amos.

Amos took a doughnut and bit into it. Way better than the coffee.

"I like to talk to some of the inmates, just in case. This girl is white I see, so how many Caucasian women are housed here?"

"Thirty," said Sisko, "They are one of our smaller populations. This includes elderly whites, so that narrows our pool to about seventeen. Only one came here pregnant, and she is now staying at Marquette General until she is due."

"I spoke to her yesterday," nodded Amos, "So, how many women are you looking at."

"Ten, but as I said, none of them will pan out I bet. However, I will set up interview times for you for tomorrow afternoon, if that's ok?"

"Sounds good."

"You also might want to look into the Latina population we got here as well."

"Good thinking. How many?"

"We got about sixty here. It's our second largest population."

"Thanks."

They finished their coffee and doughnuts.

"Alright," said Amos, once he finished, "Think I got all I need here. I'll be back tomorrow."

A thought occurred to him and he said, "Do you have a copy of the video?"

The Warden pulled out his phone and, after playing with the screen for a moment, brought up last night's video. He forwards it to three am, and Amos observed it until he reached the static portion. It only lasted half a minute before returning to normal.

Amos shrugged and said, "Nothing you can't handle, I'm sure. Have a good day Warden."

The Warden stood as Amos did, and the two shook hands. Amos was escorted out, back to his car, and drove out of the prison.

Once outside its boundaries, he pulled over, then he picked up the file and looked at it again. The report stated no abnormalities were seen, and size and weight were consistent with a healthy newborn baby just a few days old. Still, how she got into the prison was still a mystery, but in the end, it wasn't his problem. Right now, his problem was to make sure that there were no blood relatives nearby, and make sure the child was alright.

3

AMOS DROVE BACK INTO TOWN about an hour later after his interview with Sisko, his tires crunching on the old snow, now laying like a carpet across the Upper Peninsula. At a stoplight he rubbed his head, looked back down at the file, and said a silent prayer to Allah that the child would be well protected. It was a prayer he always gave, hoping that the child would be safe and that parents or family would be found to watch over the baby.

Stopping at the second of the two only red lights in town, he opened the file again, looking at it, he saw the picture of the child in the back. Cute girl. Round face, wide eyes. She is nothing more or less than adorable. Amos looked up and saw the light had turned green and was going to head straight to Belaphone home when he changed his mind. Turning left, he headed down Reman Avenue, the main road of Belaphone, and after a series of turns, made it to Lake Street. He stopped in front of Belaphone's police department in the small town square, seeing some Christmas decorations on some of the buildings but not many, the town no longer have the budget for the extravaganza of Christmas decoration they once could afford, and got out of his car, heading to the station's entrance. He passed an old woman, who gave him a strange look but just walked past without a word. But Amos knew the reason for the look.

Belaphone was the third largest town in Leon County, after Hardhome and Fair Creek, but it was a small and mainly white redneck town. It used to be a small resort town, being close to a large inland lake, but overfishing had caused a lot of tourism to dry up in the 80's and 90's. Hunting was the main revenue now, but the town was in much disrepair and the population of once seventeen hundred had dropped to about six hundred. The only thing keeping the town going was the prison, a few hunting grounds, and the Federal Dollars sent to Belaphone home, that serviced abandoned kids across Leon, Ontonagon, Gogebic, and Iron Counties. Amos grew up in Detroit, so wasn't around during the decline and many of the hardline whites blamed the few black families many times for the dwindling economy across Belaphone, making several moves away and causing more depression in the town. He never felt welcomed here outside his few friends and felt the unwanted dislike that came from many of the older folks. He felt that when he first moved here, and three white boys stared at him with unfriendly faces during his first hour in town, giving him a shiver. Who ever said racism was dead was a damn fool.

Amos did sometimes wonder why he didn't stay in Wisconsin with his father. He liked the upper peninsula and Leon County, but this town, it felt rotten, dying from the inside out. Something had to give, and he wasn't liking what it was giving into. Hatred, lack of hope, desperation, just to name a few things.

Clearing his head of negative thoughts, he opened the door and went inside the police station.

Sheldon Butler was not the typical sheriff deputy you find in Michigan. For example, he was not from Michigan, but a native-born of Texas, with a cowboy hat and all, about five foot six inches. For another, before police work, Butler used to work the rodeo circuit, riding bulls that would kick and buck, trying to shake him off. He worked it from years sixteen to twenty, until a big bad bull slung him off, and trampled him, causing internal hemorrhage from his liver and long surgery. After that, his wife then married for only six months, but very pregnant, begged him not to go back on the circuit.

After working on a ranch for about two years, Butler managed to finish night courses down in Central Texas College and graduated at the police academy in El Paso, working there for almost three years, until finding a job in Leon County Sheriff Department stationed out of Hardhome. He was at first reluctant to go North, but the pay was too good to pass up, Leon county having a well-maintained budget that allowed them to pay their price. He flew there for a weekend, and right after the interview, was offered a job. He and his family moved up a month later.

At first feeling like an outsider, his southern charms soon grew on the people and he became popular in the county. He tipped good at dinner and the bar, always helped where he could, and interacted greatly with the community. After ten years of service, Butler, with the backing of the former sheriff, and the other elected officials of the county, and the mayor of Hardhome himself, ran for the office of the Sheriff department against Deshain. He lost by one vote to Wayne Deshain, but he had a feeling for the next election year. He and his wife were campaigning across the county, and he liked his chances. For right now though, he was second in command and had driven out here to work the case out here in Belaphone.

Amos met Butler at the most unlikely of circumstances. At the Belaphone Police department. A little girl was found in a car accident, her mother was crushed after the brutal crash on the road that Butler was patrolling at the time. He managed to save the girl who, by some miracle, was unharmed. Bringing the girl to the department, Butler calls Belaphone Home, hoping they have a room. After giving the child's information, Butler waited almost two hours, and, when seeing the familiar van of Belaphone Home pulling up, was about to rip the driver a new one for being late when he saw not one, but two men get out. One was a professor at Michigan Tech, and the other, a large, bearded muscled black man. The two entered, and the Black man named Amos Diouf, explained to the Deputy that this was the child's father. The girl's cries of relief proved that.

Butler was very impressed by the man finding the father before his own investigators, and it started a friendship between the two. In fact, Butler was one of the few people Amos told that he was Muslim, and Amos was one of the few personal friends to know that Butler's daughter had been born Autistic. So, when the front called to the back office, saying that Mr. Diouf was asking for him, Butler said, "Well, send him back, ma'am, that be all."

Butler didn't usually work out of Belaphone, but he was called in by the County Sheriff, and the local chief of police after the call came in about the girl being found at Grisham's Correctional. Butler was the best investigator on Leon County Sheriff Department staff, and Belaphone had no acting detectives. He was borrowing a small office in the back to help him facilitate the County's recourse in Belaphone during the investigation.

Amos came in, and Butler stood, offering a hand, "Hey buddy, how is it hanging?"

Amos smiled and took the hand, replying, "Going good."

After Amos took a seat, Butler went around the table, and went to a small coffee table in the corner, where a coffee maker was, the kind with fountain drink tabs at the bottom. Taking two freshly clean mugs, he pressed the tab, and poured a mixture that looked like coffee with a lot of creams but wasn't. The smell of familiar spices wafted out, reminding Amos of home back in his family's Detroit apartment, when his mom made the same thing. It wasn't a Senegalese drink, but it was on his mother's liking, getting the recipe from a Pakistani neighbor, and it became a staple of the Diouf household, and Amos' second favorite drink after coffee.

"Chai?" asked Amos, with a grin, "When did you learn to like that?" He remembered introducing it to Butler when they met for coffee but got the impression that he didn't like it.

"Does wonders for my colon," said Butler, placing the mugs and sugar in the middle of his desk where there were no files, and took a swig, "This job can get to you sometimes, and I don't go to the bathroom as much with this stuff as I do with coffee."

Amos chuckled, and the two talked about sports, their families, and when the usual was out of the way, Amos finally came to the child.

"So, you working the baby case?"

"Yep, me, the locals, and the Feds will soon be sniffing around as well. They have an agent coming up from the Lower Peninsula in a few days, going to be investigating the prison, but Leon County isn't on the top of their list right now, so it's all on my shoulders right now. But I'll tell you, over thirteen years of police work, ain't never seen a case like this. Not in El Paso, and never thought I would see something like this here in Belaphone. I can't figure out how someone got a baby in there without anyone noticing. I checked the tapes again and again, but there ain't nothin' that can explain it."

"Maybe someone tricks the system."

"Oh, so a prisoner managed to disable the alarms, come outside, sneak a baby out of a hospital, climbing over barb wire, not getting a scratch, and managing to get back, undetected, and get into the Chapel undetected, and leaving a crying infant there?"

Amos had to admit, saying it out loud it was kind of a pathetic excuse, as even minimum-security prisons were not the easiest to escape from, as Sisko said. And getting back in, well, that wasn't easy either.

Butler sipped his chia and said, "Any plans with the girl?"

"Just make sure she is safe until we can transfer her to Marquette or find relatives."

"Try and do it before Thursday. The snow is coming in and it's going to be a bitch to drive through."

"Maybe for you."

"Hey," laughed Butler, "I'm a Texan, what's your excuse for bad driving?"

"My father," said Amos with a grin.

"Racist."

"Ain't racist when it's your own race. Besides, with the holiday coming up, there are bound to be delays. By the way, what are you doing for Christmas?"

"Working," Butler shrugged, "Deshain wants me in this case until further notice, you?"

"Just watched the A Muppet Christmas Carol."

"You allowed to do that? And isn't that a little childish for you?"

"I like movies, just don't celebrate Christmas. Anyways, if you're not busy, stop by if you can't make it home."

"I'll try. Thanks, man."

Cup empty, Amos stood and shook Butler's hand.

"See you next time you're in this part of town," said Amos with a smile.

"You're too. Don't be a stranger, I'll be here for a while."

Amos left, still with many questions, and no answers forthcoming.

4

AMOS ARRIVED AT THE HOME soon after he met with Butler. It was sequestered in what was once a high-end subdivision, the house paid for by both the federal government and the _____ County. It was opened about five years ago, and served Leon, Iron, Ontonagon, and a few other Counties in the western U.P., to help abandoned, neglected, or children just in bad situations. It was nowhere as bad as the facility that Amos worked at back in Detroit, but it still had a surprising amount of business. It was a bright spot in this small town, a small bit of sanctuary holding on to a thin line of hope.

The Home had three main tasks. One, sheltered abandoned children until they could be transferred up to Marquette or the Lower Peninsula. Two, try and keep families together and try and get children to fellow family members when the primary caregivers are unable to provide. And finally, the facility also helped set up adoption options when the primary caregiver does not wish or is unable to raise the child themselves.

Amos walked up the driveway. As it was a house, it felt just like a regular home in the suburbs and was designed to give any child resident there a feeling of normality. Currently, it housed two teenage girls that had been picked up from an abusive home situation, thirteen and fifteen respectively, a five-year-old boy who was being picked up by foster parents in a few days, his mother serving time in Grisham's and the father having died in a car accident years ago, and two infants, one with down syndrome, being transferred to a family in Marquette in a day or so, and the girl from the prison.

Amos saw the boy, an oriental kid of five, extremely busy drawing squares to play hopscotch, and he waved to Amos with a grin, his front tooth had fallen out yesterday. Amos, before going home yesterday, left a five under his pillow. He was a good kid and just was in a crappy situation, as most were who came here. Amos wished sometimes the States would stop letting just anyone have kids and only those who had the smarts to know not to knock around kids could, but he also knew many of these kids had come from loving home, just had bad luck that needed to be sorted. This kid's mom, for example, had been arrested for stealing some money from an open cash register to help feed her son. Just a shitty situation. She had a reduced sentence and would get the kid back in time, but it was still a bad situation to be in.

Walking inside, the place was simple but comfortable. The entrance hall leads to a large sitting room with a big screen tv in one corner, where the two teen girls sat in front of the screen on a large, comfortable couch, flanked by two armchairs.

"Hey Amos," said the younger girl, curly blonde hair in a ponytail.

"Hello girls," said Amos, giving them a kind smile, "Did Veronica and Arche get back together yet?"

"No," said the older one, "But I give it three more episodes."

Amos smiled, and walked into the kitchen when he saw Katrina. Katrina was a mix of black and Native American, her tawny skin and black hair cut above the shoulders, slightly curly. She wore glasses, and they covered over dark brown eyes. She was short but had some nice curves. She was also one of Amos' best friends, and one of the few that knew he was Muslim, like Butler. She found out when she walked in on him praying in the basement and accepted him despite it. She was a lovely person, and for some reason, Amos always felt a strange twinge in his belly when he saw her.

"Hey Amos," said Katrina, smiling warmly, as she signed bills and papers.

"Hey Kat," said Amos, "Where is our new visitor?"

"Little Jane Doe?" asked Katrina, with a small smile "I put her in Natalie's room, you know the down syndrome baby. She's asleep. I was going to make her a bottle but got caught up with bills."

"I'll do it," said Amos, walking over to the fridge and finding a premade bottle. Pulling it out, he put it in the microwave and, once it started, turned back to Katrina.

"So, any idea where she came from?" asked Katrina.

"Nah," said Amos, "None of our expecting mothers in Grisham gave birth last night. Have no doubt Cathy is going to want us to interview them so I sent it up for tomorrow afternoon, and also got copies of the videos last night, but I can't see how they could have given birth and got the kid in the Chapel without getting caught."

"The cops got any ideas?"

"No," answered Amos as the timer went off, and Amos reached in, grabbed the bottle, and shook a little on his arm. It was too hot, so he put it to the side to let it cool, "Butler taking the case for now, so we might get something soon. By the way, here is the medical report. It's only plenary but the more detailed one will come in a few days."

He handed her the file and joined her at the table. "Where is Cathy?"

"At the Mayor's home."

"You're kidding."

"No, he pissed. If this gets out, you know CNN is going to make a show out of this. This would be big news, a kid found in a prison Chapel, and he wants to keep it under wraps, like the rest of the county the way she says it, but you know it's going to get out. I can see the headlines. Baby found in prison a few days before Christmas."

Amos nodded, he knew, "Guess he is scared it will drive away from the few tourists we get around here. It was the same sentiment I got from the sheriff and the prosecutor over at Grisham's. Marquette going to pick her up tomorrow?"

"No," sighed Katrina, "They want us to keep her for now. Newborns are always the rave with foster parents, but they want us to get the full medical before picking her up."

"If she gets sick here, we get the wrap, eh? Or just don't want to be bothered before the holidays."

"Pretty much both. But they are picking up Natallie this afternoon, or so they say."

Amos got up and checked the bottle again. It was good.

"Ok, going to check on our house guess."

"Ok, but be mindful of Natallie."

"I will."

Amos headed upstairs, and went to the far bedroom, and opened the door. Two cribs were in the room. Natallie was fast asleep, while the baby girl was cooing softly, having just woken up. Amos walked over and said, "Hey baby girl."

Looking into Amos' dark face, the little girl smiled and toothless smile.

"Ah, you like me, eh?" asked Amos with a smile, scooping up the grinning girl in one arm, and walking out of the room and into Cathy's bedroom. Cathy rarely allowed anyone in there, for it was her sanctuary, but she allowed her employees to use it if the baby room had a sleeping infant and it was best not to wake the child.

In his arms, the girl looked up, and her arms bounced up and down twice, seeing the bottle.

"Ain't mama's milk," said Amos, apologetically, "But, it will do. All organic and stuff, you know?"

The nipple in her mouth, the child relaxed, drinking quietly.

"You need a name," said Amos. "How about, Amanda…nah, too common, besides, it's only a placeholder until we find out who you are."

He looked into the infant's wide blue eyes, and then smiled around the nipple, showing she was already talented for an infant. Then it struck Amos, "You know, I think I'll call you, Masira. Masir is the word for destiny in Arabic…..yes it is….oh yes it is. I think we were destined to meet....do think, eh...eh....choochecoo. Cathy will likely give you something common, but, Masira, yeah, I'll call you that. That will be your secret name. Just between us, eh?"

The newly christened Masira finished the bottle and Amos burped her. Then he went outside the room, and headed back downstairs, where Katrina was sitting with another woman. It was Cathy. She was a large woman, round, but with a face that said, "Don't fuck with me." She used to work as a parole officer, but opened this place to help kids, hoping to keep them off the streets. She was tough, but kind and fair to children. She also was the home's cook, and instead of mass meals, she made each kid meals based on their dietary preference. Amos and Katrina learned after a few years of working with her that she did this partly because she could never have children, and this was the closest she would ever have to having her own.

"How is our girl?" she asked standing and looking at the small infant.

"Oh, little Masira is good."

"Masira?" asked Katrina, smiling at the name.

"Means destiny," he looked down at the baby and said, "Sorry, so much for the secret name."

"Cute," said Cathy, "Little Destiny, sounds a bit like a stripper name in English, but it will work as a placeholder as long as we call her Masira."

"Any word on where she came from?" asked Katrina.

"Nah, the mayor wants this under wraps, but it's going to come out, whether we like it or not. We got to find the mom at least. But the Mayor's got nothing, nor does our sheriff or our police chief. God damn it. I went to the prison before I came back here and went over the video myself, but other than some static, nothing, and still saw that the damn place was empty before the static began. After the cleaning crew went through, they locked that damn thing up."

"Bit of a mystery," said Katrina, taking Masira into her arms so Amos could get some coffee. He brought a cup from Cathy as well.

"Damn coffee, I need a beer," said Cathy, rubbing her eyes, "And it's still too early. Well, you two know what to do. Start circulating, description, location, the usual on our site, and call Marquette. Let's get it out, through the U.P and the Federal data banks. Maybe we will get lucky. But try to avoid the reporters."

"Yes ma'am," said Amos, taking a sip of the black brew.

"And let's get some more diapers. Will needed them."

"Sooner than you think," laughed Katrina, as the smell of feces wafted out. "At least she is good with her bowls."

They laughed. It was one that they needed.

"By the way, while I have you two in the same room, who is going to volunteer for Christmas and New Year's Duties?"

"I did Christmas last year," said Amos, "I'll do New Year's."

"Sounds good," said Katrina, "I got Christmas then."

"Shouldn't be that hard this year," said Cathy, "Most of our kids will be gone by that time."

"Fair enough," said Amos, and stood, going to change Masira's diaper.

5

THE HOUSE OF THE LORD was a church located on Ajustant Street and Franklin Blvd. It was an old church, built over a hundred years ago, and was run by preacher Anthony Dean. Anthony was a medium-sized white man, with thick glasses, thinning hair, and an unhealthy pallid of skin that rarely saw sunlight. The rumor was he did nothing but pray on his knees all week and only moved when he preached.

In reality, Anthony was a bit of a loner, but had a wife and three sons and two daughters, who he taught the word of God daily to, and went to the Diner, one of two restaurants in Belaphone, every Tuesday and Thursday for breakfast where he met his fellow preacher, Tom Bickly, who preached in Hardhome, and worked with the ministers in Leon County and oversaw several churches financings. They were both hardline Christians, and strong in their belief and righteousness in anti-gay right and anti-Muslims, and Mexicans staying in Mexico. Illegals, as Anthony put it, were the doom of these United States. There were no compromises with these men, though to be honest, Tom was much more approachable. Anthony more than once had run-ins with the local cops, with people complaining about his so-called, it made him sick to think about, warmongering.

To Anthony, more people need the wrath of God more than the love of God. His father, once a powerful preacher himself, used that wrath on Anthony more than once. He remembers being locked in a closet if he messed up with his homework, or being forced to sit on the stairs for hours on end, and the camp, oh, that camp, the camp that still gave him nightmares, but managed to set him on the right path, finding the true love of God through the fear of Damnation.

He was confused about why Tom wanted to see him today. Today was Wednesday, which was unusual and diverting from Anthony's schedule, and also Tom brought several files. Tom stood a head taller over Anthony. He had reddish hair, freckles, and long hairless arms which Anthony for some reason found disturbing. A man's arms shouldn't remind him of a woman's legs. Tom leaned back, a look of sorrowful concern on his face, and said, "Sorry Tony, but this couldn't wait."

"No problem," said Anthony, shaking hands with Tom, "What's up."

The waitress, a young Mexican woman with a thick accent, who didn't talk to them, just pouring the coffee, and left. You might think this was rude, but Anthony had called ICE on this woman once, and after three hours of interrogation, saw she had a Green Card and was married to a man in Belaphone, had since stopped serving the two unless she had to. The incident had nearly got Anthony band from the restaurant, but Tom helped to smooth things over. Good old Tom.

"Let's order our food first before talking," said Tom.

Anthony agreed, and the two placed their order with the same waitress. They waited and chit chatted as the angry woman took their order quickly, Tom banana pancakes, and Anthony a farmer's omelet with hash browns and toast. After she left, Tom put the files on the table and said, "Anthony, you have a problem."

"What problem?"

"Well, your attendance rate has dropped by twenty percent, and for the past three months, we, the committee, have had to cover many of the maintenance bills and the rent for your church. Your donations are down, and many of the younger members have either switched or left the church life. Plus, the One Nation debacle."

Anthony winced. He had invested several thousand in a startup company to track down illegals, but it turned out they were in violation of several US laws and were shut down by the Feds. All that money was lost, and he and his church were in the red for a while. The news went viral in Belaphone, and a lot of people had stopped socializing with him. With his attendance shrinking, he didn't have the funds to cover the cost of the church. Tom had come to his rescue, but Anthony saw where this was going.

"So, what is the bottom line?" he asked.

"Unless you can raise some new capital, in three months, we are cutting funding, and you won't be able to finance your church."

Anthony's heart dropped. No, it couldn't be true.

"But my church is my life," Anthony said, shocked, his voice almost devoid of breath.

"To be honest, the committee isn't liking what we preach anymore, they feel it is sending the wrong message and driving more to the Catholics."

"Fucking Catholics," snapped Anthony under his breath, "Worse than Muslims running around in Dearborn. Preaching their pagan ways, God damn that pope. They got their foothold up here too early for us to stop them."

"Look Anthony," said Tom, sorrow in his voice, "I'm sorry, but I do see their point. We can't focus just on your church. We have other projects we need to attend to."

Their food came, but Anthony lost his appetite. "Is there something I can do? What about the prison, if I get that gig, I'll be supported by federal dollars, then they will have to keep my church open. They must."

"Tried calling them today," Tom advised, "But I wasn't able to get through to them today myself. Heard a rumor that something happened up there."

"I'll talk to Sarah, she works there. Maybe she can get me a deal with the Warden."

"Sounds good. If you get that funding, there is a chance."

They ate, but when Tom finished his meal, Anthony got a to-go box, only eating about half his food, which tasted of ash in his mouth. They stood, shook hands, and headed home. Anthony resolved for now not to tell his wife or kids about their problems. She was a good, Godly woman and didn't need that burden. He needs something drastic to happen and fast, or they would lose it all.

As he drove home, he passed the Catholic Church, and his heart swelling with jealousy. When his father had been the preacher, he had nearly driven the Catholics out of town, now they made the majority of Belaphone. It made his skin crawl with anger.

He spent the rest of his day in prayer until dinner. Dinner that night was fish and potatoes. His wife was from Newfoundland, and did wonders with cod, but all he could wonder was if this was how Jesus felt as his death drew nearer. God, please don't put me on a cross.

BUTLER WAS STANDING OUTSIDE, SMOKING a cigarette. Usually, he chewed, but once in a while, he needed a smoke. There was just something about it, the smoke trailed from his mouth, helped clear his head, and that was something he needed on this cold day. His colleagues at the Sheriff Department and the Belaphone police department had combed every inch of that Chapel, but still were no closer to solving this puzzle. He had watched the security video over a hundred times, but other than those few seconds of static, he saw nothing that could explain how the girl could have gotten into the Chapel.

Amos had called early to let him know that Belaphone home was going to start its search for a possible family member for the girl. He preferred they used only official channels, but Belaphone home was very good at what they did, which was finding family members. They needed to find the gal's folks and fast. The girl could be a kidnapped victim or an abandoned child, so establishing where the girl came from was the most important thing at the moment. He managed to get his buddy at the Marquette Forensic Lab to put a rush on the DNA from the girl. He promised to have it after Christmas or so. Maybe they would get lucky and she would be in the system. If not, well, they figure it out as they go.

The afternoon was coming fast, and he needed food. He decided he was going to get some grub and Deputy Wright, his partner on the case currently, would continue investigating until he returned. He went to the Diner. The food wasn't as good as it was back in Texas, but it wasn't that bad. He ordered a plate of steak and eggs and ate slowly, going over the case in his head. How did that girl get in there? He didn't know, and after holding her while she was at the prison, he couldn't imagine anyone abandoning such a sweet little girl. He had almost reluctantly let Katrina from Belaphone Home take her, but knew it was the right thing for her.

After the meal, Butler took his truck back to the Belaphone Police Department. He had a message from the lab. Butler called, but he doubted any DNA evidence was ready. Even with a rush, it would take a few days.

He got through to his friend, Dr. Rash, an Indian immigrant who worked at the lab.

"Hey doc," said Butler.

"Hey," he said in his thick accent, "Sorry, nothing on the DNA yet, but I found something odd in the evidence."

"What?"

"The blanket."

"What about it?"

"Well, I brought it to a friend of mine, a tailor named Arnolled. Well, that and after I examined it….my findings were strange."

That caught Butler's interest. He didn't know why but this sounded like it was going to be interesting.

"What was it?"

"Well, most baby blankets are made from flannel cotton, designed to keep the baby warm, well this one does the same thing, but it's not cotton. Cotton like, but not cotton."

"What is it made from? What did the tag say?"

"The tag was removed or fell off. I can't identify it, but its plant base, I know that much, and I'm sending it to a friend of mine in Detroit, but it's just unusual."

"Well, maybe it's a new brand they're promoting."

"That's what I thought, but I called around, to Marquette and all the way down to Detroit. They are all using the Cotton blankets. I even asked around this area. Pretty much the same material. No variations."

"Overseas?"

"Possibly, but not likely."

Butler looked down and saw his light flashing on his office phone. His partner, the Wright, was texting him.

"Hey Doc, I got to go, but keep me posted ok?"

"No problem," said Raj, "Still up for poker night?"

"Always."

"See you then."

They hung up. Another mystery added to the pile. This case was getting stranger by the moment.

After talking to his partner, and saw they were getting nowhere fast, he sent a text to Amos, asking if they could meet tomorrow night. Amos confirmed, and said he would be available around eight tomorrow before he went to visit his dad. After confirming, Butler went back to work, still trying to wrap his head around the case.

7

AMOS WAS OFF AT SEVEN-THIRTY on Tuesday and Thursday, and then eleven Monday and Wednesday, and worked overnight on Fridays and had the weekend off. Once a month, he took a three-day weekend to which he told Cathy to help his father, Abdual out. This in itself wasn't the full truth. His father had moved to Wisconsin after Amos' mother died, and Amos did visit him, but though he was over seventy now, his father was not invalid. He was healthy and still worked at a convenience store in Milwaukee. The fact was he went there to go to Mosque with his father. At thirty-six, Amos' father was often on his case about getting married and starting a family, and only going to Mosque once a month, but still, he never pushed it to the point of annoying his son, for he loved him, and was thankful that Amos made the effort, both for him and for Mosque. This was Thursday, and he would start the five-hour drive on Thursday night and be there early Friday morning and make it in time to meet his father at the Islamic center in Milwaukie before the Iman began. The holiday season was the best time as well. It was during this time he always felt the closest to his dad.

Amos was glad for the break as well, this Wednesday and Thursday have been very strange. The interviews were pointless in the end. All the women were tested, and none were found to have been pregnant or have been pregnant, save for the ones that were when they entered Grisham's Correctional. A few tried to say they were the moms, but, in the end, they were just desperate women trying to have something on the other side when they got out. None of the agencies the home reached out to had any luck, either. There were a few kidnappings over the past few weeks, but none for a few days' old infants. Amos felt so sorry for the girl but was glad he got to spend the last few days of the week with her. She kept playing with his beard, and always got well behaved when he sang her to sleep.

Amos would usually go home after he finished helping the kids with studies, counseling, chow time, and just keeping a general eye on them in their free time, feeding, bathing, and washing the two infants. It turned out little Masira loved baths, unlike Natalie, who screamed and kicked her little feet, getting Katrina's shirt all wet. Amos, seeing this, felt a moment in his stomach, seeing the shirt pasted to her skin, but it passed when Masira started cooing for attention.

After her bath, Katrina took Natalie and Amos to read Masira's stories until she fell asleep and put the infants in the crib, then went downstairs. Only the girls and Cathy were up. The girls were watching Riverdale, Cathy was with an agent from Marquette, finalizing Natalie's transfer. A family was found, a Baptist Preacher and his wife from Escanaba, who had foster kids from them before. The agent, a redheaded woman with glasses nodded at Amos and Katrina. Cathy saw them as well, Natalie in her arms.

"You heading out?" asked Cathy, sharply as usual.

"Yep," said Amos.

"I'll see you this weekend," said Katrina.

"Alright. Amos, have a nice weekend. Kat, I'll see you at eight."

Amos went forward, and put a light kiss on Natalie's cheek, saying, "You better be good to your new momma. You're going to love Escanaba, it's amazing."

Natalie gave a little baby grunt which caused all the adults to laugh.

They said their goodbyes and walked out. In the driveway, Katrina and Amos said their good nights, and headed out. Amos headed into the town square, where Butler had asked to meet him. It was the Corner Bar, close by the main road, and met Butler on the patio, who, now wearing a tan coat, plaid shirt, jeans, and boots, looked more like a cowboy than ever. Amos' own black jacket, button up green shirt, jeans, and sneakers seemed so underwhelming in comparison.

Butler was already working on a shinner and Amos saw another bottle in front of him as well. O'Dooley.

"Butler, you know I don't drink," said Amos, frowning.

"Nonalcoholic," explained Butler, but there was a sly look in his eye that made Amos raise an eyebrow, "A little loophole I found. From what I understand, you can have non alcoholic drinks."

"Cheater," said Amos with a smile, sniffed the bottle, and looked at the label. No alcohol. He took a sip. It was bitter, and the taste clung to his tongue. Oddly though, he found he liked it. He took a seat across from Butler, settling in the cold night air. Unlike other places, the Corner Bar had outdoor seating even in winter. A fire pit had been set up, to keep the patrons warm. Amos didn't like this place much. With the peeling paint and the chipping wood, it seems to weaken with the town even further, the owners not bothering with the upkeep.

"How is the girl?"

"Fine," said Amos, "Seem healthy, feeding and pooping is all working ok."

"Medical report should be in a few days," said Butler, "Got a call from the Forensic Lab in Marquette. Talked about how the blanket wasn't the same as other blankets used in the hospitals."

"That's all?"

"Yep," said Butler, "And I've been over the evidence again and again, or lack thereof, hell, I'll say it I got nothing. I don't have a God damn clue how that girl got in there. I talked to Clive, you know, the chief of Belaphone Police, and Sisko, and their guys are just as stumped."

"Well, what about the static on the video."

"Might be something there, and having my tech experts look into it, but the video just keeps going as if nothing happened other than the static. It's not a loop or anything, just a slight static that barely clouds the picture. I'm stump. Almost happy the agent from the FBI will be here soon. Will you be available?"

"No, but Kat and Cathy will."

"Oh yeah," said Butler, "It's the end of the month, you're gonna go see your pops, right?"

"Yep," said Amos with a grin, "As dad would put it, 'You've been putting off mosque for too long.'"

Butler nodded. They chit-chatted, finished their drinks, and Butler headed home, and Amos headed to Wisconsin.

Amos' drive was uneventful the next morning, but for another man in Milwaukie, he was having breakfast inside his very large office with two of his friends and having the time of his life. His name is Iman Kamal Husevah. The Imam of the Islamic Center down in Milwaukie, Kamal was a second-generation Iraqi-Jordanian American. Born from a very religious household, one would be very surprised, as Kamal was surprised, to learn how moderate his father, Jemel was in America. He moved to America during the Gulf War from Baghdad and was given citizenship for his services as an interpreter. He married his mother, Salma Malhas, a Jordanian who had come to America for college and got a degree in literary arts. Though he was seven years older than Salma, her family approved the marriage, and they were wed six months later. From what Kamal understood, his father and mother's first few months were rough. Though both were Muslims, Salma's practices were Sunni and Jemel was Shia, and was raised with much more strict practices than Salma, but her patience and kindness soften Jemel's view of the world, and they ended up finding a happy middle ground. They in the end had three daughters and two sons. The one son became a doctor, a daughter became a literary agency, the other two, stay at home moms. Though all were Muslim, only Kamal became an Iman, a fact that both Jemel and Salma were proud of. They and his other siblings talked of him with pride, glad to have an Imam in the family.

Taking after his parent's upbringing, Kamal took the middle path with his Mosque. He let all belief in the glory of Allah into the center, the main reason being that there weren't that many Muslims in Milwaukie, and all needed a place to practice. There weren't separate services for men or women, and there were also no restrictions. He had Muslims of all walks of life, rich or poor, come into the center and pray. He had women with Hijabs and women who let their hair down. He had men in traditional grab and men in t-shirts and sneakers. There was a barrier for the more traditional women, but it was only used by a few dozen women, and none born here in the states. He prays and teaches with them both.

Kamal's wife, Aysha, was downstairs in the kitchen, working with several other women, both foreign- and native-born Muslims, to set up the welcome dinner for a couple who had just moved and settled here from Lebanon with their children. He did this for all immigrants who came to the center, for it not only served as a mosque, but as a place where foreign Muslims could interact and feel comfortable being among others and a community that would help them with their needs. With the turmoil in the Middle East, centers like these were needed more than ever so refugees didn't feel as isolated. They often came from war-stricken areas, losing everything from the US occupations in Iraq, Afghanistan, Syria, and many other places, fighting the false Muslims of ISIS, Al Qaeda, the Taliban, and many others besides, praying upon the innocents in the Middle East. They were all welcomed, even when others told them just to go the fuck home. A home that was being destroyed by war.

In the past, Kamal helped with the dinners for newcomers, but his wife said, "The kitchen is my territory, the mosque is yours. Go prepare for it." So, he sat in his office, but he was not alone.

Two of his best friends were with him. Rabbi Walawitz and Father Kempt were there as well. When Kamal first came to the city, he met the Rabbi who was raising money to feed the poor. First it was a rocky start, with views on Israel and differences in Abrahamic beliefs clashing, but it blossomed into a strong friendship, each helping each other to express their woes. They met the father at a religious exchange convention in the city, and soon he joined the little band, trying to make the world better through interreligious communication. It was their duty, using the various words of God to paint a picture of peace. Christians, Jews and Muslims, working together to make the world better. And not just the Abrahamic faiths. They were trying to reach out to Hindus, Buddhists, Sikhs, Wiccans, and others as well. So far, they hadn't had much luck, but they were slowly changing hearts and minds.

On Fridays, they met for breakfast at the mosque, where the priest donated the money for the meal provided by Kamal's followers. On Saturday, they met at the Synagogue where Iman donated. On Sunday, they met at the church, where the Rabbi donated. Today's menu was a Turkish breakfast made by one of Kamal's parishioners. Fried eggs with pastrami on the side made into sausages, tomatoes, olives, cheeses of varying varieties, flatbreads, French bread, honey, and dark coffee. It was quite a spread. Walawitz, a white haired and bearded man, wearing a dark suit poured the coffee. Kempt, a thin man of Korean-Irish descent served out the eggs and sausage evenly, and, after they each prayed over the food in their own unique way, they dug in, discussing the topics of their sermons, and offering advice to make them better and improve upon the final message. God has no hate and has many faces for the children of Adam and Eve to turn to.

"Well," said Walawitz, "I changed this part here, but then again, I'm partial to Israel."

"I think it's good the way it is," said Father Kempt, biting into some bread with butter and honey on it.

"Hey, speaking of changing," said Kamal, "I was thinking of having a cross cultural exchange, you know, get the new members accustomed to seeing Christians, Jews, and Muslims living in the same city. Some more cross-cultural experience. It seems to have a positive effect on the community."

"That's an idea," said Father Kempt, "Control expositor and integration leading to the goal of peaceful coexistence for new members of our congregation. Early exposure to help the new members integrate, and old members to get to know them."

"You do realize he is just doing this to steal members from your houses," said Walawitz, smearing cheese and honey on his bread, "Because I would do it."

"You couldn't convert an Atheist," laughed Kamal.

"I'm down," said Father Kempt, "But it would have to be on a day we all agree on."

"Oh fine," said Walawitz, patting his large belly, "I'm in, as long as locks are served, besides, mosques are always great places to find Jews."

Kamal rolled his eyes while Kempt snorted. Then Kamal's office phone began to ring, and he picked it up.

"S-salam 'alaykumu," he said, "This is Iman Kamal."

"Wa 'alaykumu s-salam," responded a deep voice with a Senegalese accent.

"Hello, Abdual, how is your day?"

"Good Iman," said Abdual, his voice with controlled excitement, "Is my son there yet?"

"You know he always arrives the same time you do, my friend," said Kamal with a smile.

"I know, I just want him to meet the new Lebanese family. Heard they had a daughter about his age."

Amos, being thirty-six and the woman he was talking about being only twenty, Kamal strongly doubted that Amos would see it that way. Still Amos, though not here as much as most of his congregation, had a great impact in the community. With such an important job of protecting lost children, Abdual had nothing but pride for his son. The old man was always smiling about his son and told anyone who asked about his important role in the town of Belaphone.

"I'll call if he is here early, Abdual," said Kamal.

"Ok, bye Iman."

"Goodbye."

"Abdual?" asked Kempt.

"Always about that boy of his."

"A black guy working as a social worker," said Walawitz with a grin, "I call that progress."

"That was kinda offensive, Walawitz," pointed out Kempt.

"So was the Holocaust, but people still make jokes about that."

They all had a chuckle, each of them knowing the pain of racism and prejudice in their lives, but also learning to overcome it. Still, it was a pain the left scars, and they could run deep, but each helped each other with the pain and to overcome it. Every scar was healed by their friendship and connection.

Outside the center, about an hour later, Amos pulled up to the Islamic Civic Center in Milwaukee and got out of his truck. Then he saw him out the corner of his eye. Abdual, coming at a slow trot towards his son. He was a darker shade of ebony skin than his son, and his eyebrows and lashes were long grey with age, along with patches of grey hair on his arms. He wore a white shirt, slacks, and a Kifu prayer cap. His skin was wrinkled, and his back slightly bent from age, but all in all, he was healthy at his age and refused to cut back on the foods he shouldn't eat, or anything else that wasn't against Allah, having a love for bean pie. In fact, his eyes lighted when he saw the bean pies Amos brought for the potluck dinner tonight, baked the day before. The old man hobbled to his son, and gave him a warm embrace, Amos feeling the pure love from his father. It would never replace the love he felt from his mother, but Abdual understood that was a special love, and the two together also felt her loss even more strongly, remembering when cancer finally got her.

A minute later, the two separated, and took in each other.

"Hey dad," said Amos, with a smile.

"You grew a beard," said Abdual, with a thick Senegalese accent and smile, "But still only a little hair on top."

"Your one to talk," said Amos, patting his father's head, bald under the prayer cap.

"Your fit," said Abdual, holding him at arm's length, examining his son, "Strong looking."

"As are you," said Amos, "Taking your pills?"

"Don't lecture me," said Abdual, "Your mother would frown on you."

"She would also frown for not taking your meds, dad," stated Amos, as they walked up to the doors of the mosque.

"Ah, only God knows when I will die," said Abdual, "What pill will matter when fate always has a hand in our life."

Amos rolled his eyes, but argued no further, and pushed the door open, their prayer rugs under their arms and walked into the Mosque entrance. After washing themselves and removing their shoes, they went to the Prayer Hall. The Prayer Hall was covered in prayer rugs, and men and women were already there. While men and women were on separate sides of the room, a small barrier at the back of the female section for the more conservative women. The Imam believed in equality, but he mandated this separation of the sexes for those who came from more orthodox or stricter practices of the Islamic faith, not wanting to give new arrivals too much culture shock and chase them away. Other than this sexual divide, men and women of Arab, African, Indonesian, Caucasian, and many others were mixed in for the worship of Allah. Even the clothing was a mix. The men mostly wore prayer hats, but all the Muslims, dressed in their Friday best, all wore a mix from traditional to modern westernized clothing. Many in the congregation were first-generation immigrants, but many more were native-born, and more westernized. Muslim born American already made up one percent of the USA population, over three million, and more and more we're becoming native-born and mixing with people of other faiths. Some of the congregation had spouses who were not Islamic, though supported the spouses in their faith as they supported them, and many of those were first-generation immigrants.

Amos and his father joined the male side. The Imam began the service, giving the call to prayer. Friday Prayer, or Jumu'ah as it was called in Arabic, took most of the service, several hours, the sermon in Arabic, and finally the lesson.

"Afternoon, brothers and sisters," said Kamal, in English after several hours of speaking passages in prayer, "First, I like to introduce our newest members to our congregation. All the way from Lebanon, Ralph and Mia Khalifa, and their two daughters, Kalma and Reetou."

In the male section, a tall man of fifty in a white shirt and a greying beard stood, and in the women section, a woman of forty-four years, a twenty-year-old woman, and a sixteen-year-old girl. All had shapely figures, long dark hair, and looked like sisters took more from their mother's side than their father's.

"They join us from Lebanon and Ralph has found work at the local university as an Economic professor. Mia is a former film producer in Lebanon and produced many documentaries around the Middle East. I urge you to welcome them into our community and get to know our newest members."

There was a light round of applause, and Abdual elbowed Amos in the ribs, and nodded at the older daughter. Amos responded by rolling his eyes.

"That brings me today's lesson, the community. We all work to spread the labors of Allah, and his prophet, peace be upon them, but we also live in a multi-cultural society. This congregation is full of people who live and work differently, but all worship Allah. His prophet Muhammad, peace be upon him, teaches us that we must be kind to our neighbors, and also make your enemy your friend, by facing hate and turning it into something better. The Christians and Jews we often have historical hatred, and other religions as well, the Sikhs, the Hindus, the Wiccans, that we turn that hate and project. By being kind to our congregation, we can be kind to the others of this land and build upon positive relationships that may one day spread from coast to coast, and even across the world. Israel becomes peaceful, not through more hate, by turning hate into something else, that being love, and making your enemy your friend. But also remember, this will not reach all, and some will be offended by the idea, and will forever be a slow process, but protect yourself and others from hate, create divine love, and bring life anew."

Amos thought of those words during the rest of the service, which ended in the final prayer and Kamal announcing that a potluck dinner would be held downstairs. Amos was hungry, and he headed downstairs with his father and the rest. The food being served had many African and Middle Eastern origins. Lamb cooked in the Turkish way, Iranian rice dishes, thieboudienne and yassa from Senegal, flat bread, wat, tibs, and fit of Ethiopia. Ikan bakar, ayam goreng and tofu from Indonesia. So much more from so many places. The smell of the spices filled the room, making one's mouth water with the smell of garlic and saffron floating in the air, the various dishes making one amazed and mouths water.

Amos was eating some of the Senegalese dishes and more of the Eithiopian dishes when the Imam and his wife and son joined them.

"S-salam Wa alaykumu, Amos,"

"Wa alaykumu S-Salam, Iman."

Kamal and his family sat across from Amos and his father, their plates filled with food.

"How was the trip?"

"Uneventful."

"Your father was almost bursting at the seams at the thought of seeing you so soon."

Abdual looked up from his meal and said, "Don't tell him that, now he will expect it all the time."

"Awe, dad," Amos smiled, teasing, giving his dad a playful elbow.

"You should make more of an effort to come, Amos," said Kamal, with a grin, "That way your father is happy all the time."

Amos laughed, but deep down, knew that the Imam had a point. Sometimes it felt like he was choosing his profession over faith. Belaphone wasn't the meanest place by any means, despite its aforementioned problems, but he felt closed off there, but he never felt overly comfortable revealing his faith, especially with his skin color. He had a girl he liked when he was in late high school, a white girl, and she knew he was Islamic at the time, but then 9/11 happened, and the girl made up an excuse for not talking to Amos anymore. Since college, he rarely revealed he was Muslim to anyone he meant out a conviction of being prejudged. Though Butler and Katerina both thought he was being foolish, as did his father, it was still a fear he had deep inside. Sometimes he thought he was cursed, though he never told this to his father. He was black in America, which had its own sets of mistrust sown in by the media, but being black and Muslim, that was a double whammy. Sometimes he thought he should move in with his father, but what stopped him was those kids and the few friendships he had in Belaphone. Those things kept him going and made him work harder as a social worker. That's what he was. A protector of children and helping families stay together.

"Well," he said after a pause, "who would look after all the kids I helped?"

"How is that going by the way?" asked Aysha. Aysha was of Saudi descent, but she wore no Hijab, instead, she let her black hair flow, and accent her beautiful face.

"Good," said Amos, happy the subject had been changed successfully, "In fact, we got a new baby there. Little girl. I call her Masira."

"Masira?" asked Kamal's small son, Rick.

"Yeah," said Amos, "Masir means destiny in Arabic."

"Cool," said Rick, nibbling on his bread.

"Have some vegetables," scolded Aysha softly, making Rick take some vegetables reluctantly on his fork, a look of disgust on his face as he ate the food.

"Is she a child of those who reside in Grisham's Correctional?" asked Abdual, working on some chicken.

"Yes and no," said Amos, "Kind of a mystery."

"What do you mean?" asked Kamal.

"Well, we don't know where she came from," explained Amos, "She was found at the prison, in the Chapel actually, but none of the women in their gave birth recently, and, well none of them, outside of those few desperate for a child and make lies to have one, seemed to have a connection to her. It's unusual. Even the camera in the Chapel made it look like she came from nowhere."

"Odd," said Kamal, "Anything we can do to help."

"Pray we find the mother," said Amos, "I hope she is worried sick."

"As do I," said Aysha, looking at her son, a sad look on her face, "May we talk about something else?"

The dinner ended a few hours later, Abdual and Amos drove to his small shop and apartment in the downtown of Milwaukie. Walking upstairs, Abdual opened the door to the small, studio apartment on top of the store. It was basic, living room, kitchen, bathroom, and a small outlet for a washer/dryer unit. Abdual went to his favorite chair as Amos put the leftovers that were given to them from the dinner in the fridge, knowing full well that Abdual had slept in that chair more nights then not, ignoring the bed ever since his wife died. Like Amos, Abdual missed her more than anything, keeping a picture of her on a side table by his chair at all times.

After coffee, talk, and watching some football, Lions vs Packers, Lions losing, Abdual fell asleep, and Amos, turning off the TV, got up, and went to the bed, lying on the couch, preparing to sleep in and getting ready for his long drive the day after tomorrow. It was a few days before Christmas, and he was glad that he wouldn't be stuck in Christmas eve traffic.

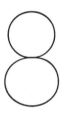

Saturday was uneventful for the town of Belaphone, Michigan, and the day turned to night, with the day filled with feedings and making boom booms as Cathy called them. Masira wasn't asleep, but was too distracted by the floating things above, her little and new mind giving her the urge to reach for it with her tiny fingers. Masira loved the floating things, as much as she liked Amos, his dark, deep tones kept the monsters and scary shadows away.

Masira eyes started to grow heavy and drift off to sleep, still reaching for the things above her, when she felt it, the cold, the cold that took her from the bright place, the cold that took her from the warm room and took her to the cold one, alone for what seemed to be forever. Masira began to scream and cry. She didn't want to go away again, for she would miss Amos, and she liked him, and didn't want him to go away like the nice lady at the warm room, the one that held her for the first time and fed her from her breast.

Then she saw the flickers. Two flickers of shadows. They moved on the walls and the floor. One came to her. A shift happened, and a shadow covered her. The shadow protected her from the cold that took her, and it said, "Close the barrier." Its voice, like that of a thousand whispers, seemed to reach out and penetrate everything in the room to its core.

A second shadow, this from the wall, reached a point above the crib where the floating things were and suddenly, the cold and the dreadful feeling were gone, and the shadows disappeared, but Masira started screaming, still scared, and crying. Her screams sounded like one being faced with something that was going to devour them, the endless wail that wanted to deny what was going to happen to them.

The door opened and light came in, and the two women came in, Cathy and Katrina, both in robes and pjs. Masira reached out her little arms, still sobbing and was scooped up by Katrina. Being held to her breast, and feeling the warmth, and the sounds of, "Its ok, its ok" calmed her, but she was still shaking,

Masira snuggled, still crying, but feeling safe as she could without Amos. Amos would protect her from the cold thing, he would make it go away.

The next morning, Katrina, though tired from the night before, was giving Masira a bottle. She had such a violent reaction to something last night but seemed to calm down when she picked her up.

Cathy came to her with hot coffee, a plate of eggs, bacon, and two pancakes the size of dinner plates, dripping in warm butter and maple syrup.

"Give the child to me, girl, and eat," said Cathy, bristly, and take the half-sleeping Masira in her arm, and bottle feeding her without disturbing her, "you been up most of the night. You need food and a nap."

"Thanks," said Katrina, going for the coffee first, and sipping it, adding milk and sugar before she did. The hot brew warmed her, and she felt a moment of relief. Well, the small kind. Katrina hadn't had a great kind in over a year. The shelter took up a lot of her time and her dating life had been lately non-existent, but God, how she missed it. She would just have to make do with Cathy's coffee, which in itself worked wonders that even the best sex couldn't solve, like waking up after being awake for half the night, Masira not wanting to leave her arms.

"Little girl got quite a pair of lunges on her," commented Cathy, then, looking down at Masira, "Yes you do, ohhhhh yes you do. So cute."

"I thought she was dying last night," said Katrina, taking a bite of eggs and bacon, "Wondered what scared her."

"Could check the baby camera," said Cathy, adjusting her large bulk on the chair, "The one in the panda on the shelf."

"When did you get that?"

"About two years ago," said Cathy, "It's in the panda teddy bear on the shelf. Got it after that mom tried to steal back her kid. Figured we needed the extra security."

"Well shit," said Katrina, "Why didn't we do that last night?"

"Wanted sleep," said Cathy with a wicked grin, "And please, no swearing in front of children."

They stood, Masira now fast asleep, and walked upstairs to the baby room. With Natile gone, Masira had the room to herself, and Katrina was thankful for that as Cathy laid down Masira. Once in her crib, they walked out and headed to Cathy's room. The rest of the kids were still asleep, for it was Sunday. A preacher from Hardhome, Pastor Obi, came in on Sundays and took the children to his church with Cathy, but that was optional and not forced upon the kids. It was only seven, and he didn't come till eight, so they had time.

Cathy turned on the computer, and opened an icon shaped like a camera. "Bluetooth," explained Cathy, as Katrina watched in amazement, remembering that teddy bear on the shelf, thinking it was just a toy, "Don't even have to take the camera out of the shelf. It will show us the last forty-eight hours."

A window opened, and Cathy punched commands on the keyboard, and several pictures popped up, the first showing Amos with Masira in his arms, and a big smile on his face. God, how handsome he looked to Katrina, seeing the smile come so easily. Katrina just couldn't help noticing the shape of his chin and how perfectly he got his beard to....."was it, Kat?"

Katrina blinked and jumped, "Sorry?"

"You ok?" asked Cathy, "I asked what time it happened?"

"Yes, yes, ummm it was about one-thirty."

"When did we get there?"

"About two minutes later."

She punched in the time, and several pictures disappeared, only to be replaced by the pictures that came up when the baby started screaming. Pressing the first picture, it began to go. Looking at the cribs, from above, it was shadowy, the only light coming from the moon threw the window. At first, nothing, but then, thirty seconds in, the camera became fuzzy. It was only a slight distortion, but it was noticeable.

"What the hell," said Cathy. The distortion only lasted about a minute, and when it ended, the baby was crying. Then the women saw themselves rush in.

"Play it again," said Katrina, placing herself a little on the edge of the computer desk, trying to get a better angle. She knelt in and watched it again.

"What the hell happened there?" asked Cathy.

"I don't know," exclaimed Katrina, "It's hard to make out anything clearly."

"It reminded me of the video I viewed with Deputy Butler when we first got the girl."

"Maybe we should call him."

"Let's," said Cathy, "And call Amos and tell him to get his butt back here."

Katrina did make the calls, and Butler was the first to arrive, Amos still going to be a few hours, driving in the snow. He viewed the video and saw the distortion. As it was his day off, he wore his button-up shirt, jeans, boots, and a brown cowboy hat.

"Yep," he said, "Definitely saw that before. I swear it's the same distortion we saw on camera at the prison."

"So, there is a connection," said Cathy, sharply.

"There is," said Butler, rubbing the back of his neck, "Just don't know what it is. Hang on ladies, give me one moment."

He pulled up his cell phone and dial the station. There was an answer on the third ring.

"Briggs," he said, "Make a copy of the video we got from the prison, and bring me the original here......Yes I'm sure.....Ok, thanks Briggs."

He hung up, and turned to Cathy and said, "Mind if I download this?"

"Sure," said Cathy.

Pulling out a USB drive, Butler downloaded the video and thanked Cathy, who agreed to walk him out. Katrina asked, "Would you like some coffee?"

"If it ain't too much trouble. Black be fine. Got a long drive."

"Only be a few minutes."

As the coffee brewed downstairs, Butler called his wife. "Hey honey, I'm sorry, I am not going to make it to church today......Yeah, work, it's that girl we found in the prison. Might have development..... Yeah, I'll try and make it for dinner.....No, I'll try not to miss Christmas......Love you too....give Sheala a big kiss from me."

He went to his truck then, grabbing a travel mug he kept there, and came back in. The coffee was ready, and his travel mug was filled. He thanked them, and went out to his truck, where Deputy Briggs just pulled up. He was an older man, about sixty, but still tough looking. He gave Butler a USB drive.

"Thanks," said Butler, "I'll see you later."

"Where are you going?" asked Briggs.

"Mass City," said Butler, "Going to see Jamie."

"You sure? You know the sheriff doesn't trust her."

"She owes me a few favors. She'll help. The Sheriff doesn't like it, he can kiss my ass."

Briggs nodded and left for his patrol car and drove off. Butler started his pickup and started to drive North. It was a thirty-mile drive, and he could be there in forty-seven minutes with the current road conditions.

He started to head North-East. He pushed the speed limit, but it was an uneventful drive save for seeing a few deer and coyotes on the way there, and he pulled into town.

Mass City wasn't much of a city. In the County of Ontonagon, it was a small collection of old buildings. It was a place for nature lovers, but not much else. The old mine had closed a long time ago, and now it seemed to be dying slightly. Butler pulled into an old home just outside of it. It was a small cabin, red chip painted, and the roof needed repair. A smell of tobacco, marijuana, and liquor was in the air.

Butler knocked on the door, hoping Jamie was sober today. He knocked again.

The door opened a crack, and a skinny, pretty face girl of twenty-three years peered through it. She was dressed in a plaid shirt on top of a tank top, yoga pants, and spikey earrings. She was pretty in a downtrodden sort of way, her eyelids covered in black mascara. She reminded Butler of the "Girl with the Dragon Tattoo." Expert hacker, semi goth, loner, but she was also amazing with computers, and Butler kept her as a contact just for that.

"Hey Jamie," said Butler, trying to give a kind smile while not wrinkling his nose at the smell coming from the cabin.

"What you want, deputy?" she asked, talking fast, "I'm on my pills, I'm on them, and......"

"Not here for trouble," said Butler, "Just come to ask for some assistance."

A nervous look crossed her face. "Assistants?"

"That's right. I need your computer skills to help me with these two videos." Butler held out the memory sticks. Jamie stared at them like a dog wanting a bone.

"What do you need?"

"Parts of the feed are, well, granny, not to a point of not seeing stuff, but making things difficult to make out."

Jamie brought up a hand, paused, and snatched the sticks, and opened the door fully.

"Come in," she said. Butler took off his cowboy hat as he did and headed down the smokey hallway to a combination of sitting, dining, and sleeping area. On three desks sat several computers, and where the fireplace was supposed to be, there sat several banks of monitors.

"Hacking the pentagon again?" Butler inquired, jokingly.

"Only did that once," said Jamie in her nervous voice, going to a computer, "Been looking into the KGB lately."

"Thought the KGB was gone."

"That's what they want you to think."

She went to one of the computers which had a dolphin jumping on the screen. Brushing the mouse, the computer came up, and Jamie put in the USBs and started going through the video. Though he had seen both of them, Butler watched them again, and they both saw the slight grainiest appear on the cameras. The one from the prison took longer than the one in Belaphone Home, about thirty seconds, but it was still not very long.

Once they were over Jamie began typing in commands, and lines of code appeared on both videos, and she seemed to go deeper and deeper into it. It made no sense to Butler, and he went to the couch, waiting for about a half-hour until... "Interesting."

"What?" asked Butler, standing, going back to Jamie.

"This was not a glitch in the security tapes, this distortion was caused by external interference."

"External?"

Jamie nodded, at the same time lighting a cigarette, the end burning, and she inhaled the smoke trail

"Something affected the tapes from the outside, temporarily distorting the feed. Natural forces, lighting, heat, and other such things can cause this, but this is a temperature-controlled environment, so, this makes it unusual, unless they were not temp....."

"No, the prison is heated, it's got a heater and air conditioner out there that's up to spec, which is surprising to me, but, eh, who knows. The home was also climate-controlled."

"So, no unnatural interference. No storms on either night of filming, I'm guessing."

"Can you fix them?"

"Give me a few days," explained Jamie, "I might have something."

"Thanks, Jamie."

"I'll text you when I'm done. You have a smartphone, right?"

"Yes."

"Good."

Butler stood and began to walk away, putting his hat back on. He met to say one more thing, but Jamie was already at work. Best not disturb her.

ANTHONY DEAN GOT INTO THE diner at about twelve o'five. Sarah was already there in her brown correctional uniform. She smiled at her preacher, who added a bounce to his step and gave her a fatherly embrace. Sarah smiled and returned the hug, Anthony not knowing her skin crawled when he looked at her.

"Sarah, how are you doing today? Didn't see you at church."

"I'm sorry Tony," she said, "I just got off of work. Had to work a double shift, and my sleep is messed up."

Anthony saw the shadows under her eyes and knew she wasn't lying. She looked haggard and worn and had been for the past few days.

"Sit, sit, sit," he said, leading her back to the booth, "I see you have already ordered some coffee."

"Yes," she said, "Long night, in fact, several long nights and days."

A waitress came, a middle age woman and poured Anthony a cup as well. They order banana pancakes for Sarah and fried eggs, bacon, and toast for Anthony. When the waitress was gone, Anthony leaned forward, his balding head and thick glasses reflecting light, and asked, "Sarah, did you talk to the Warden, about my proposal? I realize you are tired but…"

"I did," answered Sarah, "But he said at this time, he couldn't take on another preacher for the prison. He said for the time being, the Chaplin was going to have to be enough."

Anthony's heart sank. 'Oh, God, why, why have thou forsaken me,' he thought, holding back a torrent of anguish from his heart. But then, he noticed the words she used. At this time? Then something clicked for him. He remembered what Tom said, something about the prison.

"Sarah, what has happened at the prison?"

Sarah shifted nervously in her seat, looking like a child trying to find the right words as to not be scorned.

"I can't say preacher, it ain't worth my job."

"Sarah," said Anthony, sternly, "As your preacher, everything you say to me is confidential."

"I was ordered not to say," exclaimed Sarah, "I could get fired, and the prison is under enough pressure, preacher. I don't want to lose my job."

"Sarah, I promise, it won't get back to you."

"Tony," she said, nervously.

"Please Sarah. I'm your spiritual leader, and this might save the church."

"What?"

Anthony took a breath. He had hope that he didn't have to play that card, but he was getting desperate. Tom already said that other ministries had already considered him a write off, but he wouldn't be written off that easily.

"Not going to lie to my child, the church is in desperate financial straits, and if there is a way to save it, it's your God-given duty to try."

Indecision racked Sarah's features, and Anthony knew he was almost there. Just a little push.

"Please. I have to continue my work here in Belaphone."

Finally, Sarah's tired mind surrendered, and she looked him in the eyes. Eyes that said she needed to talk about this.

"There was a baby found in the prison."

The words confused Anthony, not the order or their meaning, but the phrasing. Babies were born from prison inmates all the time, but outside visitation, he couldn't see how a baby got in there, unless… yes that was it, the only logical explanation. So simple, so elegant… it was….

"So, a mother tried to hide her child from the authorities to…."

"No," Sarah shook her head, "she was found in a locked room, the Chapel, no way in or out, and from what we could tell, none of the women had given birth to her."

Anthony was shocked into silence, his mouth opening and closing like a fish for a moment, his mind working around what he had heard.

"My God," he said, "That poor child."

"A baby," explained Sarah, "Only a few days old. They took her to Belaphone Home."

"By all the apostles," Anthony leaned back in his chair and was shocked.

Sarah stood, throwing a twenty on the table, "I'm sorry Preacher, but I need sleep….and…."

"I understand," said Anthony.

Sarah rushed out, and Anthony ignored his food, annoying the waitress. God, who would leave a baby in a prison? It was a Goddamn miracle nothing….A Miracle. By Paul, it was, it was a miracle. Standing, he threw another twenty on the table, knowing the waitress was going to have an oversize tip to offset her bad mood and walked outside to the paper stand. Putting in four quarters, he pulled out the day's paper, and started reading. Nothing. Nothing about the girl in the prison. Nothing, it was quiet.

Pulling out his cell phone, he dialed his friend's number and said, "Tom, meet me tonight or tomorrow at the pub. I think I might have an idea."

10

AMOS ARRIVED AT BELAPHONE HOME about twelve hours later, his car pulling up to the curb before the house. He walked up the drive as quickly as he could. He had pushed the car more than he meant to, but, when Katrina called, it sounded serious. It wasn't a fun drive, the December snow starting to fall when he reached Michigan, but also, the quick way he said goodbye to his father upset the old man. Amos felt grumpy the whole way home, bitter about his recent and very cold goodbye to his father, his brain mulling over what was said.

"But we had plans," said his father after Amos told him he was needed back at work, "You said you weren't leaving until after lunch."

"I have to go back to work, dad, I'm sorry."

"But Kamal is having us over for lunch."

"I know, but….."

"Amos!"

"I got to go, dad."

His father then turned his back to him and said, "Well, have a good trip."

There was a note of ice in his voice, a tone Amos had never heard him use. It cut Amos to the bone.

"Dad….I."

"I'll tell Kamal you had an emergency."

Amos left not long after that, his father not uttering another word as he left, not knowing why his dad was so angry.

When he got back, he opened the door and saw the girls watching tv. He also saw an older woman talking to Cathy and holding the Asian boy's hand in hers'. He had forgotten...God what was the boy's name, Chung, was leaving today. Amos was ashamed he had forgotten it. Rushing things made one forget. And the older woman, Mrs. Fredrickson from Social Services, was holding his hand, looking ready to leave as Chung said some final words to Cathy.

"Well," said Mrs. Fredrickson, "I think we got everything here."

"Alright," said Cathy, handing Chung a brown paper bag, "Got your favorites in there Chung. You're going to love the people you're staying with."

"Can I stay with you?" asked Chung, a gleam in his eyes.

Cathy knelt, "Chung, it's going to be close by, just across the county line, and if you need anything, just let me know."

"Thank you, Cathy," said Chung, embracing Cathy. Cathy was a hard woman, but her heart was also tender, and she embraced Chung back.

"Miss Grizzward," explained Mrs. Fredrickson, sharply to Cathy as she hugged Chung.

"No, it's Cathy," said Cathy, "Chung has a right to be sad. You hear me, my boy. Don't let the mean lady tell you anything different."

Despite being on the same side, the two women didn't like each other that much. Too different, brisk and kind vs piercing and server, not a good combo to have in the same room. It was like watching a mongoose and a cobra square off. Venom was being spit, invisible venom that both wanted to poison the other for daring to have a different form of thought of taking care of children. It was intense.

Mrs. Fredrickson started walking out the door with Chung, passing Amos.

"Bye Amos," said Chung, excited.

"See you kid," said Amos, ruffling the boy's hair.

As the two left, Amos closed the door and listened for a moment as Jughead talked about Riverdale's latest problem in the background television noise. Cathy walked away and sat down in the kitchen. Her large hands rubbing her forehead.

"Well, Chung's foster parents are right across in Ontonagon. When mom gets her life together, he could go back to her quickly."

Though Amos' words were meant to invoke comfort, he noticed the water in Cathy's eye but said nothing about Chung, for that was not why he rushed home so fast. "What's wrong, is Masira ok?"

Her eyes cleared, Cathy looked up at him and said, "Yeah, but last night, something happened to the girl and she ended up screaming like a banshee. I tell you; I heard a lot of cries from infants, but I ain't ever heard one like this."

Lifting her bulk from the chair, she started waddling herself upstairs, Amos followed her to her room, and watched the video from the computer. When it ended, all he could do was stare. He felt ice water in his veins, the image searing into his mind, merging with that he had seen. For he had only a few days ago seen something like this on another screen.

"That's....that's the same thing I saw back and Grisham's Correctional," said Amos, slowly.

"Butler agrees. I'm telling you, Amos, that girl was terrified."

Amos nodded, then he looked over in the general direction of Masira's room. "Where the hell did she come from? What the hell is under that static?"

"I don't know Amos. We don't have any clear answers right now."

"Still no hits in the system?"

"None, just a few poor souls and coots calling in."

Amos looked at her, and said, "Mind if I go and see her?"

"Go, you're good. As long as you are here, you might as well do some work."

"Yes, boss."

Amos entered the room. At first, he believed that she was sleeping, but when he went over the crib, he saw the tiny arms reaching for him, a toothless look of excitement on her face. Amos smiled and picked up the child. She was cooing, and Amos held her, his hands supporting her head and buttock. Amos looked at the chart that Cathy put on the bed. It was close to feeding time.

"Alright, little girl let's get that bottle. Don't know how you can stand that stuff, but hey, it's your body, yes it is, yes it is. Goo goo ga ga."

Amos heated the bottle, tested it, and began to feed Masira. She seemed at peace. Amos smiled, feeling that there was no trouble tonight. She snuggled in his large arms, his ebony skin-contacting with her lighter tones. Her eyes didn't close the whole time as Amos fed her, looking up at the bearded man with a sweet look. Looking out the window, he saw the snow falling. It was December twenty-third, and it was going to be deep, he could tell by the size of the snowflakes. With the falling of the snow, the light of the day almost gone, and feeding Masira, Amos felt something in his body that felt like peace. Amos smiled.

"Looks like we got a white Christmas coming up honey, yes we do. You will love it. I don't celebrate it myself, but there are presents and good food from what I understand."

He wasn't the only one that saw. Katrina pulled up in her old Toyota, and, after getting out, looked up at the window, with snow falling on her hair, and she saw Amos, smiling with his bearded face, holding the baby girl with a smile that made a thousand worlds glow. It made her smile, seeing how perfect the moment was. She pulled out her cell and took a picture. Some moments were worth preserving.

She then walked inside, not noticing another, a balding man in his car, watching from a distance. He could see into the window, and he saw the child. The child. Such a beautiful little girl. The black man was holding her with a tenderness only true fathers were capable of doing.

Anthony sat in his old van, heater on, watching the child and that....that black man holding her, as if under some delusions that he was her father. He gripped the steering wheel in sheer disgust over what he saw. It wasn't natural. He would talk to Tom tomorrow, as Tom wasn't able to meet today in the end, for he knew that girl....that little girl and he had a destiny designed by God, and would be the salvation of his church, the salvation of his flock, and the salvation of himself.

11

THREE DAYS PASSED WITH ONLY small events happening of great significance. The snow came down hard, in droves. Northern Michigan is well equipped to handle such a situation, but it was recommended that one should not plan any long trips. This meant that Marquette, the most populated and largest city in the Upper Peninsula, was delaying the transfer to the social services for Masira, again.

Christmas was uneventful in Belaphone, save for the usual home festivities. Across the town, families celebrated at home or the churches. Belaphone home had presents for the children still there, and a Christmas breakfast and dinner. Breakfast consisted of cinnamon buns with icing, filled with nuts and raisins, and hot cocoa provided by Katrina. Dinner consists of baked ham, mashed potatoes, green bean casserole, chestnuts, fruit salad, apple, and pecan pie.

Butler was able to make Christmas morning with his wife and daughter for breakfast and presents. He got his daughter a new teddy bear, which she loved, and his wife, a diamond necklace. He got a new cowboy hat, a bottle of fine whisky, and new boots. He had to work for most of the day, but around dinner time, he stopped by Amos'. The snow was falling hard, the roads icy between Belaphone and Hardhome, so he was going to spend the night there, Amos and Butler watched the "Muppets Christmas Carol" together. It was pleasant, topped by, with a rare surrender to the Christmas spirit for Amos, drinking eggnog, Amos' booze-free while Butler added whisky to his. However, Amos saw he was still sad about not being home, so he suggested they went to Belaphone home. Butler, knowing it was probably the best he was going to get for this holiday, agreed and the two headed out, Amos driving, via still being sober.

They knocked on the door and Cathy answered. Her large bulk was covered by a flowery dress, and her hair tied in a bun.

"Well," she said, "This is a surprise."

Butler took off his hat and said, "Ma'am."

"You got room for two more?" asked Amos.

"We always got room in the inn," she said with a smile.

Her smile got wider when Butler revealed the bottle of whiskey, calling his wife ahead a time, asking if it was ok to bring. She didn't mind, knowing how lonely he got working these shifts and missing Christmas.

The girls were eating pie and Katrina was doing some dishes. Amos' jaw dropped. She was in a full-length black dress, her hair done up in curls, and a gold necklace rested on her neck. She turned and saw the two men walking in.

Amos went to help her, and Katrina smiled, elbowing him, and said, "Thought you didn't celebrate Christmas."

"Thought there be mistletoe," he said with a smile, "Heard that was a Christmas thing."

She laughed, and they finished the dishes.

The night ended with the two girls, Masira in Amos' arms, and all the adults watching "Miracle on 23rd Street."

However, the next day after Christmas, driving snow, a government rented car arrived at the doors of Grisham's Corrections, the ladies recovering from their own Christmas party. The FBI sent a field agent by plane to Marquette before the snow got so bad, and Agent Victoria Wilson landed Belaphone at eleven am, the day after Christmas.

Victoria was a Blonde woman, about five foot, nine inches, long legs, shapely body, and assets that could make the coldest man's heart want to reach out and dance like a fool and when they did, they would feel her coldness, and grow scared. Victoria was nothing but business and didn't let anything in her way to stop her. The big Glock on her hip helped make that point. Four years as an Army Scout, and ten years as an FBI Senior investigator, she was known around the Detroit field office as the Ice Woman.

There was one thing that Special Agent Victoria Wilson hated more than stupid men, and it was the USA correctional offices, which she despised. She hated all of them, and how they were run, and under the current and most of the past Presidential and Michigan Governor's administration, they were getting darker and uglier. More the president's side though, currently, knowing the current Governor, Carolyn Wilson, no relations, was trying to bring change. The system, and how it was run, didn't rehabilitate, it did nothing which made a cycle that made prisoners stay Goddamn criminal. When they get out, over sixty percent re-offend just to survive, and are placed back in the system they can rarely escape from. This was why when Victoria got the call about the baby found in Grisham Corrections, she jumped on it as soon as she was able to. Three investigations in Prisons across Michigan had shut down two private prisons that had abused and mistreated the populations within. They made her unpopular in Corrections but made her many friends with Lawyers and Prisoner's rights associate's programs. Wardens feared her name, and Warden Sisko was no exception to fearing the Ice Woman, now she was the bane of every Warden across Michigan.

Wilson got out of her car and looked over the notes she had of the prison as guards hastily let her into the prison. Save for the last warden having used some of the women there for sexual favors, Grisham Correction had an outstanding reputation. Prison had many jobs that could translate into real-life careers, an easy atmosphere, and the prison population had an only twenty percent return rate, lower than the national average. In fact, this was the first major incident in thirty years.

Victoria walked in, and a large guard, tough-looking and beefy, looked at the slim woman with a creepy smile, and said, "No firearms in the facility."

Victoria looked up at him with her piercing blue eyes and the look she gave turned this creep to stone, and she said, "Oh really, I thought all prisoners were allowed guns. Thank you for reminding me, dumb ass. Now, take my weapon, and make sure you don't lose it, or I will have your damn badge."

The man was still shaking when she walked into the prison and entered the warden's office. Sisko raised his large bulk and held out a hand that Victoria shook, "Agent Wilson, welcome to Grisham."

She shook, both with strong grips, that showed mutual respect. "Thank you, Warden. Just to put your mind at ease, I believe you are doing a wonderful job here in Grisham, unlike the rest of the state, I'm just here about the child, and hope it doesn't lead to anything else. Please begin."

The Warden told her everything, from the camera fuzzing, proven by a video uploaded to Wilson's phone, the discovery of the child, her pick up to Belaphone home, and the investigation by the sheriff department and the local police force. This had gotten up all the way to Governor Carolyn Wilson for ass chewing.

"So, there was no girl in the Chapel before it was locked," confirmed Wilson.

"No," said the Warden, "There is always a guard who does a sweep before locking up. One way in one way out. It's locked with a double bolt lock. Nothing in, and nothing out."

"Double-lock?" asked Wilson, "Seems a little extra for a Chapel."

"It has nothing valuable," said the Warden, "in the past, some of the girls used it to….well…have intentions with others they got close to. Intimacy, you know, they crave it in prison. Even a few guards took advantage of that with my predecessor. I installed them both the camera and the lock on my second day here to prevent further incidents."

Victoria nodded, "Makes sense. And so far, you only have three women in here that are pregnant, if I remember correctly?"

"Well, two and a half," said Warden, "One just went into labor today, so we know she is not the mother. The local police and sheriff departments have worked round the clock with interviews and with DNA evidence, but we got nothing so far."

Another note. "Any idea what caused the camera to go static?"

"No, and the technician said that there was nothing wrong with it. He suggested that it was a blip in the internal system that straightens itself out."

"But you don't believe that."

"I don't know what to believe," responded the warden, rubbing his temples "I feel like I'm walking in some lost Sherlock Holms' novel, except nobody can hear me say, "By God, Watson.""

Victoria shrugged, "So, we have limited information to go on. Where is the child now?"

"Belaphone home."

"Not Marquette?"

"Snow is too thick right now, along with the holiday, plus, the full medical report isn't in yet. Marquette likes to have it before taking kids into the foster system."

Another note.

"I'd like to talk to all staff members that were on duty that night."

"They don't come in until eight tonight."

"Then I will be back at eight. I expect you will be here."

The Warden's eyes had shadows under them, and his skin was pale from lack of sleep, but still nodded and said, "Of course."

Agent Wilson stood and held out a hand, "Thank you, Warden Sisko, see you tonight."

They shook, she left, and the Warden collapsed in his chair, and then picked up the phone, "Freeman, get me some God damn coffee, and not the shit we have here, run to the coffee house and get the good kind."

Meanwhile, Wilson called the Sheriff department to get information on the investigation and contact info to talk to the primary investigator. Belaphone, only having four local cops, it makes sense to have the Sheriff department take over the investigation. However, that call coincided with another conversation that Butler was happening to have.

This started out with a file that was hand-delivered the day before by a local doctor named Dr. Sherman, via medical currier, at the Belaphone Home. It was Masira's medical records. Amos, who was changing Masira at the time, who had a really big boom boom, was there to receive them, and reviewed them. As the child's warden, Amos had the right to review her records. Nothing seemed out of the ordinary. No genetic defects, no signs of infection. "All ten fingers and toes. Yes, you do, yes you do baby girl."

The alarm went off. It was time for prayer. He sent Butler a text, knowing that he too would have the records, and after his prayers, Butler texted back. "Can I come over?"

"Sure," texted Amos back.

Amos had just set Masira down for a nap when Butler came in. He looked haggard, and his face was unshaven. Amos, ever the sympathizer, asked, "You need coffee?"

"No, I need bourbon," said Butler, "With coffee."

"Think I could help."

Amos led him to the kitchen. He told the deputy to wait for a moment after he poured him a cup of stale but hot coffee and went to the door that led to the basement. When he came back, Amos held a bottle of Jim Beam.

"Though you don't drink," said Butler, "And don't have children live here?"

"It's also a residence," said Amos with a smile, "And it's not mine, it's Cathy. And this is the only one. Yours ran out on Christmas."

"How often does she go at it?" chuckled Butler, as he felt his phone vibrating, but not recognizing the number, silent the phone completely.

"When there are no kids, so about twice a year," explained Amos, running his hands through his beard.

Butler laughed and added a splash to his coffee. God, he needed that. Amos sat across from him; his coffee booze-free.

"Any luck?"

"Well, one theory about the videos, I got Jamie looking into it."

"How is she doing?" asked Amos.

"Got out of parole."

"Still, hacking the Pentagon?"

"No, apparently the KGB is around again."

They laughed. Jamie was smart, but paranoid, spending the better part of her late teens through her mid-twenties in and out of mental institutions. Still, that girl knew her way around computers and electronics. If anyone could solve the mystery of the static on the screen, it was her. She was magic on a computer, her fingers typing amazing algorithmic magic which few could match.

"So, other than providing our local sheriff deputy with not much needed booze, what did you want to talk about?"

"Well," said Butler, "It's not just you, because I know you were out of town, so I also have to ask Cathy and Katrina, but was there a storm the night that the camera went wanky, or a power surge, or something?"

"Not that I can recall them saying," said Amos, "but I'm sure there wasn't a storm or anything, just snow."

"What about the night when they found….what are you calling her again?"

"Masira," answered Amos, "And no, the weather that night was clear. No snow or lighting storm."

"Yeah, and I checked the weather, nothing that could explain the interference on the camera."

"Jamie?"

"Yeah, she says it's external. But everything I looked up tells me that such interference would affect the entire system, not just one camera."

"We only have one."

"The prison has over seventy."

"Dang," Amos was surprised, "Thought it was a minimum-security prison."

"Eh," shrugged Butler. He drank some more of his "Irish coffee" and continued and looked out the window, but then noticed something on the corner of the street, visible by the window. Normally, it wouldn't have caught his attention, but, for some reason, this did.

"Amos, does anyone in the neighborhood own an old, red Van?"

"Not that I know of, why?"

"Because there's one at the corner, and the occupant is sitting there looking at us through binoculars."

Amos stood, and went to the window, and saw the car, and saw a man with thin hair, glasses, and sallow skin dropping a pair of binoculars. Then Amos hears the engine start.

"Hey," yelled Amos, running through the front door with Butler behind him, "Hey!"

The car peeled in the deep snow, Amos and Butler watched as the car drove off. Amos pulled his phone out of his pocket, meaning to take a picture of the license plate, but the car had whipped around the corner, leaving a trail of snow in its wake.

12

A second car pulled up after the first. It was a rental from Marquette. The car pulled up to Belaphone Home about thirty seconds after Amos went to check out the van with Butler. Pulling up, Agent Wilson saw the two men walking back towards the house. One a muscular black man, short curly hair close to the scalp, but salt and pepper beard, the other, a shorter, thinner white man with a tough body, bald top, and a stance of a southern man. On his belt, a Glock and a badge.

Parking, and turning off the car, caught the attention of the two, and they watched the sexy, blonde woman in a suite get out of the car, wearing a blue rain jacket that was not enough for Northern Michigan winters.

She pulled a badge from her back pocket. It was a wallet, with one half showing a picture ID, the other, an FBI badge. "Hello, I'm agent Victoria Wilson of the FBI."

Both men looked at each other as if to say, "Duh fuck." Though Victoria looked between them, viewing them while not directly looking at them at the same time, to analyze their expressions, and the environmental factors that would cause this. Then, she saw the slowly disappearing remains of tire tracks, and more factors clicked in her mind. She walked forward, and took pictures of them, brushing pasted the sheriff deputy and the black man. She snapped two shots with her smartphone and saved in a file marked, "prison baby".

She stood, turned to the two, and said, "I believe you are deputy Butler of the Leon County Sheriff Department."

Butler, giving his head a quick shake, nodded and said, "Pleasure to meet you, Miss Wilson. Sorry, just some strange stuff seems to be happening in our little county, and it seems to be adding every day."

"Well, if a case of a baby is too much for your little department, the FBI is more than happy to step in."

Butler's face fell and his easy smile was replaced by a frown. Amos stood off to the side, uncomfortable.

"That will not be necessary," breath Butler, "The Leon County Sheriff department is working with Belaphone PD and getting results back from Marquette."

"Yes, I'm afraid to say yielding very little in actual evidence from the reports I saw," said Wilson in a voice that dripped with poison honey to Amos' ears, "What do you have, four local cops, and ten deputies working in the Sheriff Department. And need to remind you that federal and private Prisons are always in the FBI's jurisdiction."

Butler was about to say something when Amos spoke and said, "May I ask how we can assist you, Agent Wilson."

She turned to Amos and took a moment to size him up. Strong build, strong facial features, Senegalese descent. She had read up on everything known about Amos and the others who worked at Belaphone Home before she had arrived. As both institutions, Grisham's Correctional and Belaphone homes, were partly funded by the federal government, all employees were in the network. Amos Diouf, thirty-six, son of legal Senegalese immigrants. Father lives in Wisconsin, mother died, no siblings. Muslim affiliation but has no known ties to any terrorist organization anywhere in the world.

"I'm here to talk to you about where we are on the girl from prison. I assumed she has been sent to Marquette by now, but Sisko has already informed me that would not be the case due to the weather and the holiday."

"That is correct," said Butler.

Victoria looked unsurprised, "And the girl's condition?"

"She is healthy," said Amos, "Medical report cleared her. I have to say, you handle the road well. Don't know how you managed...."

"I'm originally from Anchorage," Victoria explained crisply, "these road conditions are nothing to me."

Amos and Butler looked at each other, a little annoyed by this woman's business-like attitude and self-importance. But she was used to this attitude from men, but she wasn't going to back down, for she knew she was better than anyone at her job, and she wasn't going to back down from masculinity.

But shit cuts both ways, and the two men, though raised in very masculine cultures, also had a life experience that had shaped them beyond being, as people would say, prone to toxic masculine. They weren't annoyed because she was a bossy woman, they were annoyed because she was acting as if she already knew everything and was assuming incompetence to overlook the facts that the facts were just not adding up.

"Care to come inside," ask Amos, keeping his tone friendly, "The cold is bitter, and we have coffee."

"That would be nice," said Victoria, following the two men, while sending the picture to a friend in the beurre to identify the tire tracks.

As for the van from early, it pulled up in front of Anthony's house, the occupant got out. Anthony was in a state of shock. His heart had been pounding since he left Belaphone Home, but he was also cramped by sitting in his car for hours and happy to be moving again. He had been sitting in his car for three hours, watching the black man feed and change the baby girl.

The girl looked like a regular baby, but there was this feeling, a feeling she was the most important thing in the world, but he could place it. It was like an echo, hitting his mind like a bell, telling him that girl, that girl was the most important person at this time, even more important than the current president of the USA, who was cleaning up the unwanted illegals swarming the streets of this once-proud country. She was the key, the key to what, he wasn't clear, say for saying that she was the key to saving his church.

He went inside. Nobody was home. His wife and children were most likely at the hill, sledding, whizzing down the hill hard and fast. They will be gone for a while. God, he needed to calm down. Please, God. Please. Nothing, well, plan B.

He went to the cabinet, and opened a half-empty bottle of bourbon, and took a swig. He took another and another. Blood turned to wine, and warmth, sweeping through his body. He then closed the bottle and worked his way upstairs.

Seeing the bed, he shared with his wife, he fell into it and fell asleep.

At first, it was unnoticed, as all those who fall asleep do, as sleep comes as unnoticed as air, but then, the dreams came.

For most humans, dreams were also like air. They came, and they went, but this one, this one was different.

The dream started in a field of stars. Stardust, forming into systems and galaxies, making a universe. What was this? Was this what heaven? Anthony didn't know. He had seen heaven as blue. Blue like an ocean with clouds. But then he began to pull out of it. A billion, trillion, beyonillian galaxies passed before his eyes as if he was in a field of fish flies, billions and billions on one spot, making a whole that was unimaginable.

But then, he hit a wall, a wall of black darkness. It was solid, but his consciousness slid across it like a water bug searching for a Lilypad in the water. A place to rest and not worry about the fishes below.

He found it, a hole in the fabric of time and space, and slipped through it, and was in, well, nothing. It was indescribable. It was unimaginable. There wasn't a verb, a synonym, and adjective that could be used to describe what was there. Nothing, absolutely nothing. No black. No white. No grey. Nothing. Was he in hell?

Slowly, the madness seeped in. Unimaginable loneliness. Was he, a man, the only sentient being in this….whatever this is. He knew not. He didn't want to know. He wanted to run. He wanted to flee. God save him. God help him. Please God, spare me from this nothingness, I give you my soul, my heart, just let it end. Please God, please.

Then it came. It was movement only at first, but in this endless nothingness, it was enough to catch his eyes. It was....it was.... darkness, pure, like a cloud in mass and texture. It was shaped like that of a cobra. It was so small it....it got bigger and bigger. Soon, it filled the void of nothing. It moved, slithered like a snake. Its mass, unbelievable. It was indescribable. It was utter blackness. Save for its eyes, its red eyes.

Anthony then felt it. The mass didn't just look dark. It was dark. Burning, searing. It was, was it hell? Anthony didn't know. All he knew was fear.

The creature observed him with those horrible red eyes, as large as two small suns, then, its back end moved. It seemed to take an eternity, but soon its tail was before Anthony, the tip reaching. Soon, it touched Anthony's forehead, and he felt something dark enter him. Hate and hope. It absorbed his very being.

Then it spoke, in a deep, horrifying voice.

"Find the girl," it said, "I will do the rest."

Fear. Oh God, the fear, it coursed through him, and yet, and entered as well. And obsession. The girl came to the forefront of his mind, taking away all other thoughts and...

"The serpent," though a voice in his head, "The second serpent is near. Revelations are near. Find the girl. Find the...."

"Honey....honey."

It was his wife. Anthony looked at her, fear coursing through her as she saw his eyes. Eyes of fear, eyes that saw what should have never been seen.

"Yes," he crooked gruffly.

"I uhhhh...." She stammered, "Time for dinner."

"Yes dear," he said hoarsely, "Be there in a minute."

She left the room, leaving Anthony with one word. Revelations. And that word only meant one thing to him. The end was coming, and he knew its name. He knew it's not from words but the feeling of cold. He would call it the great dragon, Satan, Lucifer, but a more fitting name for the great shadow serpent was…..was…..Apophis.

13

AMOS BROUGHT THE COFFEE TO both law enforcement officers, black and, in Butler's case, booze-free. They sat at the table. The girls were upstairs, working on homework assigned to them by Cathy. Masira was asleep. Other than that, the house was empty.

Before he did all of that, Amos called Cathy and she and Katrina were on their way back from buying food at the local grocery. Sitting down, Victoria opened a notebook. They went through the case, for Amos, what felt like a thousand times. The girl, the fuzz on the cameras beforehand. Their only news to Victoria was the second camera going fuzzy in the house. She viewed the footage with Amos and Butler and wrote the notes with furry.

Afterward, they returned to the kitchen. Amos and Butler's cups were drained. Victoria's was untouched.

"So," she said, "you say, Jane Doe...."

"Masira," interrupted Amos, getting a cold look from Victoria, but he returned it in kind, "That is what we call her."

"Jane Doe," said Victoria, pointedly, "had a strong reaction after the camera went fuzzy."

"From what we understand, yes," confirmed Butler.

"And she was found crying at the prison?" asked Victoria.

"Yes," said Butler, "I sent the videos to be examined by an expert I have in Mass City, about forty-five minutes from here."

"Oh, who?"

"Jamie Freeman."

Victoria picked up her phone and typed in the name into the FBI database.

"Jamie Freeman, in and out of mental institutions since she was fourteen. Arrested twice. Once for underage drinking. The other, hacking into government databases. Now on parole."

"Well, she doesn't do that in 'our' country anymore."

"You requested the assistants of an ex-con with clear mental health issues?"

"Her expertise I felt was essential to the solving of this case."

"We will see."

Amos found the cold tones from this woman very impersonal. Butler had been working his ass off to find even a scrap of information to help Masira, and this agent was treating him like a rookie cop. Butler may not look like the east coast version of a cop, but in Texas and Leon County, he was one of the best, his Texas charm being only one piece of Amos' complicated friend. This city woman was just snotty and had one hell of a chip on her shoulder.

She stood, and said, "I need all the files you have on the case."

"I'll drive you to the office," replied Butler, standing.

They walked to the door, and Amos walked them out, with Victoria turning and saying, "I will be back to talk to the other employees of this establishment."

'What the hell, am I running, a bar?' though Amos, but out loud he said, "Ok, have a good day."

She nodded, and Butler felt his phone buzz. It was Jamie.

"Finally," he said, seeing attachments to a text message, and a message that said, *"I think I need therapy after seeing this shit."*

Victoria came back annoyed.

"What's the delay?" asked Victoria.

"Just got the videos. Hang on."

The three crowded around the Deputy as he played the first video. It was that of the prison, the end where the section of fuzz was, the picture, though still dark, was clearer, and what they saw made all three of their jaws drop.

It was shadowed, moving, moving without objects to cast off them. They moved like phantoms or ghosts, around the podium, ethereal and otherworldly. They cast themselves on the walls and floor, and yet, interact with the physical world as men do. The shadow things were humanoid in shape but seemed to be both flat and three dimensional at the same time. They stuck to the walls like shadows but were able to touch things in the room. The nightmarish ghouls moved almost fluidly, almost like water. But it was their eyes that caught Amos' breath in fear. Two round holes where human eyes should have been, but instead, only showing the objects they were casting off of, the walls and the floor, like holes in their heads. In one of the shadowy things' hands, it held a buddle. And it was set on the floor. Then they disappeared as if evaporating into thin air.

Without prompting, Butler opened the other video, and shadows moved again, two of them, and above the crib, there was.....was a shift, like a heatwave, small over the crib. Masira was screaming her lungs out as the shimmer seemed to only get closer and closer. Amos' heart went out to the little girl, who was screaming in fear. One of the shadows protected Masira, the other went to the wave above her, and seemed to crush it with one dark hand.

"What the fuck," said Butler.

Victoria's analytical and high-speed mind tried to process this. Amos only stared at the screen for a time and looked upstairs where Masira slept. A deeper mystery had opened up more questions than answers for all of them, and the question Masira's origins had become, even more than before, deeper mystery than ever. What did those shadow things have to do with her, or perhaps, what did they want with Masira?

Amos' mind was dreading what he saw, God the horror. What were these things, and why did they bring Masira here? The better question was, were they protecting or harming her.

14

Amos showed the videos to Cathy and Katrina after they put the food away. They both had the same reaction he did, which would loosely translate to, "What the fuck."

"What are they?" asked Katrina, clutching at her legs upon her second viewing. There was horror in those eyes of theirs', horror and fear that came from gazing upon the other worldly things. These shadow things reminded her of Lovecraft creatures she had read about in old pulp magazines her father collected. Gazing upon unknown, cosmic horrors, and driving one to madness.

"Don't know," said Amos, his own thoughts surprisingly echoing Katrina's, "but I have my own crazy ideas."

"What?" asked Katrina with curiosity.

"It's crazy-sounding," said Amos, "but have you ever heard of Jinn?"

Both women shook their heads. Amos continued. "In Arabic myth, later picked up by Islam, but it goes there were three races created by God. First was that of light, angles. The second was man, made from earth. The third was those of fire, the Jinn. The myth was what Aladdin was loosely based on."

"What are they?" asked Cathy, "Like demons in Christian myth?"

"Yes, and no," explained Amos, "More like humans then Demons though. They have free will, so they can be both good or evil, or even neutral. I don't know much about the myths myself. They're like the Nephilim in Christianity. They are only mentioned a few times and rarely go into deep details. There's only one section dedicated to them in the Quran and a smattering of stories, but most of the stories of Jinn were pre-Islam."

"You seem to know a lot about Islamic myths," said Cathy, eyeing Amos with a newfound interest.

"College," Amos explained quickly, "Took a few courses."

"These look more like shadows than people of fire," observed Katrina.

"It's the only thing that came to my head," said Amos, "And even I don't believe it."

Cathy leaned her bulk back on the chair, resting her hands behind her head. "This girl gets stranger and stranger every minute that goes by. I mean I feel like we walked into a Goosebumps book, slowly burning to something we are not going to like. You know what, fuck Goosebumps, we are getting Lovecraftian up here."

"You don't know the half of it," said Amos, "Before Butler left, he explained to me that the blanket Masira was wrapped in….well, they couldn't identify the material. Can't tell what kind of animal it came from, or plant. Not even synthetic materials were a match."

They looked at each other. Curiouser and curiouser, like Alice exploring wonderland, the deeper they went, the more insane the situation was.

"So, what does this all mean?" asked Katrina, "the static, the shadow men, that….that wave, the blanket. What are we looking at?"

"I don't know," said Amos, "But don't you find it odd. A seven-day-old kid, missing, and not one hospital or parent reports. Yeah, true kids going missing every day, it's a sad fact of life, but a seven-day-old baby. And unless they took a plane, I cannot see a way they could have driven this far out, and just to drop a baby in a prison chapel. Now we find these shadow creatures seem to have dropped her off in the prison. Something isn't adding up here. And worse, what is adding up doesn't seem like it should be real."

Cathy looked up where Masira slept, and said, "I don't think it matters in the end. It is not our job to investigate like this, that is the police's job. We just have to make sure the child is well and protected until she gets fostered. I know this stuff is strange, but we can't waste time on Jinn shadow creatures and fears of the unknown. We have to do our job, which is protecting the child."

"What if these....these shadow things are hurting her?" asked Katrina, "You heard how she screamed that night, she was terrified. What if she was also in pain?"

There was a pause as the other two thought about it, but then Amos pointed out, "I'm not too sure they are hurting her. Think about it, they drop her off in a prison where she would surely have been found, and that one in her room....well, it seemed to me that it was protecting her."

"We don't know anything about them to make that call," pointed out Cathy, "As I said, all we can do is protect that kid before our guys in Marquette comes and picks her up."

There was a knock at the door. The three jumped, nobody expecting visitors. Amos' head turned to the door and his stomach dropped. Who was it? The three sat nervously, frightened at what could be on the other side. Visions of shadow men, reaching out with dark fingers plagued their minds, causing inaction, fearing for their and their charges safety. A second knock came, and they all started at each other, and Amos, stealing himself, stood, slowly walking to the door, his feet feeling like lead weights were on them. One step, two steps, each one made his feet feel heavier and heavier, until he reached the door handle. He reached a shaking hand out to it, and....turned the handle and let the door open.

In the door stood Iman Kamal. Instead of his traditional Iman clothing, he wore a button-up shirt and khaki pants. His thick beard and olive skin seemed to put him out of place, showing him to be foreign and an outsider of Belaphone. Stranger still, though from Iraqi and Jordanian descent, it was amazing how much he looked Amish right now, and Amos' mind imaged him in a straw hat and suspenders, and he had to hold in a laugh. Relief hit Amos like a battering ram, and, not realizing he had been holding his breath, gasped in relief with almost painful exultation.

"Imam," gasped Amos, breathing hard, "What are you doing here?"

"Came to talk to you," he said, "Your father hadn't heard from you in several days. Is all well?"

"Yeah...just, not the best time."

"Amos," said Kamal, calm but like a scolding parent, "Talk to me please, your father is worried sick."

"Oh God, it's only been a few days."

"Don't use his name like that," said Kamal sharply.

Amos sighed, looking at the guy with a mixture of annoyance and humility. He knew the Iman was probably here about the argument he had with his dad before he left from his last visit. The two hadn't said goodbye on the best terms, and neither had called each other. He also knew his dad had asked the Imam here for a reason but right now.... now....a thought entered Amos' head. He had a lot of questions that needed to be answered and he needed some ideas to help him take care of Masira, maybe the Iman could give him some clarity.

"Ok," Amos reached into his pocket and handed Kamal his apartment keys, "Just met me at my place. We'll talk there in a few hours."

Kamal nodded after Amos gave him the address and went to his car. He drove off slowly in the winter light. Why people insisted on driving hundreds of miles on icy roads, Amos had no idea. Then again, he did it all the time so who was he to judge.

Amos went back inside, and looked at the time, almost time to go home, but also almost time to check on Masira. He started up the stairs when Katrina caught up with him.

"Everything ok?" she asked.

"My Iman is here."

"Kamal, why?"

Amos shrugged though he had his theories. One was that he wanted him to talk to him about the fight he had with Abdual. Then another idea came to his head, and that odd feeling in his stomach came up as he spoke it.

"Don't know, hey you got this evening off?"

Katrina's eyes widened in surprise, but she also looked a little excited.

"Yeah."

"Want to come?"

Katrina's heart fluttered. Did he just….Oh my God….he did, he totally did, he……stop….stop it, you Goddamn brain.

"Yeah," she managed to croak, then, she managed to clear her voice, "Yeah, sure."

"Yeah, I'll pick up some pizza and we will head back after work."

Katrina nodded, but her heart was fluttering right now. She walked like on clouds. She only felt this way a few times. Once in middle school, when she was fourteen and was asked to dance by the captain of the football team. Another time in High School when she graduated. This was the third time.

Their shift ended two hours later, and Cathy waved goodbye to them as they headed out. Katrina's cloud walk continued after work and when they drove to the pizza place. Mancenes Party Store was the best and only place in town to get pizza. It was a small liquor mart in the square of Belaphone. But it made the real money in Pizza. The crust was not too thick or too thin, and the toppings were piled on. Amos ordered a large vegetarian, not being able to eat pepperoni or ham by the tenants of his faith, but he also ordered a small pepperoni and onion for Katrina.

As they waited, Amos showed Katrina a copy of the video again. The images of moving shadows were still haunting their memories. It was like a nightmare given form, or the images children saw at night, with shadows becoming horrific monsters at night, and the ones cast from the closet were like monsters with teeth. Or the ones from bookshelves become that of evil demons from hell coming to take you away from your mommy and daddy.

"God, that scares the shit out of me," Katrina said, "That isn't natural. Shadows aren't supposed to move like that."

She looked up into Amos' dark eyes, which also held fear for the shadows on the video. "Do you really think they are Jinn?"

"No," said Amos, shrugging as he said it, "But in truth that's the only thing I can think of. But that's just my way of thinking. You probably think they are demons."

"I don't know what they are," said Katrina, "I just hope they are not hurting Masira."

Amos nodded gravely. The pizzas were brought out in two pizza boxes and they got in their cars and headed to Amos' apartment.

They took separate cars. The snow was thick but the roads in the town were finally salted after the Christmas holiday. Amos pulled up in front of his building, and Katrina pulled up into his guest spot. They walked up, and Amos pulled out a spare key, and unlocked the building. They climbed the stairs and entered Amos' apartment.

Katrina looked around and saw a picture of Amos with an older man on a side table just in front of the fully opened door. It looked like Amos' father. Another pictured, that looked like it was taken during the late seventies or early eighties, showed a picture of a young, beautiful, Senegalese woman on a boat with a man who also looked similar to Amos, holding a bundle with a baby inside, a tuft of black hair poking out. Katrina assumed right that this was a picture of Amos' mother.

Amos heard sounds coming from the living room/dining room, and so went over to put the pizzas on the kitchen counter that acted as a border between the two areas. Amos saw the Iman sitting there, watching an episode of "One Day at a Time" on Netflix. Amos rolled his eyes. He really hoped this was a rerun and not the next season. He hadn't gotten to that yet.

Looking up at the pair, the Iman came forward and embraced Amos like a long-lost brother. Amos returned it, actually happy to see his old friend.

"As-Salaam-Alaikum brother Amos."

"Alaikum-As-Salaam brother," responded Amos as the hug was broken.

Kamal turned to Katrina, surprised but not displeased, and asked warmly, "And who is your charming friend?"

Katrina couldn't help but smile at this as Amos responded.

"My friend, Katrina."

Katrina smiled again, a warm welcoming smile, and held out a hand. Without hesitation, the Imam shook it. It was firm and warm, the grip saying, 'I have you, and will help you up, always.' Katrina smiled even wider. She liked the feeling of security the man gave her.

They set up the pizzas on the small dining table, and after pulling out some juice, they began to eat. The food was very tasty. Katrina loved her pepperoni, and the two men went to work at the larger veggie pizza. It paired well with the juice Amos had in the fridge. It was a pomegranate, his mother's favorite when she was alive. It always reminded Amos of her.

Amos was on his second slice when the Iman leaned forward and stated, "Amos, from what your father has told me, other than trying to marry you off, is that he hasn't heard from you in a few days and is getting worried. Everything ok?"

Amos highly doubted that was the only reason why the Iman was here. He sometimes went over a week without calling his father, and his father rarely called him. No something was up.... something.....'He is trying to marry you off.'

"Who is he trying to hook me up with?" asked Amos.

"Kalma," said Kamal with a smile, knowing Amos was embarrassed right now at this father's meddling in Amos' life, "I really should just get straight to the point."

Unknown to the men, Katrina's heart had just felt like it was being squeezed by a man with iron hands. She kept it together, but deep down, in that cold darkness of her heart she....well to be honest she wasn't sure what to do. Her head was in a haze. The thought of Amos getting...... Voices came and interrupted her thoughts.

"With all due respect to you and my father, Iman, I have been too busy with my work here to think of family obligations put on to me, with, may I remind you, without my consent. The girl we are taking care of here is taking up a great deal of my time."

"What is so important that you ignore a request from your father about marriage and Halah?" asked Kamal, still with a kind and humorous look, but also pointed out, "Amos you're in your late thirties, it is something you should start thinking about."

The TV was still playing in the background, a commercial for a new name fantasy game called "Etam Kingdom". It played with an eerie music that reminded Amos before a terrifying moment in a horror movie, or a great surprise of a jump scare that would end in something horrifying happening to the cast. His next words would decide what the tone of the music would lead to. An overall good ending, or a crushing ending that ended with no happiness for anyone.

Katrina watched as Amos pulled out his phone, and as it slid from the pocket, a light came on. On the screen was a picture that Katrina took when Amos held Masira in the sitting room. She had shown him the photo that night when she got inside. He had loved it and asked her to send it to his phone. And now, he showed the phone to Kamal who now viewed the special picture. Kamal looked at the picture, and a look of tenderness came over his face. Being a father himself, the picture brought memories of him holding his own child, seeing him so small and frail, and yet, watching him grow taller every year, he seemingly changed by the hour it seemed. He looked up at Amos and said, "Oh, Amos, she is so.....oh I don't know. She is just adorable."

"That's the girl found in the prison."

Kamal looked up and back down, and Katrina and Amos both knew what he was thinking. Who could do this to a baby? Children were a gift from God, a part of their mothers and fathers. How could one harm or discard such a great gift? It was something he couldn't fathom or understand about people, and each story of a harmed child or a kidnapping chipped away at him, hurting his very soul. He, Walawitz, and Kempt had each had to, once or twice in their career, console a grieving family who lost a child, or scold one who harmed a child. He remembered doing a funeral for a five-year-old who got run over by a car, and he was silent for almost a month after having done that, his wife spending that time holding him, bringing him slowly day by day back to himself. He hated it.

"There is something else," said Amos, interpreting the Imam's thoughts, and went back into his phone, and pulled up the videos of the moving shadows on his phone. Kamal's eyes filled with the same emotions as all who saw those two videos with Little Masira in it. They were filled with fear, no understanding, a great and powerful dread, leading into disbelief, for what he was seeing could not, no, cannot be real. Shadows don't move on their own.

"By the love of Allah, peace be upon him, what are those things? They are…my God. Amos, where did these come from?"

"From the cameras in the prison and the baby cam in the room."

Kamal looked at them for another moment, but then pulled out his phone.

"Please send them to me."

Amos did, and Kamal had watched them four times to accept what he saw. The cold hard shadows just…..they were unreal. He had read horror novels and watched many horror movies, but for Kamal, this was the first time his blood ran cold with fear.

"I would like to say they are Jinn, but, these…..these shadows, but God, these things, they cannot exist."

"I know the feeling my friend," said Amos, "You think you know what they are?"

"I don't want to guess," said Kamal, "But I will do research."

"So, not assuming they're some kind of cryptic creature?" asked Katrina.

"I don't want to guess," said Kamal again, "As a Muslim, I would want to say they are Jinn, but I would be biased via my beliefs.

However, there are myths and legends far older than my people, older than all the Abrahamic religions in fact, though most Christians, Jews, Muslims, Hindus, and others would deny this. Spirits and Demons that would match these creatures to a T. Every mythology has something like these creatures. Things in shadows that take children. I believe in the Quran, and thus, my mind goes there naturally. But a Zoroastrian would say it was something else, as would every other religious scholar, so I also have to look at all the facts, and the lack of them as well. We don't know what they are, but we all know that they have taken a special interest in the child."

A quiet moment followed, but the thoughts of the creatures were still on their minds. An hour later, Kamal stood, and Amos escorted him out. Kamal turned to Amos once he was out the door and said, "I'll tell your father you will think it over. Should keep him out of your hair for a bit. I should start heading home. It's late, but if I leave now, I can be home before my son has breakfast. I'll see what my research can bring up."

"Thanks," said Amos, embracing the Iman.

"I'll pray for the girl."

"Thanks," said Amos, again.

Kamal looked over Amos' shoulder at Katrina for a moment, and looked at Amos, not saying a word, but when he left, he had a small grin on his face, walking to his car, and saying to himself, "Well, I think that boy has a love for another on his mind."

Unknown they were observed for a second, Katrina helped Amos clean the dishes. She was oddly quiet, much on her mind. However, when the last dish was dried, she asked, "What is Halal?"

Amos was surprised, and said, "Well, their kind of laws that Muslims obey. They differ slightly via region, but in general…."

"They involve marriage?" she asked, her voice quiet.

Amos felt himself grow hot, but, he continued, "Well, yeah. Many Muslim marriages are arranged via Islamic law. But Halal law isn't like USA law. Halal is more about cultural preservation. Here in America, Halal helps Muslims keep in touch with their culture and lets them live as both Americans and Muslims. And arranged marriages are more of first-generation Muslim's style. Most native-born Muslims marry like most people in America. We date. We cohabitate, and we experience, and we mix. I know several Muslims who married outside their religions. One was a Muslim man who married a Catholic. Another was a Muslim woman who married an Evangelical."

Katrina's heart lighted after that. "So, you're not interested in arranged marriages?"

Amos chuckled, "Nah, just my dad."

"Your culture can be strange sometimes."

"Sometimes it can be isolating."

"I know how that feels."

"What do you mean?"

"Amos, I'm half black, half Native American. You think I am fully accepted in Belaphone anymore than you?"

Amos never thought about it that way. He always saw Katrina as beautiful, kind, some who….stop it Amos.

"Yeah, guess we are in the same boat."

Katrina grinned, then a text went off. She checked it.

"New arrival at Belaphone home. The girls are being picked up by their aunt, and some kid named Sam was just brought in. Mom was sent to Grisham."

"Oh, ahhh, you want me to come?"

"I'm fine," said Katrina with a smile, "You have a good night."

"You too."

As she left, Amos didn't miss her smile, and Amos felt that swooping feeling in his stomach.

15

ANTHONY FINALLY SAT WITH TOM. Their meeting had been delayed until after Christmas. Both had family obligations of the usual kind during Christmas, time with the kids, presents, dinner with the wife, and Christmas Night Mass. Now they were there at dinner. The same diner, but thankfully, were served by a far different waitress. A young woman, college-age, blonde, soft on the eyes, wide waist, and high breast. College girl. Tom and Anthony were drooling over her.

While she smiled and put up with their drooling orders, as she got to the counter with those orders, she put the order on the computer, she muttered to her older colleague, "What creeps. Well, I won't hit them if they give me a big tip."

Oblivious to her secret conversation to the staff, the patrons waited on their food, each one in the back of their minds imaging the girl in lusting positions.

"So," asked Tom, sipping at his cola, "what you have for me?"

"A miracle, here in Belaphone, which, if we play it right, can raise attendance at the House of the Lord, as well as all churches across the UP we are associated with."

Tom leaned back with interest. Catholicism wasn't the dominant religion in the Upper Peninsula, that honor went to the Protestants, but it was the dominant religion in Leon County. Of the over two billion Christians in the world, the majority were Catholic, and Protestants were left trying to convert those leftover. Then again, as Anthony often said, better Catholic than those Goddamn Muslims, Hindus, Sikhs, or Buddhists. Terroristic Asian bastards a lot of them. They were all the Goddamn same, like those on 911. The country should kick their terroristic asses out of this grand, Christian nation as foreseen by the founders of the United States.

In the time it took for their food to come out, Tom, a burger, Anthony soup and salad, to go through everything he heard and witnessed. The baby was found in the prison, her staying in Belaphone Home until the roads were better, and everything he saw while he spied on it.

The food came out, and Tom picked up his burger and chewed slowly, like a food critic trying to describe what he was tasting. Anthony was on the bridge of his seat, not yet daring to touch his food, which sat there, the soup steaming, and the salad covered in ranch.

When he swallowed the mix of bread, meat, cheese, and vegetables, he looked at Anthony, and said, "Ok, so, they found a girl inside a prison chapel. Sounds like a Stephen King or Clive Barker novel in the works to me. But what does any of this have to do with saving your church?"

"Don't you see?" explained Anthony, in the voice he used to move people to find the true spirit of God, "She was in a Chapel. All will see it. The Chapel is a sanctuary and the girl just appeared there. It's a sign of a miracle."

"Prison Chapels are neutral in religions," explained Tom, "Muslims, Wiccans, Jews, hell, any religion can use them."

"But they are meant to reflect a Christian church," said Anthony, "And I looked in the papers and the internet. So far, this has been kept quiet for over a week. But if we get on top of it right now, I'm telling you, we can spin this as God's great work, and the masses will flock at our doors."

Tom took another bite. He chewed for a full minute, then swallowed, and said, very slowly, and non-committedly, "It's possible.

But, Anthony, this could also blow up in our faces if not handled delicately, and we need to inform the commission."

Anthony inwardly shuttered. The commission was a council of Christian Protestant Leaders across the U.P. It had a lot of sways over churches across this fine land. Anthony had tried for years to get a place on the council. He never got voted in. He blamed Obi, the head of the commission. He was a black man, and Anthony hated that it was led by him. It should be led by a pure man, a white man. But Anthony knew Tom wouldn't go against him, so instead of complaining that a damn black face, a spineless bastard was in their way, Anthony put on his kind mask, and explained.

"I have a member of my folk who works at The Belaphone Gazette," explained Anthony, "And he has friends in Marquette Mining Journal. I'm telling you, if we play this right, we can spin it to get more in our churches and spread the word of Jesus more effectively."

Tom rubbed the top of his head with the palm of his hand. Finally, he said the words that Anthony wanted to hear.

"I'll call the commission. Call your friends. We will need to get this out before anyone else does. You know the other churches outside our council will want to use this as well, so we need to spin it carefully. The girl would help as well. Where is she staying? Belaphone Home, right? It would help a lot if we get a good picture of her. Maybe you can visit."

Anthony stood and shook his friend's hand, smiling like a child who just got the biggest piece of chocolate in his life. Sitting back down, he finally attacked his food.

However, deep in the bottom of his soul, he felt another twinge of joy. But this joy was darker, more evil, and not of him. It was a separate thing, a thing that terrified him, but also, he felt would save his church.

16

THE IMAM DROVE HOME, WHAT he saw still on his mind. Normally, he would rest after such a long trip, but after seeing what he saw on the phone, Iman knew that he won't be able to, not til much later. Such horrors. He remembered a similar feeling after reading a story by Lovecraft, "Nyarlathotep", and the fear that the story invoked in his mind. Those shadow creatures gave him the same feeling.

After thanking his disciple for the hospitality, and driving off, that fear continued to hit his mind. He was able to distract himself by playing the Sick Puppies song "Going Down," and speculating the relationship he saw brewing between Amos and Katrina. While he believed they were not conscious of it, he had seen the long looks they gave to each other as he shut the door, watching as the two began to talk a second before it was closed off to him. He saw the smile though, the shared smile. The kind that he shared with his wife in their private moments, where he wasn't an Imam, but her husband and her lover. He smiled. Many religious leaders didn't allow mixed religious marriages, but Kamal believed they should mix to build a stronger foundation. He knew many Muslim men and women who intermarried with people of the Christian, Jewish, Sikhs, and other religions and have long, productive relationships. These interfaith unions were surprisingly productive, as it was common for both parties to still retain their faith and yet still commit to each other. Kemed, an Egyptian who immigrated to Milwaukie about forty years ago now, when he was only eighteen, had been a hardline Muslim, who believed that there were only Allah's and Muhammad's words and no others, fell in love with a Catholic woman. The woman, named Anna, didn't convert, but supported the mosque her husband attended, and he would go with her to church every Sunday to help support church events. This mix proved to Kamal that interfaith unions did fit in with Allah's vision. Don't hate your enemies and replace hate with something better and make them your friends.

He arrived at Walalwitz Synagogue at four in the afternoon. He did manage to get home, join his family for breakfast, take a nap, and tell his wife he was going out for a bit, then arrive at the Synagogue. It was a large structure with a blue dome roof, with large white wood doors, which he pushed and then he walked inside. The area reminded Kamal of Christian churches, but the front dais held the podium and on it, the Torah. He had been to many chanting and found them interesting. He called in the vast room, and the rabbi heard him, and he and Kempt came out. It was ironic how much Walalwits reminded Kamal of Santa Claus, even with that Yakama on his head. Kempt mixed features looked at his friend with worry, seeing the slowly fading expression of horror on his face.

"What's wrong?" he asked, grabbing his friend's hand, and leading him to the bench at the front row.

Kamal explained everything he saw and showed them the video that was equally terrifying to them as it was to all who had seen it so far. For a while, they said nothing, needing to process the girl, the shadows, and horror they saw, the screams, everything. It was like an extreme nightmare they were living, almost as visual as an Edger Allen Poe story, his word creating visions of fear in their heads, filling them with dread, and endless anxiety, darkening this house of God and all it stood for, and replacing it with Eldredge horrors. The visions were so vivid, they all shuttered involuntarily.

"So, this girl," said Kempt finally, "She just appears in the Chapel in Grisham Correctional?"

"So, it seems, and these…. these shadows, they appear when the camera's go fuzzy." Kamal shuddered at the faith of this poor child. Where does this dear come from, a question on so many people's mine and yet is not yielding any answers.

Walalwitz was oddly silent. His usual chatty self was sitting like an old teacher after work, thinking over all that was to be said at tomorrow's lecture, and countering points established beforehand. He pulled off his Yakama, put it on his knee, and rubbed his eyes.

"What is it?" asked Kamal, knowing these were signs of Walalwitz having an idea in a certain topic.

"Nothing, just….just," he paused, took a breath and continued, "thinking of a story that I was told long ago. The man of Taured. Ever heard of it?"

The Imam and the priest looked at the rabbi, looks of confusion and interest on their faces. Walalwitz sighs and says, "One of my members, Benjamin, he told me this story. The story goes that in Japan, a man on a business trip was traveling to meet with a company for investment opportunities. However, when he arrived, the man's passport said he was from the Principality of Taured. Everything, his passport, license and even his checkbook confirmed this, everything."

"I've never heard of a country called Taured," said Kempt, thinking it over in his head.

"That is because there isn't one," said Walalwitz, "Nowhere on this earth is there is a country called Taured. Anyways, the authorities tell him to point on a map where his country is. He pointed to the nation of Andorra. It's a country between Spain and France, so small you can't see it on globes without a magnifying glass. Anyway, seeing that it had a different name, this caused the man great distress, so the Japanese authorities took him to a hotel, as for that moment, they were not sure what to do. The next day he, and all his documentation were gone. He just vanished. The security officers guarding the door never saw him leave. The window wasn't broken or opened. The man was just gone. Nobody has seen him since."

They looked at each other, and Kamal shuddered. He never drank a drop of alcohol in his life, not even in college, but by God, he felt he needed one. They were entering the realm of the supernatural, and in religion, that was a dangerous path to go down. It felt like snakes slithering down his spine, the stories and thoughts clouding in his head with thoughts of Jinn and Vampires, the predators of humanity.

"Sounds like that man and this girl came out of an alternative earth novel," muttered Kempt with a frown, his hand unconsciously fingering his cross.

Walalwitz looked at him, and asked, almost incredulity, "You don't believe in the supernatural, in our line of work?"

"I believe in the divine," said Kempt.

"Which involves Angels, men with wings, fiery demons, golems, Jinn, and who knows what else beyond human intelligence."

"It was created by God," said Kempt, pointedly.

Walalwitz looked at Kamal, and he and Kempt silently agreed to stop for now. Their friend was still upset. Then Walalwitz said, "Let's have that conversation over breakfast tomorrow."

Kempt nodded, stood as he said, "Where is this child now?"

"Belaphone, in Michigan."

"I will pray for her tonight."

"I will too," said Walalwitz, "But may I ask your reasons?"

"I have a feeling she is on a rough road ahead."

"Well, then I will pray for her to have a sweet life full of flowers and wonder. Think that's what girls like. Don't know, I had two sons, so I'm not familiar with what girls like."

Kempt shrugged and said, "Don't look at me, I ain't got no kid."

They both looked at Kamal and said, "I only have a son, but I have been told that daughters have wondered about them that their sons lack."

The three men nodded, but they had no idea how right Kamal was going to be.

Amos was up. He went to work to find Cathy talking to the new fifteen-year-old kid with a bad attitude, and authority issues and a leather jacket, and imminently was brought down two pegs by Cathy. It was Amos' night to work the night shift, and already caught the boy, whose name was Sammy, trying to sneak into the fridge. He babbled and complained, but Amos sent him packing to his room. Now he was just sitting at the table, looking at YouTube on his phone.

He didn't know why, but he soon brought up the video of the Shadow creatures. He viewed it several times. He saw, faintly, that the creature's humanoid look made them even more terrifying and its familiar visage clutched at Amos' heart. God, he wished he still smoked, like he did in High School, for this was so serious. The more he viewed it, the more he wanted to fling his phone away. But he didn't, he needed to know if Masira was in danger, what was sleeping in her crib with her. Day after tomorrow she would be going to Marquette, the twenty-ninth of December, and that made him hope she would be free of the creatures, the literal nightmares that were stalking her. Still, he was going to miss her. She had brought him so much light, and happiness, that it would hurt his heart to see her go. But until they picked her up, he was going to be working more night shifts.

There was a knock at the door, and Amos went to the spy hole. It was Katrina, and when he saw her, his mouth dropped, opening the door to get a better look.

Katrina was a beautiful woman in general, but right now, she looked like a knockout. She wore a sleeveless, black, tube top, with shorts, cut jeans, and high heels under her long winter Jacket. Her dark hair was curlier than usual, and her makeup was light but only highlighted her natural beauty.

"Hey," she said, "Thought you could use the company."

She held up a six-pack. It was O'Douls and Amos smiled.

"Butler told you?"

"Yep," she said with a smile, "When you last went to Mosque."

Amos invited her in. In truth, the coffee was hurting his stomach, and while he wasn't sure about O'Douls alcohol content, he needed something new in his stomach other than black coffee.

Katrina opened two bottles, and they started to drink. The cold liquid felt good. He wasn't sure if it was better than coffee's acidity, but God felt good. He was glad Kamal was back home. He didn't know what he would say about Amos drinking beer, even the non-alcoholic variety. Still, he was home, and Amos took a moment to enjoy the social norms of most Americans. Drinking a beer with a friend. A very, very attractive, hot friend, who wasn't wearing a bra and her nipples were erect due to the cold she just escaped from and....by Allah, he and his hormones right now, he felt like a teenager.

"How is Masira?" asked Katrina, smiling, and leaning back with her legs crossed. Another wave of heat hit Amos, and this wasn't coffee heat, the beer having longed killed it.

"Sleeping," he managed, "But I am worried about her. She has been through a hell of a lot, stuff that no child should go through."

"Amos," said Katrina, putting a hand on his forearm, and he swore his dark skin was on fire, "She is alright. She is going to be alright."

Amos lifted his bottle and gulped down more of the beer, in the hope to cool the heat building inside of him.

"How..ah, how is it going for you, Kat," stammered Amos.

"I'm ok," she smiled, "Just worried about you. You've been sleeping?"

"When I can," said Amos.

She began to rub his forearm and Amos prayed to Allah that he did not screw this up. What he was screwing up, he didn't know yet, just that he didn't want to screw it up.

"Amos, are you really thinking about arranging marriage at all?"

"No," said Amos, his voice low, "I am not. Thinking of another woman in fact."

"Who," asked Katrina, her voice also lowering, and leaning forward on the table.

"She is here right now," Amos' voice was almost a whisper, and his body leaned forward almost on instinct. It was almost animalistic but had some forethought in it.

They slowly lean forward. Closer, and closer. They were on automatic, and couldn't stop, like a river current.

"Kat?"

"Yes."

"I think this is happening."

"It is."

Their lips touched, and it was soft and tender. It was the first kiss. An experimental kiss. And it felt right, it felt good. Their lips slid across each other, full of soft passion. It was the right thing, and Amos felt it for it felt right, almost like something just locked into place. This kiss was meant to happen. This was.....

A scream came from upstairs, and Amos and Katrina broke their kiss. It was a scream of fear, of terror, that of a baby waking up from a nightmare.

"Masira!" yelled Amos, and he and Katrina ran upstairs to her room. Amos slammed the door open. What he saw, it made him almost lose his mind. He saw a shadow move, and then, it melted into the wall, and Masira was screaming. Amos went in, and picked up the child, and said, "Shhhhh, it's ok, it's ok. I'm here baby, I'm here."

Katrina came in too and put a hand on the child and together she and Amos calmed the baby and each other. What the Hell was going on? Then the two adults felt it. The cold, the cold coming through like a knife. It surrounded them, chilling them to the bone. It felt like their blood turned to ice water. It was in the air, it was inside of them, unwanted as a rapist. Then, one on the ceiling and one on the floor, two beings appeared. The shadowy apparitions of the creatures seen in the video, more terrifying in person than in the video. They appeared only 2-D, but they seemed to interact with the 3-dimensional world, reaching out, touching, feelings. Then the voices came. Loud but its tone was that of a whisper, coming from the walls, the ceiling, the floor, vibrating in their skulls.

"Get out. Get out."

Amos struggled to think. For a moment, he felt frozen to the ground, replacing the heat caused by Katrina. But then the voice came, seeming to help him unlock and began to move.

"Take her far from here," they said, "The serpent flees, but the other can still sense it. Take her far from here."

Amos ran downstairs, with Katrina, and they made it to the kitchen, a dark shadow appeared out of nowhere, and Amos quickly turned on a light and saw….and saw…..

"Sam!" he yelled.

Sam looked up from the fridge, a half-finished sandwich in his hand. "Ahhhhh," said the boy stupidly, "Is this your?"

"Get out!" yelled Katrina.

"Oh," the boy noticed Katrina, and started to flex his nonexistent arm muscles, "Hello mami."

Amos grabbed the boy by the arm and pulled him out of the kitchen.

"Hey," he moaned, like a child half his age, "I was eating."

"I see you in here one more time, I swear I'm going to make you clean every inch of this kitchen!"

"My mom didn't make me do chores."

"Well, start in the bathroom."

"It's like two in the morning."

"Then you have time to earn your food after you're done."

Amos went into a cupboard and pulled out a spray bottle of tile cleaner, cloths, and a brush, stuffing them into Sam's arm, who looked terrified, "Go."

"You can't….."

"He can," snapped a voice that made Sam jump. It was Cathy, looking like an angry hippo right now in a bathrobe, looking pissed and as if she just woke up.

Fear on his face, the boy ran upstairs, and a door slammed. She looked at her two employees, and asked, "What is going on? And

Katrina, why did you dress like a stripper? That stuff can't protect you from the cold."

"Cathy, we need to see the camera," Amos told her quickly, and then Cathy saw the bundle.

Cathy's eyes narrowed at the two of them, but then Amos' words came into her skull.

"Come on."

They got her room, and on the computer, brought up the camera. Five minutes into the film, they saw it. The grainy static. Under it, cold creatures of darkness, moving around, terrifying a baby girl and her guardians.

17

BUTLER AND VICTORIA MEANWHILE WERE burning the midnight oil. Only the night shift desk operators and one officer were on now, and only one out of the two of them were in the office right now.

Butler was going over his notes with her, and she attacked them like a harpy, trying to find a reasonable explanation of how shadows move on their own, refusing to believe in fairytales as she put it. She looked at electromagnetic levels, storms in the area, atmospheric disturbances, Solar flares. Nothing. Nothing. God damn, good for nothing, nothing.

Butler rubbed his closed eyes, and almost said "Hallelujah" when the phone rang. He snatched it up.

"Hello."

"It's Rash."

A new wakefulness hit him when he heard the Indian Doctor, and he sat straighter, Victoria not missing the change in posture.

"Doc, how is it going?"

"There have been some developments in the blood work."

Butler reached over his cluttered desk and pulled out Masira... titled Jane Doe's medical report.

"I got the medical report...."

"It is not in the medical reports, and I won't lie, what I found, it disturbs me."

"I'm all ears Doc. Hang on, I'm going to put you on speaker. Got an FBI agent investigating as well."

There was a long pause until Butler put the phone on speaker, then Rash said, "Very well. Hello agent...."

"Victoria Wilson."

"Agent Wilson. Nice to meet you. Well, putting it bluntly, in the blood samples, I found trace elements in the girl's blood that, well, don't exist."

The two law enforcement agents looked up.

"What does that mean?" asked Victoria.

"Depends on what you mean. In a biological stance, trace elements come from our diet, you know, iron and zinc for example, but from a chemistry standpoint, all humans have very small amounts of elements that come from the environment. The girl's biological elements are normal, but some of the chemical ones are, well, not on the periodic table. I discovered at least ten new elements. This development is baffling."

"Forgive me, doctor," said Victoria with a smile of, can you believe this guy, "But are you saying that our girl is from Krypton or something?"

"Sarcasm aside, Agent Wilson, I am not saying that. Her DNA and blood work are clearly human. What I'm saying is what I found in her blood samples, isn't found on Earth, or at least hasn't been discovered."

"Thanks, Doc," said Butler, seeing Victoria's eyes widen, "As always, owe you one."

"Good day, deputy Butler. I'll email you the results."

The line went dead, and Butler stood, started to walk outside.

"Where are you going?" yelled Victoria after him.

"To make a phone call."

He was outside and dialed Warden Sisko. He answered on the fifth ring.

"Hey Warden, it's Deputy Butler."

"Deputy, what can I do for you?"

"Wanted to ask a favor."

Butler asked it, and a long pause followed.

"Don't know, Butler, that's a tall order."

"Come on man, you owe me from the last golf game. We will call it even."

Another long pause. That was a lot of money he owed Butler.

"Ok, tomorrow afternoon ok?"

"Sounds good."

"Ok see you there."

The cell phone went dead, until a second later when it started ringing again. Amos.

"Yo," said Butler.

"Butler, it happened again," said Amos, his voice frantic.

"What happened?" asked Butler, concerned.

"The shadows, they….they came back. This time even more active."

Butler's eyes widened in realization, only taking the time to say, "I'll be there as soon as I can, don't move."

Before heading in, Butler shot a quick text to Jamie and ran inside. Victoria stood and asked, "Where are you going?"

"Belaphone house."

"Send a deputy," she snapped, "We have too much to do."

He whirls on her and snapped, "I am going personally, and calling two of my fellow deputies in from Hardhome. You can either follow, or get out of my ass, and stay here and look for grains of sand. I'm going right now!"

Victoria was shocked as he turned. A second later, she stood as well. Victoria did follow behind in her rented car, following the deputy car, which was soon joined by another. They parked in front of Belaphone house about ten minutes later. Two deputies, one older man built like an ox and one woman in her twenties, came flying out and joined their fellow deputy, Victoria trailed behind them.

Butler knocked on the door, and it opened. Cathy was there in a pink bathrobe. Butler heard a baby crying behind her.

"Thank God," said Cathy, letting them pass her bulk. The four officers came in.

"Terry, Franky, look upstairs in the baby room," said Butler, "Cathy, show me the…." And then in the kitchen, he saw Amos. Amos had shadows under his eyes, darker than his ebony skin, holding a softly crying baby, who was holding him around his neck, Amos slowly rocking to calm her. Katrina was in the kitchen, making a bottle. Both looked like they saw some Eldredge abomination, and judging by their faces, they most likely had.

"You ok?" asked Butler.

The two adults gave non-committal shrugs. In short, yeah, not sure. Butler didn't know what they saw, but what it was, well, it shook their souls.

"I'll be back as soon as I see the video."

He did and saw what he expected. Static. In an hour, he hoped, that would change.

Butler came back down and saw Victoria making coffee. Amos and Katrina, Amos holding Masira, had thankful looks as the coffee began to brew. Butler, for the first time, saw genuine kindness in the FBI agent's looks, as well as concern. It was the first, well, human expressions he saw on her face.

"What did you see?" asked Butler, sitting down next to his friend.

Amos and Katrina slowly explained what they saw, felt, and eventually heard in the room. The descriptions made him shutter, and even Victoria gave them looks of wonder.

"Call Jamie?" asked Amos

"Yeah."

"Let's wait for her."

They did, in silence, for an hour. Nothing was said, no chit chat, no friendly banter. None were in the mood for it. It was just pure, pregnant, silence. The tension was built, for what needed to be talked about couldn't be talked about, and yet, it burned in all of them, like a fire, and if not released, it would consume them.

The door received a soft knock and all six of them in the kitchen, including the baby, jumped, causing another, but short round of crying.

Butler and Amos were the first to rise, but as Amos was still holding Masira, relented the task of opening the door to Butler, but all had relief. Soon, soon something would happen to help clear the air. The thing that needed to be talked about would soon come to light.

The door's handle twisted under Butler's grip, and it opened. Jamie stood there, her bald head, thin, attractive, shapely body, and glasses, with leather jacket and skirt, between two deputies, with a look that said, 'Please don't arrest me.'

"Let her in," snapped Butler, and the Deputies stood aside, "and for the love of Jesus, go back to the squad car to warm up."

The Deputies were grateful for the reprieve and walked back to the squad car. Jamie eyed everyone nervously, and Amos handed Masira off to Katrina. She held her with tender care and love.

He and Butler escorted Jamie upstairs, who's eyes were moving so fast that they appeared to blur. When they got to the computer, her face went from nervousness to outright annoyance.

"That's it? The whole network is operated through that?"

"What?" asked Amos, "We are a shelter, not NASA."

Jamie went to the computer and pulled the equipment out of her bags, plastic devices with a lot of wiring, and chained them together and plugged them into the computer, reminding Amos of the ship in "The Matrix," with wires everywhere.

She brought up the videos and began typing commands, and within a period of fifteen minutes, the static cleared.

"Jesus," murmured Butler.

"By the prophet, peace be upon him," said Amos, whispering it so not to be overheard.

The image of the shadow creatures came back, and while Amos had been witnessed to most, he missed the first three seconds. They were around the crib, on the ceilings, and walls, like Peter Pan's shadow, and above the crib, a soft cloud, like a dark mist was above it, less than a foot, but it reached for the baby. The shadows defended her, pushing the whips back to their origin point. At the end of it, Jamie rewind, and began fiddling again. They waited and a minute later everything was green, but the shadows were purple, and above them, where the mist was, there was….well, a portal. A breach. One of the Shadow people came to it, and closed it with its hands, but looked as if it was struggling to do so. Finally, it closed, and then Amos and Katrina charged in. Amos shutter, being now an outside observer to his own life, and viewing the perspective of the outsider was more unsettling than someone then actually witnessing it.

"The fuck?" asked Butler.

"I saw those things on the last videos this morning," explained Jamie, "Now I know I am not crazy."

Butler turned and started walking away. Amos followed.

"Where are you going?" asked Amos.

"The prison. I need to see something."

"What?"

"You saw what was in that video. My guys are going to sweep the room. I'm going to prison. We were there for hours, but there has got to be something. It's where we found her, so there just has to be something."

"I'm going to," said Amos, defiant.

Butler looked at him, "Amos, I can't. This is an official police business, and I'm going to federal prison. I won't be allowed to…."

"Masira is in danger, and I need to find a way to protect her. It's my duty as her guardian, so you get me into that prison or by God, I will do it myself."

Butler was silent for a moment, but then nodded. "Ok, but you do exactly what I say, got it?"

Amos nodded.

Butler sent a text to his wife, another late night. He wasn't going to make it home again and told her to give his daughter a kiss from him. He then asked Victoria to supervise the search of the room. She nodded, having seen the video, and went outside to get the deputies. Butler sent them a text as well, and they imminently obeyed her. He and Amos jumped in the car and took off into the night.

18

THE SAME NIGHT, ANTHONY AND Tom were at Giovanni's, one of the best restaurants in Leon County, Michigan. Located in Hardhome, serving Italian style home cooking, its bottom was brick, and around the doors and on the second floor was red paneling. The inside was comfortable, its food, artistic, rustic, and filling all in one. The burrata caprese was to die for. The gnocchi, almost too beautiful to eat, only to be the best in both flavor and textures. The salads, amazing. The soups, all classical. The wine, almost too perfect with each meal.

Six men and one woman sat in the dining room with Anthony and Tom. The Protestant Commission. Four whites, two blacks, and one Latino sat in the room. They were a coalition of churches in Leon, Newberry, Marquette, Houghton, Iron, and Ontonagon counties, Michigan. They were, save for Anthony, richer than sin, their collections worth more than some celebrities, well, those in Michigan at least, nowhere near LA levels.

They sat, ordered, and chatted. Anthony was silent, answering questions when they came, but his mind went back to the dream... the serpent...Apophis. The only thing he could find on Apophis was a dark, serpent God of ancient Egypt. But what about the second serpent. Another serpent of corruption, like the one that corrupted Eve in Eden, and this was the second. Were revelations coming? In revelations, it was said a dragon would come, but weren't the words serpent and dragon interchangeable, intertwine. And how did this girl play? Was she the second mother? The whore of Babylon? Could Belaphone be Babylon or New Jerusalem? 'God give me answers.' What was this girl, what is her destiny?

"My brothers and sister," said one of the black men, a tall preacher from Hardhome named Obi, formerly from Mississippi. Called the Great Kenobi by his congregation, Obi Gerald was a Lutheran Minister, which some in the council were surprised to learn when he joined up. He was well versed and incredibly wise in scripture. When he spoke, all eyes were drawn to him, and his commanding presence was almost at king levels. Anthony hated him. This black man shouldn't hold that much power. Descendants of slaves, wasn't it clear to the others that he and his kind were dragging down America. Didn't people see that it was people like him, the blacks, the Arabs, the Orientals, the Latinos, and the Natives who were responsible for the degeneration of America. But the power of his words was like electricity, and nobody, not even Anthony could deny it, "I love starting a business with a fine meal and a fine wine, and so I would like to call this council meeting to order."

The oldest man, an Anglican Preacher, sipped some wine and said, "Agreed." He was Hamish, a former Amish Bishop, but he and his wife left that church after they had their first child and went to Toronto for a time. He came back and built a church based around Anglican teachings. He was considered to be the wisest of the council.

Megan, a Calvinist, and a severe-looking woman, looked over at Tom and asked, "So, what is this about Tom?"

Tom stood and started talking. "My fellow preachers, priests, and teachers of Jesus Christ, I have gathered us here to hear the Words of Anthony Dean, who may have found true proof of a miracle of God."

Anthony stood, and gave a small bow. All eyes were upon him. He felt the power of God in those eyes. Let them hope that they use that power well and see the light and.....and then he realized what he had seen, and knew what to say.

"My brothers, and sister, I stand before you, a humble man of the Lord, to tell you a story. Over a week ago, a child was found in Grisham's Correctional, locked inside the Chapel. She was found by the Guards and am now staying at Belaphone Home."

"Praise is given," exclaimed Obi, "Hallelujah."

Anthony was indignant of being interrupted, and even more so Megan, head of the Calvinist Bible Church in Houghton spoke next. Women, learn your place.

"Was the Mother found?" asked Megan, "I can't say I blame her for hiding her child, but a prison is no place for a baby."

"None of the women there gave birth to her," explained Anthony, stretching the words as far as he could, "She just appeared, it seems from thin air."

The group looked at each other. Now he had them.

"It in itself is proof of a miracle and God's work. This baby came from the church, a literal child of the church."

Hamish leaned forward, forearms on the table. "With all due respect, Anthony, the Chapels in the Prison are designed to be neutral, to allow all spiritual practices within the Chapel, and it's not just Christian practices."

"Then the other part of my story will sway you away from your flawed thinking. I saw the coming of Revelations, and the coming of the dragon. I was in hell, and I heard the voice of the beast. The second serpent is coming for this girl. He comes. I believe this girl is the Woman of the Apocalypse, for foretold in Revelations."

There was silence in the room. Then Sam, of the Stand-Up Church in Newberry, leaned forward and asked, "And what evidence do you have to back up these claims."

"'Behold, I have set before you an open door, which no one is able to shut. I know that you have but little power, and yet you have kept my word and have not denied my name.' Revelation, three-eight. A door from heaven has opened and the first has walked through it. This girl, the child."

"I read nowhere that baby girl would appear in a prison," said Megan with a small smile of humor.

"Yes, but there are two women said to come during that time," explained Anthony, as if speaking to a slow child, "The second virgin, and the whore of Babylon. I do not know which is she, but I know....I know she is a sign of the end times. We, my brothers and sister, must take this child in the church and prepare for the coming apocalypse, for soon, the chosen will be brought to the kingdom of heaven, the nonbelievers left behind."

There was silence, and Anthony swore they felt the holy spirit around themselves as he did, and certainty of Jesus' return. Tom just stared, mouth agape, for this was not what they talked about earlier.

Then the laughter, first coming from Obi, then, more and more, it spread to the others. The men and the one woman were all chuckling. Obi stood, and waved down the waiter, who nodded, and began to type up the checks.

"The end times, all because a girl was found in a prison, and a dream. Tell me, Anthony, how much did you have to drink and how desperate are you?"

Anthony's mouth opened. "How could you be so blind?"

"You want to use this girl as a beacon, a tool of the lord. That is God's call, not ours. How could you even think about this? Using a girl like that before she can even think for herself. The Commission forbids using child preachers, and that's what you want to use this kid for. A Preacher. That thought sickness made me take away the girl's choice at such an early age."

Sam spoke next. "This organization stands against child preachers. They have been proven to do more harm than good, especially to the child. And you're talking about taking in a baby and using her as a prop. We got Coronavirus overseas, and we have more tension in this country than ever. All this would do is divide us more than help us. You think this is an original on your part? And you think Muslims and Jews can't make the same claim, not to mention the other Christian Sects. This will do nothing but harm."

"Do us a favor," said Megan, as she and the others stood, snickering, and giving Anthony dirty looks "Lay off the booze and leave the child alone."

Anthony was a dumb struck. How could they be so blind, as they slowly stood to pay their bills, and take their leave. In a minute, only Tom, Anthony, and…..and Hamish were left. He was the only one who didn't take his bill, and asked, "I like some coffee please."

The waitress nodded and went to make a pot. For a long time, he was silent, but said, "I have over two hundred people who come to my church. They are always looking for a sign. I think you gave me something I can give them. You sure you can sell this to the masses, you two?"

"What?……" started Tom.

"Yes," interrupted Anthony, "But why are you helping us?"

"Because Obi is a coward, and the others are fools."

The coffee was delivered, and he asked, "So, what is your plan?"

Amos and Butler arrived at the prison about a half-hour later, and the snow was falling again, fast, and thick. Road conditions would soon be undrivable again. About an hour or two. The clock turned to midnight, turning the twenty-eight into the twenty-ninth. They would have to move fast.

Butler's radio went off. It was from Belaphone PD, and the male voice over the radio waves started saying, "Calling all units. Calling all units. Do not, I repeat, do not leave the city unless it is an emergency. It's nasty out here boys, and I won't have anyone injured by the weather. Assist all government services to keep the roads clear. Sound off."

The radio squawked five times as the local officers and sheriff deputies on the line acknowledged the call. Afterward, they got out of the car and entered the prison. No others would be joining them tonight, or day, as dawn would be coming in an hour, or two, or three. God damn it, what time was it. So much happening in so little time. How, how did this all begin again? In a prison. Amos looked at it and thought. He lived in the real world, but often felt like a prisoner. He lived in a world which for almost twenty years, or what if felt like, in his lifetime, had vilified his religions, and for almost most of history, his skin color. When he was a child, he felt no fear of being a Muslim. In fact, he felt like most Americans had never even heard of it. But after the towers fell, it became a sigma. Then the wars, the news. He lost a friend, who, before then, didn't mind that he was Islamic. When he got to college, he didn't tell any but fellow Muslims. Only brothers and sisters who followed the path of Muhammad knew and many of them didn't admit it as well. Some of the women just threw away their Hijabs, and pretended it was not part of the various cultures they came from, even vilifying them, and though some were justified, many came from countries that were mostly peaceful. He was jealous of those who had the courage to say, "I am who I am, Fucking deal with it." They stood tall, even when put down and dragged in the mud. What kind of man should be afraid in his own home?

Then these thoughts went to Masira, and he realized she was a prisoner too, trapped in a world without a place to call home. A world without a mother or a father. The world had treated this girl so coldly, and she had done nothing to deserve it. Amos' fist clenched. He would be her rock if no others would stand. He would not let her be brought low as he was and show her how to stand tall. He would stand tall for her, the way he had to in this world where both the color of his skin and faith he practiced made the world turn its back on him. Until she left Belaphone home, he would stand tall for her.

Butler's feet crunched as he walked through the snow. Amos followed. A guard, a large one, stood and opened the door. He nodded at Deputy Butler. He didn't acknowledge Amos. Amos knew this guard well, and often heard him mutter, "Dirty nigger," under his breath when he passed. He heard it tonight as well, but he stayed calm and walked behind Butler, resisting the urge to punch the guard in the face.

They found the Warden, who nodded and said, "I am pushing wake up back an hour. You're lucky the ladies love to sleep in."

"Thanks, Sisko," said Butler, "We won't be long."

"Four hours, no more," nodded the Warden, then nodded at Amos, "What is he doing here? Wasn't told a civilian was…"

"I deputized him for the night," explained Butler, giving a little lie sense only the Sheriff could deputize, "Amos is helping."

The Warden shook his head, but let them in, and they followed him down the empty halls to the Chapel. It looked like a school auditorium, with rows of descending chairs heading towards a center raised dais. God damn, it was depressing.

They walked down hard carpet stairs to the center stage and Butler looked behind the pulpit. He moved his hand over the cheap laminated wood. His hand ran over the grain, feeling it, tracing the design in the wood.

"What are you doing?" asked Amos.

"Feeling for anything," said Butler, "hot, cold, I don't know."

"Why?"

"There has to be something. Something to explain what is going on."

An hour passed. Then two, then three. Nothing. Nothing to feel, nothing to say. Amos sat in a chair waiting. When hour four was almost upon them, Amos stood, and said, "Look, man, I don't know what you are looking for, but it's been days, what could you have missed?"

Butler had worked his way from the podium to the wooden stage, to the stairs, and only muttered back, "There has to be something."

The sun was starting to rise outside, though neither men knew it, save for their advancing tiredness. Amos' eyelids began to heavy. His head nodded, the cold is the only thing keeping him…..the cold. The cold that hit him like an underpowered train, hitting down to his bones. They were coming.

Amos stood, awakened, and shaken. The room was being warmed by the heater. There shouldn't be anything remotely cold in there. He looked around and saw Butler, stiff as a board, petrified with fear. He felt it. The cold. He picked up a phone and asked, "Warden. Is the chapel camera fuzzy again?"

Silence, then got an answer, which he gave to Amos in the form of a nod. "Thanks."

He hung up. He was joined by Amos, and the two went back to back. Their breath began to fog, and then, movement. The first flash. Out the corner of his eye, Amos couldn't make it out. He turned to it, and....nothing.

He saw another, but upon turning his head, nothing. Then, the flash, the flash of darkness. Amos took a step back. Butler's hand reached to a gun that was not there. And then it came clearly.

The thing clinged to the wall like a shadow and had a humanoid shape. It had no mouth, no nose, but its eye. Large circles they were, and the wall's tan pant coloring stared through them, the circles disconcerting in the light.

Another rustle, and the two men saw another on the ceiling, then a third, flat against the stairs.

Fear gripped the two men's hearts. These other worldly presents in front of them shook them to the core. It twisted their minds against what they perceived as the orderly universe. But then Masira came to their minds and helped them stand. Amos was breathing hard, as was Butler, but clearing his throat, Amos asked, "Who are you?"

For a moment, nothing, then another came. Then another. Then they talked. It was one voice, but it was the sound of many, neither male nor female. They spoke in echoey voices, close but far at the same time.

"We are watchers. We are listeners. We protect the portals. We prevent the worlds outside the worlds from touching."

"Huh," grunted Butler, his brain not fully functional at the sight of these dark things.

"The Serpent of the Dark Universe has touched your universe, a mere touch. But it has already caught the interest of the Serpent."

"What are you talking about?" asked Amos.

"The Seven Universes, each housing infinite possibilities and times. But each unique, surrounded by one of the seven serpents. They are watched by us, watched, and separated, but sometimes, they occasionally touch, and interest is brought. The portals here have attracted the Serpent of the Dark Universe. The girl came from there, and the Serpent seeks her like a moth to a flame."

This talk of another universe made both men stare, feeling like they were experiencing out of body events. Amos himself felt like his body was on autopilot, and he only was an observer in this material realm. And then something came to Amos' head. Could Masira be from....

"Why?" asked Butler, interrupting Amos' thoughts, "And what is this Serpent you speak of."

"It matters not."

Amos rolled his eyes. Such a stupid line. But then he spoke.

"The girl, she is not of this world, is she?"

"No, she was from a world in the Dark Universe. The Serpent sent her to the void, knowing we would find her. We took her to this world, to keep her safe, safe in the Midgard Universe."

"Ok, why can't she go back home?"

"The serpent can use her to find your serpent. If united, chaos will ensue, and will attract the others. The girl must stay in this world but be away from this region of this world and time."

Then the walls switch, to that of an endless forest, to a dark void, to a land of flowers, to a golden desert. So much landscape, familiar and alien. God, what was all this? Their world, other worlds, other planets, and version upon versions ongoing.

"We close the doors, not among the separate universe's own doors, but those that are between the serpent, and we stop them from finding each other."

"And if they do," asked Butler.

"It will be the end," said the shadows, simply.

"Oh."

"Send the girl, far away from here. We can stop the doors, but the Dark Serpent is getting more and more drawn to your Serpents' location."

"Wait," Amos interrupted, "Why are you telling us this now? Why wait so long?"

"The storms have calmed, now we must be ready for the next probe. Take her soon. The longer she stays in this area of the world, the more risk there is to your serpent, your universe, your world."

They disappeared, vanishing in the wall, ceiling, and stairs, melting away into the surfaces, and were gone.

Amos and Butler looked at each other, only noticing the heat about fifteen minutes later, and went out to go back to Belaphone.

19

It was a Monday summons for Sarah. Monday was a rare day off for her and she was not happy when she got the email from her church. Still, it was in the early morning, and since she worked the night shift, she figured she could spend an hour there with a large mug of coffee from Monique Mcall's Coffee, and still get plenty of sleep and go out with her friends for the night. Like all who worked nocturnally, she lived a life of boring afternoons and that of work. On these days she had off, she would dress up, drive to Houghton, go to Continental Fire Co., or the Downtowner Lounge and party until the sun rises. God, she needed the day shift, and a Goddamn social life that didn't revolve around drinking and ending up in Jackson's bed, or Perries'. Gods above, she was thirty and still partying like a teenager.

She entered the church and went to a pew in the rear. She hoped here that if she nodded off, she would not be caught. About seventy-five people answered the Preacher's call. Quite a turnout. Fewer and fewer were attending the church every Sunday, and Sarah felt it would get worse. She was considering leaving herself.

She saw the Preacher's family in front and thanked God for that. Meant this shindig would start soon. Which was good because the coffee wasn't working, and her eyelids felt like lead.

He did come, dressed in his Sunday best. A white button-up covered by a brown sport coat, with black slacks, and black loafers. He went to the pulpit and surveyed the crowd. He was like a master eater looking at the spoils of a Thanksgiving dinner. It made Sarah cringe slightly. Creepy guy sometimes.

Anthony spoked, and his voice was as rich as the Kings of old. He spoke with a power she felt he had lacked for some time.

"Brothers and sisters of Christ. Thank you for answering my call and that of the Lord, amen."

"Amen," the responses were soft and lacked feeling. It's been like this for months.

"I called you here, for I have witnessed a true miracle here in Belaphone Michigan."

Some of the crowd moved, but mainly it was the older folk. The old had witnessed many miracles. The day, the end of Vietnam, Martin Luther King, Gandhi. So many old heroes, so little time to go through them in this story, say thank you. For the young, a miracle nowadays was finding a charger for your Kindle or your IPHONE. Fuck, the ignorance of the youth was so sad now. Sarah, stop it, you're thirty years old. Stop lamenting.

"Let me not speak, but let the facts speak for themselves."

Two people stood, and from the two sides of the stage, they each pulled up a bundle of newspapers. Jesus, what's going on?

It took five minutes to get to Sarah, and she looked at the paper, and the headlines cured her of a lack of sleep.

'Child Found and Saved at the Chapel of Grisham's Correctional.'

Sarah started. Oh God, please God, no. Fuck, fuck, fuck. God damn it, why. Oh shit, she was so going to lose her job. If the Warden....she read on.

"On December 20th, 2019, a child was found in Grisham Correctional chapel. The child, now only a few days old, was found in the center of the Chapel's......" She read and learned more. She knew where this was going. It was not going to end well for her career. Better get ready to find another job.

"My brothers and sister, I believe Revelations are upon us," exclaimed Anthony, "My brothers, Tom and Hamish gather their flocks and prepare for the coming of the beast. It's our duty to bring this girl to the church and bless her. God had called us to bring this child to Christ and prepare for the second coming. I know this, for God has given me a vision, and I saw the dragon of Revelation, the second Serpent, coming to destroy mankind. I see it coming from hell to earth, and thus, we must be ready to be raised by Christ, and brought to heaven for judgment."

At first, Sarah thought she was safe when nobody responded, then, a chant came. It came slowly. "Miracle," it said. It started weak, but slowly got stronger, edged on by the Preacher. "Miracle. Miracle. Miracle." But there was a darkness Sarah had never felt before in there, a controlling, something that had slithered its way into the congregation, and was using it further its goals. The chanting, the praying, unknown to the rest had a dark undertone to it. Soon, the band played, people felt the holy spirit, and all Sarah could do was send a quick text to her boss. Too little too late.

Sisko sat filling out new transfer forms when he got the message. Looking at his old flip phone, his bored expression turned to horror when he saw the message.

"The Press Knows."

"Oh, shit," murmured Sisko, feeling his whole world crash around him. Quickly, he sent Deputy Butler a text.

Butler and Amos made it back to Belaphone Home around six am and there was a surprise waiting. The original plan was to just drop off Amos, whose car was there. However, another car was waiting. One Butler recognized. A green van, which he hated, but his wife insisted they got. They got inside, and were bombarded by the smell of eggs, turkey sausage, crispy hash browns, sausage gravy, biscuits, butter, and grits. Sheldon Butler smiled, and saw his wife bustling in the kitchen, Cathy gave her a grateful hand.

"Amanda," exclaimed Butler with a smile, "What brought...."

"Well, it's almost New Years," she said, with a pleasant smile, "and since you've been working late, and I would guess come back here first, I thought I would save you a drive and get you a real breakfast for a change before you got back to the office. Oh, and Sheala is here."

There was a squeal of excitement and a little girl came running out of the room. Sheala, Butler's autistic daughter, came running for him. He scooped her up in his arms and planted a kiss on her cheek.

"Hey, baby."

"Thought you forgot about me," she said, laughing as her father spun her around.

"I never can forget about you baby," said Butler, going in and kissing his wife, gratefully, "But thanks baby."

"We will leave after breakfast," Amanda said with a smile, "Going to my parents' house in Dodger Ville until New Year."

"I'll try and make it."

"You better try," she said, kissing him on the lips and going back to cooking.

"Where's Sam and Masira?" asked Amos to Cathy.

"Sam is upstairs, sleeping," explained Cathy, "and Katrina has Masira in my room. Breakfast isn't quite ready, but we have coffee if you need it."

Amos smiled and poured a cup. Then headed upstairs and saw Katrina with Masira in Cathy's room, the two sleeping in the middle of the bed, Masira snuggled against Katrina's breast. She just looked so peaceful. Actually, they both did. Amos sat on the end of the bed, putting his coffee mug on the table. He put a hand on Katrina's shoulder, and she felt warm. But the touch brought her slowly back to life, and, smiled, seeing Amos.

"Hi," she said, with a smile.

"Wa s-salam 'alaykumu," said Amos, with a grin. They leaned forward and shared a soft kiss. To a man who might happen to walk by, he would see a family, a beautiful one. The baby protected between them, and Amos and Katrina providing each other comfort. But this was far from the truth. The two had only begun their relationship.

The baby wasn't theirs. But at this moment, at this moment in time, it didn't matter. They were a family right now, together and happy.

"What happened?" she asked.

Amos took a deep breath and explained what he saw in the chapel. Katrina's dark eyes lit up in horror and wonder upon the descriptions of the encounter they had.

"So, they aren't Jinn or Demons?"

Amos shook his head.

"What are they, aliens, angels, something else?"

"Don't know," said Amos, "It's just, what they talked about, I don't understand half of it. I do know this; we have to move Masira away from here. She needs to go to Marquette, soon."

Katrina looked down at Masira. "And she is from a different world."

"Sounds like a different universe," said Amos, "Wasn't really clear on what they spoke of. All I know is we better get her out of here.

Katrina held little Masira close to her, the baby still snoozing. "I'm going to miss her Amos."

"As I will......"

"SON OF A BITCH!"

Amos and Katrina jumped slightly at Butler's cursing, both jumped up and ran downstairs, carefully leaving Masira on the bed before they did. Victoria was standing in the kitchen with the rest, and Butler was holding a newspaper in his hand, anger filling his face. "How, how the fuck.... fuck. Fuck."

Amanda was covering Sheala's ears as Butler swore, looking at the newspaper with daggers in his eyes.

"What's up?" asked Amos. Butler shoved the paper in Amos' face, who grabbed it, in fear that Butler may use it to break his nose. He saw the headline.

Amos' ebony face turned a lighter shade of brown as the blood drained from his head. He opened the paper. It was a short story, explaining the facts about Masira's discovery, and her stay at Belaphone house, but the interesting bit was at the end.

"Pastor Anthony Dean claims this child being found in the Chapel should be called the Miracle of Belaphone. Nothing like this has ever happened before in recent times, and Pastor Anthony Dean is claiming the child may be a child sent by God too ...."

"Who the fuck is Anthony Dean?" asked Cathy, fiercely.

"Some pastor who runs House of the Lord. It's a church located on the outskirts of this town," explained Butler, "He often called in to the local and state departments about susceptible illegals. Guy is an asshole."

"Mean man," said Sheala, breaking her parent's illusion's that covering the ears will protect one's child from profanity.

"We have him on the watch for being part of suspected white supremacy groups in Upper Michigan," explained Victoria, "but, he has caused little trouble over the years. The worst he has been is a couple of unpaid parking tickets and some shady business deals."

They all stared at her, and she said, "I looked him up before coming here when I saw the paper."

"Now what?" asked Katrina.

"Marquette should send someone today," explained Cathy, "Masira should be safe this afternoon."

"Sooner the better."

Butler turned to Amanda and said, "Sorry honey, but after breakfast, I like you and Sheala to head to your parents' house as soon as possible. Got a feeling stuff is going down."

"We will," said Amanda, but then said, "Frist you need a proper breakfast."

20

DAREK, A SOCIAL SERVICE AGENT from Marquette, drove down the street at a rate of sixty miles per hour, about twenty minutes outside of Belaphone. God, he hoped his pickup wasn't one of them retarded kids. He hated the retards. He didn't condone mass murder, just take warning labels off everything, and let natural selection do its thing. Get rid of all the retards.

The drive was slow. Jesus, there was nothing out here, why not got like eighty for most of the way. Jesus fucking Christ, why can't he go….well why not. No cops were around.

He put his foot on the gas and took off like a bat out of hell. He laughed with pleasure as he felt the speed of his vehicle press him lightly into the seat. God damn, it felt good.

"I got the power," he sang with the radio. He had it. He had it until he reached the outskirts of the small town, until….

There were twelve of them and a barricade made of four vans and two pickups, and he saw them dressed in winter clothing. His mouth opened and he saw a couple of the men with guns. Jesus, what the…. they were walking over, and Derek felt like he was in a horror movie where the crazy cult tore him limb from limb. His bladder almost let loose as they did so.

A large, bearded man with a red plaid shirt, looked at him, and all Derek could fully see was the large knife on his belt and the pistol in his hand.

"Where are you coming from, mister?" he asked, in an aggressive voice.

"Marquette," gulped Derek.

The man looked at Derek like a dog surveying a small mouse. "You look like a child fiddler."

Ok, to be fair, Darek, in the dark recesses in his apartment, and using his cell phone's camera he used to take pictures of the pretty girls at the facility so as to use them to masturbate to. Still, in their tight clothing, why wouldn't he. Still, best not to mention this. After all, it's not like he did use these girls to fulfill his sexual appetites physically.

"No, I work for social services."

"This road is closed, dude," said the man.

"Well, ummmm, if you know of another way through…"

"All the roads into Belaphone are blocked," snarled the man, and the rest of the group moved forward. They were barring on him, wolves on a lone sheep.

Out of fear, Derek reversed his car and drove off. The man lit a cigarette and muttered, "Fuckin' child molester."

"Where the fuck is that car?!" asked Amos, annoyed. That earned him several stares and that when he realized, it was the first time they had ever any of them had ever heard him swear. He felt kind of guilty about that. Allah help him.

But they were all on edge. The car from Marquette should have been there over two hours ago. Where the hell was it? And why was he so on edge? 'Well,' he thought, 'it's just me being paranoid. It would soon be over.'

Chief Benny Clive was Belaphone's Chief of Police. He was two hundred and eighty pounds of officer, with an overhanging belly, caused by a love of cheap beer, over-sugared coffee, and doughnuts. His blood pressure was high, he was on the tipping point of diabetes, and alcoholism was right down the corner. However, he always came into the office at seven am, and left at six pm, and had a remarkably successful department. His three other full-time officers that respected him, and his four reserve officers understood him as well.

Entering the station, he saw a tired June, a Korean American, originally from California, but moved out here to raise her daughter. Now, she was married, working the night shift this month, and tired. Two more hours until she was off, and the day shift was on, along with Moe who was on patrol, replaced by Steven and Dean.

"Hey June," said Benny, putting a black coffee from Biggby in front of her.

"Hey, chief."

"Any calls?"

"Not much, car crash took out a power line, but that's it. Came back up in a few hours."

"Good," said Benny, looking at the snow plowed streets, and he went into his office to look over reports. He did, for three hours. Then it was time for breakfast, with lots of eggs, bacon, and pancakes. He headed for the door. It was a tradition he had. Night shift guys, he always bought breakfast for. They worked the hardest, and so, deserved some extra help.

He walked and saw June still at her desk, with only one of the morning shift already here and....and no Steven.

"Hey, Dean," he stopped his officer, a young black kid who was on the day shift, "Where is Steven?"

"Said he had an early morning at his church."

"Probably on top of some drunk hooker as well," muttered June, rubbing her eyes.

A car pulled up, and a tired officer named Moe, the only currently active reserve officer in Belaphone, stumbled out of his car. He was called in after the debacle at the prison. He was tired as hell and gulping at coffee.

He got inside and yelled, "Where is Steven? He is supposed to take over patrol."

Clive Benny looked at the time. Nine, no ten o'clock. Ok, that can't be right. All his guys got to work ten minutes early. Often, they would take home the night shift guys so they could get some sleep without driving while tired. This was unusual. He looked over at the dispatch girl.

"Suesy, dear," he said to the dispatcher, "Can you call or text him?"

Suesy, whose real name was Susan, did so for officer Steven Shanks. Both went to voicemail. She did again three times, and still no answer. Finally, in order to avoid insanity, she said to Benny, "Nada chief, sorry. He isn't answering."

"Keep trying," said Benny, trying to sound unconcerned while thinking, 'Hope he is ok.'

Finally, an hour later, Benny said, "Ok, let's see if we can wrangle some more Reverse Deputies. Let's get these tired officers' homes. I'll drive them."

Grateful, they piled up in Benny's car and he dropped the night shift off. One at a house, the other at an apartment. They were grateful, their spouses, scornful, and the children, a mix of excitement to ambivalent.

He got back, and his officer still wasn't there. Concern, he called Steven's wife. She told him that he went to church early in the morning.

As Benny waited back in his office, Dean taking over patrols for now, Suesy walked in and said, sir, "Sir, have reports of roadblocks on the College Ave., Woodland, and Belaphone Canal Road."

"By whose orders?"

"Nobody by the looks of it. Happened just a little while ago. It was blocked by cars and trucks."

"Shit," snarled Benny, "Ok, get those reserve officers here, and hell, call the sheriff department again, now. We need back up. And keep trying Steven. I'm going to fire his ass if he isn't in the office in the next five minutes."

Suesy nodded and Chief Benny Clive sat down, and looked at the crawler on his desk, for the first time, not feeling like eating it.

Amos paced now. He had been for half an hour. They called Marquette, but they insisted that they were sending someone. God damn it, where the hell was the driver?

Then Butler's phone went off. He answered. "Yeah.... huh...ok, I'll go check it out sir. I'll be right over.....Yes sir, thank you." He hung up and sent a text.

"That's odd," he said, "A local officer is missing, and apparently the roads are blocked off."

"City order?" asked Katrina.

"Not that I have heard," said Butler, looking concerned, "Better get out and find out what's going on."

"Honey," admonishes Amanda, "You're dead tired, and you haven't slept in...."

"I got to know what's going on, honey, you just get to Dodger Ville. Take the backroads."

Butler leaned in, kissing her on the cheek.

"Ok baby," said Amanda.

Sheala ran to her father, her autistic mind not knowing trouble was brewing and said, "Love you daddy."

"Love you too baby."

They left, waving goodbye, five minutes after that, then Butler looked at Cathy and said, "I'll see if I get some back up here later."

"Thanks," Cathy smiled, "Amos, go upstairs and get some sleep. Kat, you're in charge."

The two nodded.

"I'll go with the Deputy," said Victoria with a smile. Oddly enough, it was not comforting, but they all nodded politely.

Amos did head upstairs, but he realized he missed prayers, twice. He looked to the sky and figured Allah would forgive him. He prayed quickly, and stripped his boxer, and fell into bed. He slept for six hours.

Butler had eaten breakfast and showered at Cathy's and changed at the station, suffering the Chief's whining, then took off. In his fresh sheriff deputy uniform and cowboy hat, he drove out to Low Woods Ave, Victoria joined him along with two deputies that were patrolling near the park. His Deputies drove out to the other two blocked roads, but he was getting reports from over the radio of crowds gathering near the churches across the city of Belaphone. Odd, for a Monday.

Butler drove to the edge of the city, where he saw the block. Several vehicles were sitting there, mostly vans, and a patrol car. It was Belaphone PD markings. So now they knew where the missing police officer was. The rest were civilians. About twelve of them. They were armed. Ok, this was different. Hunting rifles are common in Belephone, but there was a pistol too. A feeling of foreboding came over Butler. This wasn't good.

Butler got out of the car and walked forward, Victoria by his side, the two deputies behind them. Then he heard the voices. It was a big blonde dude, he came to Butler and the others.

"You've been ordered to clear the roads," said Deputy Butler, face set in a stoic determination, his eyes giving off a look of steel.

The other blond man blocking them said, "We are here on holy orders, you can't stop us."

Butler recognized him. "Steven, what the fuck man?"

Steven stood there, all six-foot blonde hair and blue eyes and said, "We must keep out the outsiders."

Butler was confused. "And who are the outsiders?"

"All those who don't see the end of days coming sir."

Butler felt a flashback to the prison. End of Days. End of everything. "Uhhhh, ok, what are you…?"

"Book of revelations sir," said Steven, and Butler noticed his badge, and the spare pistol on his hip, along with a pump-action shotgun. Oh shit. This was not the time to play the hero, as the cop and the public officer were planning, this was a time to pull back and rethink what was going on. This was reinforced by seeing the mix of weapons on the other people. Oh shit.

"Ok boys," said Butler, "Let's check with the town."

"But sir," said one the deputy, but he was silent with a look from Butler.

Butler got back with Victoria to his car and called a number. "Sheriff, Butler, I need some help. I suggest calling in the state police."

Sheriff Deshain of Leon County, and Butler's boss, who never liked calling in other law enforcement agencies asked, "What do you need?"

"Back up, a lot of it."

"Ummmm, Butler, what's going on in a Belaphone that you can't handle?"

"Something you can't believe."

Amos awoke with a touch of fingers on his back. They were Katrina's, who was smiling and said, "Here I come."

Amos chuckled, but felt where she was touching, and felt intense pleasure going through his body, and muttered, still only half awake and not sure if this was real, "I don't know if I like this."

"You are not supposed to."

Amos pulled her in, and kissed her hard on the mouth, pulling her into the bed, and under him. They kissed, softly, enjoying each other's company, laughing, and playing. They did not go further than that, but they did cuddle and take a well-needed nap. It was nice, almost making the darkness creeping in their minds just go away for a few sweet hours. Amos held her to him, and slowly stroked her hair as she fell asleep. When he finally slept, he dreamed of having a family and watching a child grow up.....up.....the dream shifted. Shadows began to move, and shift. One in the shape of a dragon, the other, a satyr. Thousand more, different shapes and sizes, coming stretching. Amos woke up, and saw he was back in the bedroom, Katrina still cuddling with him.

Amos felt her, resting on his chest, and he felt all their problems, everything, just melt away, both from dreams and reality. It had been, oh God, since graduate school, since he had last been with a woman like this, and further. Allah, almost ten years. The last time had been a girl from Spain that was studying at the university with him in a shared class, and the two got close during a study session. They even dated, though, Amos grew tired of her party lifestyle. She had been twenty-two, he twenty-six, nondrinker, and had only ever experimented with

147

cigarettes and weed. Amos walked the path of the prophet the best he could for most of his life, but there were time's where temptation had led him astray, due to feelings of doubt. But here with Katrina, there was no doubt, only an amazing feeling of love and closeness.

Today, with the help of her and his God, he handled a lot in a rather short amount of time. Upon seeing the shadow people, their message of doom if they didn't get Masira out of Belaphone, without them, Katrina and Masira, his mind would have shattered. They kept him whole, despite feeling like he was in a Stephen King or Neil Gaiman novel. He had loved growing up, but now he lived in the world of those author's characters, and it scared him, and often, as he remembered, the black man didn't survive long in those stories, at least in the movies. In the book, black men had better chances. What was it with film producers and killing the black man in horror movies? No brother, as his old pal AJ once said, would have done any of the shit that those crazy white folks did in those movies.

He then looked at Katrina, and felt safety and faith coming back to him, and felt the power come back to him. He got up after another hour, brushed his teeth, and got on a t-shirt and jeans he found in the bathroom, waiting for him. Before leaving, he put the blankets over Katrina, and kissed her on the cheek as she slept, but as he went to the door, another wave of tiredness rolled over him. He looked back at the bed. Ok, maybe another hour.

He climbed back into the bed, rolled over and soon was asleep, his mind drifting to the void of rest.

The dream came to him. He felt like he was leaving his body, floating into the clouds. But he didn't stop there. He moved passed the atmosphere, passed the stars, passed the galaxy, passed unnumbered galaxies until he seemed to reach a barrier, then like an octopus fitting between two rocks, he slipped passed the barrier into an endless void. There was nothing. No color, no description, nothing. Amos' heart filled with fear.

Then he saw it, like a looming universe before him. It was ahead. It was reptilian shaped, made of grey smoke. Its eyes were as blue and as vast as the ocean, and it looked at him. It was vast. Vaster than any horizon he ever saw and was unable to see where the head ended in this immense nothingness.

Then a voice. It was both chilling and warm at the same time. It rattles his very being and it spoke in a voice deeper than any ocean on his beautiful blue world he called Earth.

"So, you are the guardian."

Amos couldn't speak for a long time, lost in the vision that was before him. The thing was overbearing, and it hit his soul. Finally, he forced himself to speak, not realizing it was with his mind, not his mouth.

"Who are you?"

"I am the serpent of your world. Some called me the Midgard Serpent. In other worlds, I have other names that I call myself, brother Amos. The vastness of my being cannot be summed up by one title alone."

"How do you know me?"

"I am the guardian of this universe. I see all, know all, and I know you care for the girl from the dark universe. You were easy for me to find in my cosmos. Your heart shines brightly in this vastness held in my coils."

Amos' felt like he was being revealed slowly to himself, like an onion, his layers being peeled back to reveal himself, his true self.

"Why is she here?"

"I had the Watchers bring her in, for she was lost, and the Watchers needed to bring her somewhere safe. I offered that safety, though it put me at risk."

"What do you mean?"

The Serpent, the Midgard Serpent seemed to regard him, then said, "Once, in this void, I and the other serpents were one. We were alone. Traveling the endless void. Then the one above us, the one who made the first true life, brought the Watcher. They divided us and gave us matter. Through this matter, we created life. We created our universe, or perhaps it's more apt to say our multiverses, for that which is in our coils is endless and timeless, as we are."

Amos started, unable to believe, and asked, "Are you, Alllah?"

"No," the entity said, "Allah, Yahweh, Kooomotoa of the planet Vedu, Chewmia, Buddah, Jesus, they are all just beings in my coils, moving life as it is needed. Life, the life we see live and die, that is our blessing and curse. But the dark Serpent, Apophis, Ahriman, Nyarlathotep, Coomoko, Balamantha, and many other names of many other worlds, he wants to reunite us. He hates life. He used the child to make me act and tell the Watchers to bring her to me. She is a beacon. A weak one for now, but the longer she stays in where the barrier has weakened, in that place you call Belaphone, the risk becomes greater that the Dark Serpent will find her, and with her, me."

"What happens if he finds you?"

"We will unite. Then the other serpents will come. We cannot help but seek each other if this happens. You must stop the one he influenced. You must leave your place. Find another before Masira becomes too strong of a beacon."

Then, Amos saw her, Masira, wrapped in a blanket, resting comfortably in her little cocoon, seemingly floating before the Serpent.

"I brought her here because she has a great destiny. Her descendants are meant to save your world from the coming Green."

"Green? What is Green?"

"It matters not to you. It will happen after your life is but a forgotten flame. But she will be the catalyst of your salvation. Protect her Amos."

A light flashed before him, and Amos awoke, Katrina still on his arm. He never told anyone about what he saw. He also didn't know, or at least admit to himself, even on his deathbed, whether what he saw was real or not.

Butler watched the crowd, waiting for the state police back up to come. It had been six hours, and he watched, but no new movements came from the crowds, and he continued to block the roads. The other officers in the city were doing the same. For now, it was calm. And this made Butler even more worried. Where the hell was his back up? Damn it Deshain, you stubborn son of a bitch.

"Strange," Victoria was echoing his thoughts, "They're blocking the main roads, and yet making no move against anyone yet. They are even letting some people leave town. It's almost as if they are waiting for something."

"I don't get it either," said Butler, "If this was an attack or some kind of protest, there would be chaos in the streets. But Belaphone is not a major city. It's barely home to six hundred people year-round. Maybe goes up to about two thousand during summer and fall, but that's it. Not the profile for something like this to happen."

Victoria's eyes, wide, "Unless, this isn't an attack. It's a distraction."

Butler's brain activated, years of being a cop kicking in, "To hide their primary motivation."

"The paper," exclaimed Victoria, "They're going...."

"To Belaphone House," moaned Butler. He was an idiot, he should have realized, and he picked up the radio, barking, "All units all unit. Get to the Belaphone home, I repeat. Get to the Belaphone home."

"Sir we got people still blocking...."

"Don't matter," snapped Butler, "Get to Belaphone House, now."

Revving up the car, Butler took off, like a bat out of hell. He dialed Amos. He hoped he wasn't too late.

Amos came downstairs, with his step slow and somewhat heavy. The dream. That Goddamn dream. It was on his mind like a leech on his skin. Every step and sound brings him back to it. From the moment he slept to the moment he saw.... Katrina. The thought of her drove the serpent from his mind. He slept with her, holding her the whole time, and he realized something. She was the one. That was what he needed to bound down the stairs, a smile on his lips. It even helps him push thoughts of that smokey, cloud-like, grey Serpent. It put a bounce in his step. That Cathy didn't miss. "What got you all happy?"

Amos was about to say, "Well Cathy, it's just a lovely afternoon," when the words were taken away by the sight of a baby in her arms. Masira.

"Marquette still MIA?" asked Amos, using military slang he learned from an old marine friend he had.

"I called," explained Cathy, her face becoming that of annoyance of a situation that should have been resolved by now, "They said the driver should have been here hours ago. Don't know where he is. Fuck, Amos, I have no clue about what's going on. Today's been all levels of weird."

Amos nodded, and took Masira from Cathy, who smiled a joyous, toothless, grin at Amos, who responded with the smiling declaration of, "Hey baby girl, no bad shadows today, eh?"

Cathy laughed, tiredly, and Amos said, "You should get some sleep."

"I think I will," said Cathy, "Have you seen Kat?"

Remembering Katrina was asleep, and tucked in upstairs, Amos said, "I'll go get her, you wait right here."

Cathy nodded, grateful, and Amos trotted upstairs, Masira enjoying the movement with babyish giggles. God, she was already getting bigger, and it only been a short time when he met her.

Amos reached Katrina and shook her shoulder, gently. She awoke, and seeing the baby, pulled the covers down, revealing her pink sweater and jeans.

"Amos," she said, sharply, "what...?"

"It's Cathy, she needs sleep."

Katrina, realizing the time, quickly adjusted her clothing to make it less wrinkle, and said, when done, "I wish I could have showered."

"You smell nice," said Amos with a smile.

"I smell like you," giggled Katrina.

"That's why," said Amos.

She swung at his shoulder, but he caught her wrist and pulled her in, and they kissed. Amos knew they had a lot to talk about, she being Christian, and he being Islamic, but, he felt....he felt....he felt his phone buzzing.

"Crap," muttered Amos, "Hang on. Can you hold Masira."

"Sure."

Katrina took Masira and Amos picked up the phone. "What's up, Butler."

"Amos," Butler yelled, "Lock the doors until I get there. I'm two minutes out."

"What's going on?"

"I think you're going to have company. The roads that were blocked, Victoria and I think they were just a distraction. I think people are coming to Belaphone Home."

Amos' life just froze. He looked at Katrina, who saw something was wrong.

"Butler, you sure?"

"I'm positive."

"Butler, hurry up, man."

"On my way."

Amos hung up, and started downstairs, Katrina on his tail.

"Cathy," he yelled, "Lock the doors!"

"What's going on?" asked Cathy.

"Butler said we might be…." then he saw it from the front window. Hundreds of people were coming down the road leading to Belaphone Home. It looked like half the town. It was almost too late.

"Close the doors," yelled Amos.

Cathy and Katrina saw as well. The three ran to the main entrances. They got the front, back, side, and sliding doors. Then they locked and bolted all the lower windows. The crowd was coming closer and closer all the while.

Amos then saw a cop car screeching down the road, the opposite side of the marching crow. Its back end swung out, nearly spinning them out, but they managed to get control again, followed by two other patrol cruisers. They beat the crowd and unloaded in the driveway, and two other cop cars, one deputy and local, and four other officers joined Butler and Victoria. Butler gave orders, and two of the officers ran to the back and station themselves there. Butler, Victoria and the two other officers ran to the front door and Amos let the Deputies and FBI officers in. The door was locked three seconds later.

Then the crowd moved in, being led by a balding man with glasses. "Anthony," explained Victoria, and Butler took a picture of the man who was going to be trouble for them for the next few days.

Amos stared out of the window, angered and not sure what was going on. He looked over at Katrina, who was still holding Masira. They both nodded, both ready to fight and die for their child.

21

ANTHONY LED THE FLOCK FROM his church to the street, the lord's prayer going through his mind. Hamish's plan worked like a charm, but he was surprised how well his speech worked at the church. Honestly, coming out, it sounded to him like an actor giving a false motivation speech from a Christian movie. But it worked. Something worked, threw them, the power of the Lord, or....or something else. Something slithered in the congregation and now he had power over it like never before. And he liked it. He would purge America from sinners, and purge it of the unclean, the colors, whether black, tan, yellow, red, or whatever, and he would bring the USA under God, starting with Belaphone.

They gathered and stood in front of Belaphone house. four hundred from Belaphone, Big Rock, Fair Creek, Dodger Ville, Hardhome, and many other small towns in the Upper Peninsula Leon County area. Soon, as Hamish promised to throw his contacts, others would come to protect across both the upper and lower peninsula. They would come. They would come and help build the new Jerusalem and bring the wholly love of God here to Belaphone. They just needed to have the people inside bring out the child.

Then he saw the cars rushing at the other side, three police vehicles, pulling up to the driveway of Belaphone home, and six persons rushing to the house. Two went around back. Four went through the front.

It mattered not, for soon they would see the light of God, and step aside. 'This', he grimaced, 'was only a delaying action.'

They stood waiting, praying and singing in the background. Anthony turned, jester, and the crowd quieted. Again, that power slithered through the crowd, influencing them to listen to their most wholly leader. The power of this worship was almost physical, and he channeled that worship into the power of the one high above. But then, for just a moment, he felt something else from the house. It was a power. One like his, very similar, but different, less aggressive. He was about to turn, but something stopped him, and he shook his head, clearing his throat to cover for his momentary lapse. The power had hit him lightly, but it was noticeable, but he had a mission from God to complete. The darkness was coming, and the girl was needed.

"My brothers and sisters, I must go to the house, and retrieve the child, and bless her in the name of Christ. Today, the Revelation will start, and it starts here, in Belaphone, the new Jerusalem. Amen."

"Amen," the crowd echoed. Men and women raised their arms and hand in hope and jubilation of their trust in Christ.

Amos watched the fat man at the front of the crowd, talking and overheard the Amen they shouted to the sky. Then he saw him walking towards the house. Cathy looked troubled. Katrina looked scared. The officers looked ready to kill. Amos thought back to his karate lessons he got when he was just a kid. Don't kill, save in self-defense. Basically, for Amos it meant, don't pick a fight, and don't harm unless it's the last thing to do. He knew these lessons, so he also knew that he wasn't going to harm the fat man coming up, not unless he tried to harm Amos or anyone else, not least, Masira.

The fat man lumbered up, with the arrogance of righteous on his shoulder. Fucking prick. Too much pride, not enough down to earth thoughts. Amos stared. He did not know the man, but he felt mistrust and dislike for the man. He also sensed something, something

156

wrong. It was like a trick of the light, playing tricks on his eyes. For a moment, he felt a sort of dark force on the man, and swore he saw a shadow winding around him, starting from his ankle on his left side, and working its way through his crotch, up to his torso, across his chest, and neck and across his neck, the shape vaguely resembling a cobra. Amos blinked, and the vision was gone, but the dark force reminded Amos of the thing in his dreams, the thing he tried to forget. The creature was dark, but his vision of the creature he encountered in the dream was not light, but more grey, neutral, and caring. Victoria's voice interrupted his thoughts.

"That's Anthony," explained Victoria, "this wasn't part of his profile. He has an inflated ego, but poor social skills. His preaching skills shouldn't have done this."

"Well, he did," said Butler with hidden, but deep, satisfaction in his spirit at Victoria's inability to understand what was going on, "Now we have to deal with it."

The man walked closer. Amos' urge to protect grew, the spirit of Allah driving him to action, and to defend Masira, Katrina, everyone in the house, even Sam, who was sniveling in a corner. They didn't deserve this. He wouldn't let them be harmed. He stood as Anthony disappeared to the front door.

"Let me answer the door," Amos announced, making the rest stare at him, even Sam, who was so selfish, he made Caine look like a misunderstood brat when it came to his relationship with Able.

"No," responded Victoria, "We have to establish..."

"Yes," interrupted Cathy, "I don't want these bastards stopping our work. We need to keep the road clear. You're worried about our safety. I'm worried about my kids. If you have a problem with it, bitch, step aside, or I will roll you down. And I have enough rolls to do it with."

Victoria was jaw dropped in disbelief, but Butler, at this point, willing to try, stood, and said, "I'll be right behind you."

Amos nodded, and the two men walked to the front door, just as the doorbell rang. Amos looked through the peephole. Amos stood there looking at Anthony for a long moment, a small, curved spec, an enemy who was too much bust and not enough brains.

Amos opened the door. It was like in the horror movies of Alfred Hitchcock, where the door slowly opened for the grand reveal of the terror behind it. A terrible, unspeakable thing. A Poe horror, a Hitchcock dread, and so many others, and yet all those movies couldn't have prepared Amos for this. He saw the man as a snake, a cobra, ready to strike, but waiting for the flute to come closer and closer, luring the charmer until it was too late. But when the snake spoke, he spoke as a man of confidence, of true divinity, or so he thought.

"Hello sir," he said, a smile meant to light up worlds, but instead, for Amos, it bathed them in darkness, not knowing Anthony also sensed something from him. It was different from what he felt but similar. "A glorious day this is, peace be upon the Lord."

Amos looked over his shoulder. There were a few times he enjoyed embracing the Islamic side of him in public, but the African American side, oh boy, this was going to be so fun. It always brought these fools down to do a double-take.

"Bitch, what is this crazy nigga talking about?" asked Amos, in a higher than a normal voice, looking at a shocked Anthony, Amos smiling inwardly at the shaken look that Anthony gave now, unsure how to respond. For a white man, any use of the N word was provocative, and it was not a good weapon to use in arguing his case, no matter how much hate he had. But for Amos, it was a weapon, to off-balance Anthony, and Amos needed all the weapons he could get.

The man, now offset, shook his head, and said, "Ahh, sir, I wish to be able to come in and explain our intent. We mean you no harm. We come in peace and to bless the child."

"Fine with me," said Amos, and saw a look of overwhelming joy on the man's face. Amos looked over his shoulder and yelled, "Sam, it's for you."

"I got diarrhea," yelled Sam, scared as a deer in headlights.

"Oh shoot," said Amos, "Well don't look like he wants to come out."

Butler, hidden behind the door, had to put a hand over his mouth to stop himself from laughing. This can't be real. Victorian, in the other room, was ready to throttle Amos. Anthony, on the other hand, said, still with a smile on his face, "No, I'm afraid you misunderstand, sir. I am speaking of the girl."

"Oh," said Amos, "Well, I'm afraid you came at a bad time. You see, little Masira is fast asleep and won't be up for a while. Maybe later. I mean if it's not inconvenient for you."

Anthony had a look of frustration and annoyance on his face. Amos looked smug, but deep down, he thought he might have gone too far.

"Sir, I am here to perform a right that cannot be delayed, and if it is, it could...."

"Sorry bud," said Amos, "But I'm afraid she is sleeping. Please, come back tomorrow. Come on man, give it the night."

Anthony had a look of pure anger for a moment, but then relaxed and said, "My congregation will be here for the night. Tomorrow, we will talk."

"Breakfast is at seven," explained Amos, with a smile.

"See you then."

Anthony left, and Amos closed and bolted the door. Butler looked at him, a smile as wide as a banana on his face.

"That," he said, "Was both stupid and awesome."

Amos nodded. "We won round one. Let's get ready for round two."

22

ROUND TWO WOULDN'T COME FOR several hours, after midnight on the Thirtieth of December. It would take until seven in the morning. Until then, the visual stood in front of Belaphone Home, candles lighted, all in silent prayer, four hundred souls, praying for a girl who was in a situation against her will. She wouldn't want their prayers, even if she knew what prayers were. All she wanted was to be held by Amos and Katrina. She liked Cathy too, but she was too large and soft. Amos was hard, Katrina, light.

For Amos, it was a sleepless night in the baby room staying up with Butler and Victoria, who were in the living room, little Masira in his arms, Katrina, snoozing on his shoulder. For Sam, it was scary him, hidden under the blankets, not knowing what was going on. For the Deputies, the local cops, and the FBI agent, it was a watchful vigilance, with two awake at any time, patrolling all entrances. The rest of the department of Belaphone PD and the Sheriff office were keeping an eye on the crowd from the outside, having arrived about an hour later after Amos talked to Anthony. Some wanted actions, but most wanted this to end. For the Mayor, it was a feeling of uneasy as soon as he got the phone calls from the sheriff department and the papers in Marquette, Hardhome, Fair Creek, and Belaphone.

But for Liedy Diosa, a reporter from New York, she would be the only one happy in any way shape or form about the situation. Liedy was a reporter who originally worked for El Diario Nueva York. She was Dominican-American, and grew up in New York City, her mother supporting her with a food truck company ran by her and her second husband, Liedy's father being killed in a car accident a long time ago, selling Dominican food and drinks from those trucks throughout New York City. Soon, they were running a fleet of five trucks across Manhattan and Liedy was living a good life. Unlike her mother, she went to college at NYU, and became interested in Journalism. Soon, she got a good job at the El Diario Nueva York, a hot, Cuban boyfriend, and a son. Then the internet started to trump real world reporting, and she soon lost her job due to budget cuts. Her boyfriend left, she and her son were forced to move out of their apartment and Liedy had to work on the food trucks, moving back in with her mother for a time.

Then, two years, working the food trucks and failing to get back into journalism, she found an internet channel on YouTube that was being run by her former Haitian American editor, a man who was now in his fifties, George Mikey, who was making six digits every year when they met back up. Liedy went to meet George for dinner, and got to talking about his reporting style, as he went to the ground every day, going across the country, covering stories that affected America. He hired her, and she served as a secondary reporter, and her Dominican feature and curvy body and her deep, serious, down to the bone reporting, got her tens of millions of views every year. She ended up living full time with George, who, though older, was healthy and strong, became her lover and a father to her son, and a literal father to their daughter. Leidy was back on top and financially stable again to take a hell of a lot of vacations. This year was Belaphone Michigan for Christmas holiday, but they also went to Houghton and Marquette a lot. Her son, now sixteen, was looking at College, and asked Liedy if they could go to Michigan Technological University and, seeing it as a good spot to take a vacation, Liedy agreed. She and her daughter enjoyed the snow sports while her son checked out the college in Houghton during the day with George and later, NMU in Marquette.

Liedy was seven days into a nine-day Christmas-New Year's vacation in Belaphone. They choose this area because of the lovely camp lodges they had available at a small year round campground. It wasn't the most exciting vacation they had, but it was peaceful. That was until, after driving into town for some coffee, she noticed the main roads being blocked. Weird, but, as she had her four-year-old daughter with her, Liedy didn't want to investigate, though it gave her a bad omen. It wasn't until the four of them were at dinner at the local Diner when she saw the marchers.

"Weird," commented George as he saw them holding signs and crosses, "Is it a religious thing?"

Liedy watched them marching. She saw groups like this before, religious people protesting some law or right that didn't match their faith. But this was different. No chanting, just following an unseen leader. Well, this was different, and journalistic instincts kicked in, and she looked at George, who nodded, and said, "Might be a story."

Their daughter gave an innocent, confused look, while Liedy's son, used to this from his mom, said, "Hey, sis, when we get back to the cabin, you want to watch "Moana"?"

"Yay," screamed the girl, as she tackled her brother in the chest. So excited, the magic of movies. Liedy grinned, and nodded at George, who, now that their daughter was well distracted, stood, and took her to leave. She was very skilled at slipping out now, but she felt guilty for she loved her daughter, and hated sneaking away while she was distracted. But it was a story, and it was her job.

She walked into the town's center, a fur coat, and high heel boots clacking on snow-covered sidewalks. She walked a short way behind the crowd, marching like an army parade. She walked for fifteen minutes until they reached a subdivision. It looked normal until they reached a house, a large brick and white panel one with a sign in front of it that said "Belaphone Home."

Confusion hit her like a brick. Belaphone Home was a sort of way station for foster kids and orphans who were later taken to Marquette, getting them out of bad situations. She did a piece on it a long time ago, about three years. Pulling out her high end, digital camera, which was connected to her phone, she started to record, watching the crowd, and seeing three in deputy uniforms and one, a blonde woman in a professional suite, all running to the house, as if trying to protect it from the coming horde. Strange. Stranger, a black man with a thick beard, met them at the door. Progress, a black man trusted at a foster care center. Half-way house, sure, but not some place with kids. Real progress, even with the fascist fool in the oval office.

The one pudgy, balding man stepped forward, and she knew who he was. Anthony. She went to his church the first weekend she was here in Belaphone, and never again. In fact, from what she heard around town, most people tried to avoid him due to his views on race, religion, and women. She notices the women in the crowd, dressed in conservative clothing and lacking makeup. Liedy shook her head and looked down at her body. Though covered by a winter coat, her large breast and wide, curvy hips stood out from them, pushing against the cloth. She smiled, remembering the way George's eyes flick to them bound in a tank top in the warm car. She smiled wider at the memory. Women should be proud of their bodies, not have to conceal them away under heavy garments, well, at least when it was warm.

She watched Anthony knock on the door, and she moved through the crowd, though darker than a lot of these crackers, she moved unnoticed between them, and got close enough to listen, and hear something about….a child? A baby. What the hell?

She pulled out a phone and sent George a text. "Something happening at Belaphone Home. Something big."

Inside the house, Sam saw the Dominican woman standing behind the crowd, and turned away. God damn, she was so fine. That ass, so big, plump, and seems to go on forever. He started to get an erection, like he did when he saw Katrina, and felt another moment in the bathroom might be needed.

"Sam," snapped Cathy's voice that immediately killed his boner, and seeing her made him run as fast as he could upstairs. Cathy, kills joy. For the love of God, the woman actually made him do chores. Chore? Mother figures shouldn't make their sons do chores; God damn it. The only good thing about this woman, she made the best banana pancakes ever, with butter and maple syrup. Mmmmmm.

However, what Sam failed to realize, in fact all teenagers, boy, girl, trans, or whatever genders there were nowadays was that adults were teenagers once too. Adults know what teenagers thought, and what changes they are going through, so, when Cathy saw the lustful look on Sam's face, and the lovely, busty Latin woman outside, she quickly put two and two together, and put the brakes on it, no need for horny trouble teen on top of everything.

She would make banana pancakes though, for the fridge, freezer, and pantry were all full, and hygiene supplies.....supplies, when did she start thinking they were under siege? They were not under siege God damn it, they were in a house, her house. This wasn't a fort, this was a home, and those hundreds of people outside were ruining it for the children who needed homes. As long as they were there, she couldn't bring the lost souls here for the time being. God damn those people.

She felt like a mongoose, being wrapped by a giant cobra. Cobra. What made her think of snakes? God, she hated them, the thought of them wrapping themselves around her body, the thought sent chills down her spine.

When Sam ran upstairs, embarrassed, Cathy looked out, and saw hundreds of candles lighted, and some metal barrels stove fires burning, and people gathered for warmth. Dumb asses. Out in the cold, only a few fires for warmth. She almost took pity on them, wanting to bring them in for some hot coco. They followed an idiot and were manipulated pawns. Still, her Christian duty told her to take care of others, so she brought out the biggest pot she could find, and two gallons of whole milk, sugar, and a tin of cocoa. She put together the ingredients, and let them combine and cook in the pot, and yelled to Katrina to give her a hand real fast. Katrina did, wearing a robe and no socks, hearing her from the room she was sleeping in with Amos that night. It was Masira's room, and they slept on the floor together.

She helped Cathy bring the pot to the door, along with two officers. Putting it down for a moment, Cathy slowly opened the door and she and Katrina took the pot and a few stacks of strophes cups and put them on the porch. The two cops provided security, hands on their guns, ready to draw until the two women were done. They slammed and locked the door and went back to the window. Anthony came up, saw the pot, which was given to him by a deputy, and brought it to the crowd, who looked at it hungrily. Then, using both hands, Anthony turned the pot over, and poured it on the ground. The brown liquid melted the snow it landed on.

Cathy shook her head. Fools.

Liedy watched the pot being brought forward, and by this time, her lover had joined her, having hired a babysitter she and George met in hard Hardhome. The girl was from the country of Georgia, named Annika and was studying computer engineering at Northern Michigan University, in Leon County with a friend for the winter break. They met her during an interview performed by Liedy and George, and they had dinner with her multiple times over their vacation. Once, she even stayed for breakfast. Liedy's son had a hard-on for her, though she was twenty. Her daughter loved Annika.

It was getting interesting out here State police started to arrive, along with other officers from the Leon County Sheriff department, the crowd allowing them to set up a sort of human barrier around the house, knowing, though there were more protester then cops, to not mess with people who carry firearms. Fifteen patrol cars and even a command truck were brought in to monitor the situation, a State Police Captain taking charge.

George was now watching with Liedy from outside their van. A camera was in his hand, which was connected via Bluetooth to his iPhone. Using headphones, Liedy adjusted the sound, focusing on Anthony, who held up the pot that was given to him earlier by a Sheriff Deputy.

"My brothers and sisters. This pot came from those inside preventing us from performing our holy goal. You may see this as an act of kindness, but this is the fruit of the devil, for he prevents righteousness by disguising their evil in good deeds. Will you eat poison fruit?"

"No," yelled the voices, though Liedy sensed some disappointment in their voices. She rolled her eyes. This guy, Anthony, as much charm and charisma as a slug. Why were these idiots following him? It was like she always said to her daughter, never drink the Kool aid. She watched as he dumped the pot, and the brown liquid being tossed away with the same regret in his eyes he would have about throwing away shit.

She looked up at the house. For now, she had a story to figure out, but it was past midnight, and her daughter was asleep. George called an uber, and Liedy got in. George was going to get a few hours of sleep later and continue covering this story from the van. Liedy would go back to the cabin and hold her daughter for the night. Maybe Annika would help as well, with editing the story. She did have a good working ethic, and it was George trying to convince her to pursue a writing career after seeing some of Annika's poems.

23

THE DAWN WAS COMING. SOME slept that night. Amos was sleeping on an air mattress in Masira's room, not noticing he had drifted off around midnight, and Katrina, who had been sleeping next to him, heard him moan something that sounded like, "Serpent, why?" Thinking he was having a nightmare, she rolled over and held him, and in turn he held her in his sleep. But then she heard Cathy's call. She helped her with the coco, but after seeing it thrown away, she went back upstairs to join Amos, only to find him awake. Masira was in her crib in front of the bed, fast asleep, and Amos was watching her like a hawk.

When she entered, wearing a robe, the sound of the door getting Amos' attention, and when he saw her, all he could think was, 'God, she is beautiful.' She grabbed his hand and pulled him into the large walk-in closet. Then, she kissed him. He pulled her in and held her. He could also feel that she had no clothing underneath. God, he was tempted, but Masira was asleep in the other room, and he just felt weird about that, though he admitted to himself when they pulled apart, and the left side of the robe slipped down her shoulder, revealing a bit of flesh, that he would have if there wasn't a baby.

"Should get back to the baby," she said with a smile.

"I think she can survive one more kiss."

"Oh yeah."

"Yeah."

They kissed again.

They held each other, not noticing the van, the cops, the crowd outside. They only let go when little Masira woke up, and after sneaking off with one last kiss, they got out of the closet, and went to her small form, crying in the crib, then silencing and smiling when Amos cradled her in his arms. She smiled at Katrina as she readjusted her robe, and she smiled back. Few hours later, they headed down to breakfast where the deputies, Butler, Victoria, Sam, and Cathy were sitting around the very full table. Eggs, bacon, hash browns, banana pancakes, and hot coffee. God, Amos wanted some chai tea, but had to take what he could.

He took a little of everything, except for the bacon and began to eat. They were all silent as they ate, pretending not to notice the crowd. It was hard, with the feeling of being constricted was palpable. Victoria was on the phone, trying to get FBI hostage negotiators out here, but that would take a few hours to get together. Belaphone police had put up a barricade sometime in the night, with four officers, two deputies, and nine state police were using to defend the house. From the news and the outside officers, they learned the barriers blocking the roads were removed when the state police arrived, arresting all who were involved that day. They also knew that they haven't yet arrested anyone from the crowd yet because a few of them were high ranking people in Belaphone, Fair Creek, Dodger Ville, and even Hardhome, and it was a powder cake waiting to explode, and they had no wish to cause any more violence, and, in Amos' mind, in those places where dark thoughts were born, it helped that they were all white. Every last one. 'Where were they,' Amos thought, 'surely this wasn't America.' His father had told him stories of things like this happening in Senegal, but not here in America. This wasn't ever supposed to happen. Crowds gather here to make changes, not keep hostages, for that was what the people inside were in the end.

Butler's phone rang. He put it on speaker phone.

"Deputy Butler."

"Butler, four guys are out here, they want to talk."

A moment of silence. "Check them and keep an eye on them."

"You got it."

Butler hung up, and silence was oppressive for a time. A knock came. Round two. Amos, Victoria, and Butler all stood, and headed to the door.

"Wait," Victoria stopped them, and went to the window, unlocked it, and rolled it open a crack.

"We can talk through here."

Amos nodded, and Butler, this time, took the lead. He went to the window, and yelled, "Yo, can we help you?"

The group came forward, Anthony in front. Four men from the crowd all together. They looked cold, miserable, and...and mesmerized. Anthony looked like the only man who was not suffering and had his wits about him. He came up and said, "Blessing be upon you."

"Thanks," said Butler, "Mighty cold out there. Mind telling us what is going on and how we can help you?"

"We are here," began Anthony, his voice powerful, "To bring blessings upon the child inside. The child of the Chapel in Grisham Correctional, for she is a tool of the Lord, and will bring upon our salvation."

Butler shrugged, "Sounds fun. And then?"

"Then we must take the child. She must be taught how to perform her destiny."

"Uh huh, uh huh," breathed Butler, "Well sir, there is a process for adoption, so, if you head down to...."

"This is destiny," declared Anthony, "This is beyond that of man's own laws. Only God's rule will apply in this instance."

"Yeah," said Butler, "Ummmm, sir with all due respect, you can't just come to a foster care center and just demand that you take a child. Masira....."

"Who?"

"Masira, that's the girl's name, we are still trying to locate parents for her. That takes time. If not found then we have to start the process of....."

One of the men, a large one with a missing ear, came up to the window with such aggression, Butler had to step back, and pull out his gun, aiming at the man's face.

"You will not deny the will of our Lord," he yelled, "You will not..."

"David, back," snapped Anthony, seeing the gun.

Amos stood behind Butler and David and turned to look at Anthony. Amos yelled, "You're not getting your hands on her, period. Help is coming."

Anthony came close to the screen and said, "You have no idea what we are capable of."

"Nor you with us," said Victoria, "Pray we don't show you."

"Poor, Godless child," said Anthony, "You have no idea what is coming."

"You aren't coming in the house," said Butler, flatly.

"God will provide away, when the time is right."

He and his group turned and walked away.

On the other side of the street, Liedy looked at her tall, handsome lover, and asked, "Did you get all that?"

"Oh yeah," he said, "I think we got a story."

"Let's go through the papers," said Liedy, excitedly, "I can't believe our luck."

They got in their van and drove for the library, but were back soon, forgetting the library was closed for the holidays. So, they did the next best thing. The digital library.

24

AGENT MAKAVOY GOT THE CALL to drive to Belaphone, Michigan at three in the morning. Stationed in Wisconsin, Makavoy asked why he was going to Michigan. The FBI explained that where he was, he would be there in half the time as someone from the Michigan office. It wasn't until he reached the Upper Peninsula he understood why. Fifty-five miles per hour, bullshit, even in this snow driven hell he was driving on.

Makavoy served as a hostage negotiator for the Northern USA for almost twenty years. He was good at his job, as he was able to....well, he didn't know, feel his way through to the criminal mind. He could almost sense what they were genuinely wanting. Most of the time, his instincts were right, and ninety-nine percent of the time, everyone got out. But there was that one percent of the time, the Green Clover incident. That one time, he misread it. It was a man in a bar, holding the place up, wanting his children back, which had been taken by social services. So, using his instinct, he tried to feel his way to the man's mind. It failed and the perp and three hostages were killed.

Makavoy saw the barriers, and state police outside the subdivision, and was met by two burly cops. He liked the MSP officers, and found they were professionals, and in general, good cops. He got out of the car, and the cops came forward. Showing off badges, they shook hands and the cops briefed him. So far, no violence. That was good, so the plan now was to keep it that way.

He saw the crowd ten minutes later. He was shocked at the crowd around the house. This was the first time he could think of that the hostage holders were on the outside of the house instead of inside. They were holding signs and candles. The signs read things like "Christ comes again," or "The chosen Child of God."

Religion, great. Then he saw them, two in the background on the other side. It was a curvy Latin woman, and a black man, sand with cameras on tripods and in hand. Makavoy nodded to them. The woman saw him. While normally Makavoy avoided reports, this woman had seemed to have been here a while and might know something.

The two approached each other, and Makavoy, well he sensed a playful yet serious stance in the woman. He couldn't explain it fully, it was just something….strangely a mix of committed journalist, and a playful, sensual woman.

"Who are you?"

"Start with you," said Makavoy.

Instead of answering, Liedy pulled out a wallet from her jacket, and said, "Together?"

Finding this fair, they both open their wallets at the same time.

"FBI," nodded the woman.

"Liedy Diosa," nodded Makavoy, "From Liedy and George Reporting."

"Heard of me?"

"First rate reporting online, and stories are newspaper quality. I enjoyed reading your piece on the urban decay of Detroit and how it came to be used to support the tourist and movie industries to bring Detroit out of the red."

"I've heard of you too," said Liedy, "The Green Clover incident was a low point, but fuck, you're good."

"Can you tell me what's going on?"

"Something about a kid. Other than that, they haven't really moved. Been here all night."

"Who's leading them."

Liedy pointed, and he saw a balding, glasses-wearing man. "Anthony Dean, local preacher, but not very popular around here with most people. Seems to have some xenophobic and radical views that many don't like, even among other preachers. Seems like his congregation and the congregation of a few others around here. A few from a couple of other churches from around the state."

Regular people with jobs, holding up a house. This was a new one for the books.

"Sir," said another voice. Turning, Makavoy saw a man in a blue uniform and a captain rank on.

"Awe, captain," said Makavoy.

"Sir, if you follow me, we are about to make contact with the people inside."

Mackavoy nodded, and walked towards a large truck, only turning to see a disappointed Liedy, writing stuff down on her pad.

Amos heard the phone from downstairs, as Katrina did. Realizing something was going on, they changed, but Katrina was going to stay with Masira while Amos rushed downstairs. He reached the bottom and saw Butler on the phone. He nodded at Amos and continued talking.

"Yeah, there are nine of us, four deputies, one agent, three civilians, and two minors, one an infant..... We have service pistols and pepper spray..... Not clear, has to do with the infant.... No, no terms yet......"

Butler hung up and turned and said, "That was an FBI Agent. Someone named Mackavoy. A hostage negotiator."

Victoria looked excited. Amos frowned, not happy. It was official now, they were hostages.

Amos looked at the clock. Six-thirty, Anthony should be back rather soon.

But he wasn't back soon, not even at midnight, when the Thirtieth turned into the Thirty-first, and a heavy snow hit Wisconsin. Across Michigan, hell most of the world in general, New Year's Eve was being celebrated by fireworks and dancing people, even at that early hour. Children waited all day for the ball to drop, one of the few times they were allowed to stay up past midnight and take full advantage of it. But not for Belaphone, nor for Abulal was sitting in his chair, a second before the day change, groaning as he did so. He looked at his landline phone, thinking over whether he should call Amos or not. He looked at the time, and decided against it, though he still had a heavy heart from when Amos last left. He sighed, picked up a remote, and brought up YouTube on his tv, typing in Liedy and George. He loved that channel. Hard reporting, on the ground, hard facts, nobody did that anymore, and by Allah, Liedy had a rocking body. Though he knew Muslim women must be modest, thank God most Latin women were not. When he was younger, he took a vacation in the Dominican Republic. God, those bodies. If his wife knew his thoughts on the beach, she would have beaten him, but by word of God, it would have been worth it. He sometimes wished his late wife would have worn a bikini. She had the body, but they never got the chance. He hoped Amos was enjoying life as much as he did. It was at the heart of why he got so angry at Amos. Amos was in his late thirties, not young anymore, but still able to have a family. He wanted to introduce him to the new Lebanese family's eldest daughter. He had even arranged a lunch with the Imam when Amos got the call. It was a surprise for him. Abulal was going to tell him when Amos told him he had to leave, leaving Abulal embarrassed and not wanting to talk to Amos, but when he left, all the old man felt was shame at his actions. He later asked the Iman to talk to him, being too old to drive himself, but also not ready to admit to Amos his feelings of embarrassment over his son leaving. He looked over a picture of his wife then, as Liedy's page loaded, and, seeing this, said in French, "I'm sorry honey," then went back to the TV.

The title of a video title came up and made him pause. "Crowd Gathers in front of Belaphone Home."

Belaphone Home….but that is where Amos…..

He clicked on it. It was a live stream and Liedy stood in front of the camera, and behind her, a house. "No change, but as you can see, hundreds have been standing out here in the cold and snow all night, waiting on something yet unknown to us dear viewers, however, they…."

They're….in the widow, it was for a second, but Abulal knew his son. He saw him, there, oh God…Amos.

Abulal went for his landline phone and picked it up. Nothing but static. Phone lines must be down due to the weather. Damn it, why didn't he go buy a cell phone like Amos told him? The Imam…. the Imam would have one. He didn't live far away, in fact, only two blocks down.

Grabbing his boots and jacket, he walked from the apartment on top of his store, down to the bottom floor, and went out the back, locking the door behind him. The snow and wind were harsh on the bones of the old Senegalese man. God, why didn't he move to the south where it was warm. His boots sank into the snow, the white, wet stuff cling on and add weight. God fucking damn it, sorry God, but still.

He made it ten minutes later, swearing that his underwear was frozen to his crotch. He got to the front door of the small-town house, and knocked, and rang the doorbell. Two minutes later, the door opened, and a tired looking Kamal answered.

"Abulal?" asked Kamal in surprise, "What are you doing out in this weather?"

Abulal tried to speak, but his jaw would only chatter with cold.

"Come in, for the love of God," Kamal grabbed the old man by the arm, feeling how thin it felt, even threw the jacket, and helped the man out of his boots. He took him to the fireplace and sat him down. The man was shivering, and Kamal helped him out of his coat.

Aysha was dressed in a green robe over her pajamas, and saw the old man, shivering.

"What happened?"

"Got caught in the snow," explained Kamal for Abulal, "Please, make some tea."

Aysha nodded and went to work as Kamal pulled up a chair. "Abulal, what has happened?"

"Do you have a phone, a...uhhh...smartphone?"

Kamal pulled it out. "Bring up YouTube." He did, and Abulal brought up the video. Kamal watches, a look of concern on his face.

"Did you call Amos?" asked Kamal, his jaw slack.

"Phone is down, I couldn't...."

"I will call him," said Kamal as Aysha brought some tea. Kamal brought up Amos' number, and pressed the call icon. It began to ring.

Amos saw the call. The Iman, what the hell did he want? Amos answered.

"Hello."

"Amos, it's Iman Kamal, are you ok?"

Amos, for a moment, feeling like a caged rat, chose to say, "Yeah, everything is..."

"Bullshit."

Amos was shocked. He never heard the Iman swear before.

"You're on YouTube. A cameo production to be honest, but still, you're there. What the hell is going on outside Belaphone Home?"

Amos was shocked and asked the question, "What video?", so Kamal told him about the video on YouTube. As the live stream had ended some time ago, Amos was able to get to the portion with himself in the window, no problem, and his father must have seen it.

"Is my father there?"

"Yeah, right here, Amos." There was a moment of silence, then, in French, "Amos, you ok?"

"I'm fine, dad," responded Amos in kind.

"Son, what is going on?"

Amos bit his lip and told his father everything. There was a long period of silence, and then... "I'm going to be there first thing this morning."

Amos' stomach dropped, and Katrina noticed his face turned a lighter shade of brown. Butler looked and saw it as well in the reflection of the window, and his own eyes went wide.

"No, dad," snapped Amos, "There is nothing you can do. We got an army of cops outside protecting us, and your old rust bucket couldn't make the journey. Just stay…."

"No," yelled Abulal, Amos hearing him jumping to his feet, "I am coming and that is final. You do…."

"Dad," snapped Amos, in English, "You can't….."

"Don't tell me…."

Then the line sounds went quieter, and Amos heard two muffled voices over the speaker, when suddenly they both came into focus. Kamal had turned on the speaker phone.

"Amos," said Kamal, calmly, "I will drive with your father out there. He may be old, but he is still your father. Show respect."

"But what about the store?"

"We will handle that. Here is your father."

There was a clicking sound, and Abulal came back alone. "On my way son, I promise."

"Dad…" began Amos, but there was a tired, defeated sound in his voice that Abulal heard.

"Allah is with you son," said Abulal kindly, "Be strong, I will join you as soon as I can."

"Ok, dad."

"I love you."

"Love you too."

"Amos."

"Yeah."

"On your mother's grave, I am sorry for getting mad at you last time you were here. It was…."

"That's ok dad."

Their phones clicked off and Amos rubbed his head, finally noticing Butler pointing. Three men were walking towards the barrier.

The cops had their hands on their pistols, seeing a large megaphone in Anthony's hand.

"Where da fuck did he get that?" asked Amos, looking over at Masira in Cathy's arms.

"About to find out," said Butler as the megaphone was raised.

25

THE COILS OF THE FAITHFUL bound them in the cold. Bound by destiny and by God's will, the faithful stood outside the barrier around Belaphone Home. Others, not bound, but destined to observe this wholly activity had gathered as well. A Dominican woman and a Haitian man were watching, and soon would see that God didn't smile on them as they did the people out here. Officers of the law, standing on the side of the devil and not realizing it. Curious neighbors had poked around, men, women, and children. And the people inside the home. Anthony didn't like them at all, especially the black man. There was something off about the man. He wasn't Christian, that was for sure. What was he, what kind of infidel was he?

"Infidel," he snorted to himself, "That's what they call us, the followers of Christ. Now it's time to take back our birthright."

Anthony walked forward; a megaphone brought by one of his people in the police department was in hand. He raised, and like the voice of God, commanded all around to hear and obey it's called, like that of the prophets of old. Like how Moses led the Jews out of Egypt, or how Jesus called his disciples. He would be like Jesus, Anthony's own sacrifice perhaps eclipsing his.

"To the people inside Belaphone Home, you are hereby charged by God, bring the child before us so she can be Baptized in the Glory of God."

"Amen," yelled the crowd.

"Brothers and sisters, let us bring forth the lord's prayer."

Together, the crowd of hundreds bowed his head, and said, "Our Father, which art in heaven,

Hallowed be thy Name;

Thy kingdom come;

Thy will be done

in earth, as it is in heaven:

Give us this day our daily bread;

And forgive us our trespasses,

as we forgive them that trespass against us;

And lead us not into temptation,

But deliver us from evil:

For thine is the kingdom,

the power, and the glory,

For ever and ever.

Amen."

He turned back to the house, saw the black man, the deputy in the cowboy hat, a blonde woman that was another agent, and the fat woman who brought out the hot chocolate.

A voice, the voice of God, or something else, in his head, said, "The child, bring the child, and the glory of God will be revealed."

Raising the megaphone again, and said, "When Jesus told his disciples to walk across the water, the disciples failed, for they had no faith in him. Will you make the same mistake?"

"Not how I remember the story from the nuns," huffed Cathy, causing the others to laugh. Yeah, not exactly how the story went. Didn't Peter manage a few steps before falling in? Even Amos knew that.

Butler looked over and said, "Let him chant, don't change much."

"The failure to obey God is the greatest of man's sins and…"

"God," murmured Katrina, "That man loves the sound of his voice."

'Yes', thought, Liedy, listening to the religious rant, 'that man loved the sound of his voice.' She looked over at the command center van, wondering what the Feds and State boys were planning as the city and county boys secured the outside of the house.

"Hey Liedy," said George, and she turned to see him on the laptop, going through the comment section. Looking over, she saw various messages, but George had one highlighted and pointed at a comment sent about ten minutes ago.

"Is Amos ok?" it asked. Already responses were flowing in. "Amos, who is Amos?" "Is he inside?"

Liedy typed in a response.

"Who is this?"

Ten minutes later the responses came. "Abulal, Amos' father. My son is inside the home."

Liedy bit her lip, then typed in her business number. She would either regret this or have one hell of a story.

George looked at her and nodded his approval. Liedy pressed enter.

Kamal drove. It was seven am, but he had already got responses from the text he sent to Kempt and Walalwitz, and Mr. and Mrs. Kenesh, whose son agreed to run the store. Abulal then used the iPhone to continue to watch YouTube, using a login password to get full access.

'A password he's got, a cellphone he does not,' though Kamal to himself, not noticing Abulal struggling to type on the phone.

Twenty minutes later, they pulled up to a very nice subdivision, the kind with Christmas decorations out even after the holiday passed, and a festive jolly in the air for the coming new year. However, one colonial home that sat apart from the others. Where the others had red, white, green, and blue lights, this one had only blue lights. Where others had depictions of the birth of Christ, Santa, Rudolph, and Frosty the Snowman, it had a Star of David, a giant inflatable dreidel, and a depiction of the ten commandments. A man came out. A man with a thick, grey beard, a Yakima, and a dark suit. Abulal looked at the man and then looked at Kamal, who said, "Walalwitz."

Walalwitz opened the rear car door, and, after getting in said, "Shalom everybody, off to an adventure, are we?" His beard and natural smile made him look like Santa more than any man Kamal had seen before.

"Walalwitz, thanks for coming," said Kamal, while Abulal still had a confused look on his face, not understanding that the Rabbi was his Imam's friend. The Rabbi, unfazed, simply held out a hand to Abulal and said, "So, you're the man who Kamal said needed help. Rabbi Walalwitz is the name. Hero for the little guy is my game."

Abulal still shocked, still confused, but assured by the Zionist kind look and warm touch. Walalwitz looked at Kamal. "Kempt will be ready in a few, just drive to the church."

Kamal nodded, then asked, "Who is covering you on Saturday?"

"Sammy, he's good, a little rough, but insightful. You?"

"Gibreal has me on Friday. Aysha will bring him my notes tomorrow."

Walalwitz nodded, then pulled out a small buddle from his coat. For a wild moment, Abulal thought the buddle held bread or a snack but then saw what it was when the cloth fell. They were CD's. Kamal, seeing this, looked at Walalwitz, and snorted, "Really?"

Walalwitz shrugged and smiled, "What, we said if we all go on a road trip, we would play these."

Kamal sighed, but then asked, "Santana?"

"Of course," said the Rabbi, handing Kamal a disk, which popped in the vehicle's CD player, "What do you think? I'm an animal?"

He wasn't. As 'Black Magic Woman' boomed through the speakers and Abulul, learning a new side of his Imam he liked, one that laughed and smiled at simple jokes, they pulled up to a church as the sun started to shine. In front of the said church was a man, of Oriental Asian descent, dressed in a leather jacket, jeans, and a Notre Dame jersey with the number fourteen on the front. Walawitz rolled his eyes. "Show off."

The man walked in and looked at his two friends wearing the wears of their faith while he looked like the wholly football player bad boy for God.

"What," asked Walawitz, pointing at the jersey, "is that?"

"Where I went to college," said Kempt with a smile.

"Dude, you're such a stereotype."

"So says the Rabbi."

"Hey, at least I'm not ashamed to be...."

"Knock it off you two," groaned Kamal, "I'm putting on AC/DC, and that will be the end of it. Ok?"

"I want Ted Nugent," whinnied Walalwitz.

Abulal couldn't help but snicker as he watched the three religious leaders bicker over old time Rock and Roll. Who said religion was on the only topic that mattered for these men?

As the three continued to talk, Abulal saw a reply on his message. It was a phone number. Curious, he dialed it, and let the phone ring. It was answered on the fourth ring.

26

MACKAVOY WAS WATCHING THE CHANTING crowd outside of Belaphone home, but another crowd was forming as well. That was the crowd of disapproval. Other church leaders' faithful with signs that said, "This is unchristian," or, "You sin against the lord." Regular towns folks were also gathering as well. Just regular people, young, idealistic kids, neighborhood chums, even Town officials were on the outer rings. This was getting crazy, and Mackavoy wanted to arrest everyone. But he felt an arrest now will just make matters worse. It was time to talk to the ringleader.

The three men were at the barrier, talking to two County Deputies. Mackavoy sensed the tension, and walked over with his escort, over hearing what the man was saying.

"The command of God cannot be denied. Please move the barrier aside."

"Sorry man," said a County Officer Doyle, "Nobody is going inside, period, not til this crowd clears out. Now, why don't you tell me what you are looking for and we can talk….."

"Do not interfere with the way of God. For his wrath is beyond that of which you can understand."

"Yeah, sir could you please….."

"It's alright officer, I got this."

The men turned away from the County boys and saw Mackavoy, standing there behind them, a blank expression on his face, though he studied each one of the men before him. He recognized the ringleader, Anthony, not the others, but they didn't matter.

"Why don't you come with me, sir," said Mackavoy, "We can talk."

Anthony looked at his boys and nodded for them to stay put. They crossed their arms and nodded.

Anthony followed Mackavoy to the command truck, noticing Liedy eyeing them from a distance, scribbling notes on her pad. He really needed to get a gag order on her, but right now he had bigger fish to fry.

They went to the side of a police command truck, opened the side door, and entered. There were two guys with glasses, windbreakers, and bad haircuts inside, but Mackavoy ignored them and took Anthony to a center table. In the tight space of the computer banks, the table was a small thing, but handy. Quick meals and all. Mackavoy sat in the front of the table, Anthony at the rear.

Mackavoy looked at the man, balding, mousy, and yet, leading hundreds of people, disrupting the town, and causing a county wide emergency.

'The world belongs to the nerds,' thought Mackavoy.

That thought died when....well, going into the metaphysical here, he saw the shadow. A normal man would have blamed it on booze, or weed, but, he saw, he saw...the Serpent. It coiled around the man, like a shadow, a mist shaped as a cobra, going from his waist, and going up to his neck. No one else has seen this snake and yet, Mackavoy did. He saw it, as clear as seeing a cloud in the sky, a blot in the blue, and this, this thing, it had a presence, something....foul, evil.

Mackavoy blinked, and the mist snake was gone, and Mackvoy rubbed his eyes. 'Fucking seeing things. I need either sleep or coffee.'

"So, Mr....."

"Please, call me Pastor."

"Ok, Pastor, how is your morning going? I think a few of the guys are getting food, would you like some?"

This was a rare thing for him. At this point, he would arrest this man, but the crowd was still outside, and so, he wanted to see what was driving them. What was so special about this child they kept chanting about?

"No, I do not. I am here on a mission from God."

'God', how was a being of love and compassion the cause of so much madness in the world. He was glad most people who use God as an excuse to commit crimes were Christian or Islamic. Hindus had over three hundred and fifty million Gods to choose from, that would be a headache. One God was enough to handle.

"I was to meet them hours ago, but your goons won't let me."

"Seems like the people inside don't want you in either. I think they feel threatened."

"They feel the coming of the second serpent, and the devil holds me outside those doors, the illusion of man's defiance against God's will."

Illusion of man's defiance, what the fuck was this guy….know what, didn't matter, all that did was protecting the people inside, and stop the madness outside. Mackavoy was going to speak, but then he swore he saw darkness in the man's eyes. It was a flicker, only lasting for a second, but made his eyes look pure black. It wasn't…..wait, it was gone. Must have been a trick of the light, but it made Mackavoy shiver. That was creepy.

"I command to be let in, by the will of our Lord," Anthony's voice had changed, it was becoming that of command, and authority, a strong extension of power which wasn't there before….Mackavoy stood, feeling sick, and went outside, Anthony followed behind, and went back to his flock without another word.

Mackavoy took several deep breaths, and saw the Serpent around him, so vivid it was, made of mist and shadow, coiling around. What was he seeing on the man, he had never seen such a thing, something horrible. He felt it, so strong. What did he feel, what was this?

27

ANTHONY RETURNED TO HIS FOLK, and his three goons joined him, and began walking through the street. The snow was building up, the plows unable to go through due to the police barriers and unmoving brothers and sisters of Christ. He felt his Lord's power, as this wasn't the first time. When Anthony was a child, he had a friend, Marcus. Marcus was full of life, and free, and he and Anthony would often play outside. Slowly, Anthony, when he was ten, he had the urge to kiss Marcus. He did. When over the shock, Marcus, with a look of disuse on his face, ran away from him. The next morning, Marcus's mother called Anthony's parents, and being from a strict, old testament religious family, was hit by his mother and father, and sent him to a reeducation camp to turn him straight. After prayers and hard labor for almost twenty days, Anthony was saved by Christ, but he forever lost his friend. He was forever saddened by this, but at least he was saved from damnation. Now he was given a mission from God, and he would not be led astray as he was in his youth. He would crush the Muslims, the Hindus, the Jews, and others with false beliefs and bring them to Christ. For Christ was American freedom. There was a reason that it was "One Nation, under God," for this was God's country, not Allah's or Buddah's or Shiva's. It was a Christian's God country.

Anthony, embolden, marched forward with the megaphone that was brought earlier, handed back to him by his goons, and yelled into it at the House, "The Child must be blessed. Bring her out, and we will baptize her in the name of our Lord."

Inside the house, Amos rolled his eyes as he chewed on a turkey sandwich, annoyed by the man with the horn, as he was making him feel on edge. This was getting crazy, with Butler constantly on the phone, the four cops at the front and back doors, Victoria's insistence on checking the upstairs, and worse of all they were running out of diapers for Masira, and she was going through a lot. By Muhammad's word, they had to get this kid to slow down on the formula.

Cathy was watching TV with Katrina, Masira in her arms. They were both calm, but Amos knew they were worried. They all had a sense of dread, and Amos had a feeling that was soon going to fester and then they would all break down, and yet, he had to hold strong, and they weren't desperate yet.

Butler came in, opened the fridge, looked in, then closed it. "I'd kill for a beer."

"I like some Chi," said Amos, rubbing the bridge of his nose.

Anthony's voice came back over, "Oh, say the lord on to me…."

"Wish he shut up," muttered Butler, "I mean, I believe in Jesus and the message, but this is just ridiculous."

Amos nodded, then saw it. It was not even a second, but it was clear. A flicker of shadow, moving autonomously. He looked at Butler, who nodded, indicating he saw it too. Without a word, the two men stood, and moved to the stairs.

"What is it?" asked Katrina, worried.

"Just seeing what's going on, honey," said Amos with a smile, "We will be right back."

Katrina smiled back and continued rocking Masira. Amos was slightly jealous and swore to take over Masira duties as soon as possible. Until then, Amos had another mission to attend to. Something he dreaded, but something that had to be done.

"Honey?" asked Butler with a grin.

"Shut up," said Amos as they reached the door.

Slowly, bracing themselves for what was to come, the two entered the baby room. It felt cold, the same cold they felt in the prison. It seeped into the bones, and both men saw the shadows. They formed on the wall their eyes formed by empty sockets that revealed the wall behind them. Creepy.

"The barriers grows thinner, and the child is still here. Why the delay?" asked one of the shadow's hissing, echoing voices of many.

"We have some issues," explained Butler, looking at Amos with annoyance at the question.

"What is the situation?" asked the shadows.

"We got over three hundred people outside wanting the girl," explained Amos.

"Flesh matters not," said the shadows, "Apophis grows stronger, and is getting a hold. If he finds your serpent, it will attract the others, and reality will be ruined."

"You know what," said Amos, standing tall, anger in his voice, "We are not some higher beings. We are of flesh and limited to where we are. We can't magic our way out of here. You say you're trying to stop reality from crashing, but all I see is a lot of bitching."

The shadows shifted and expanded, "We are between the walls of the universe, keeping the Serpents from touch. Failure on our part will be not only the end of you but also the end of us, with only the beast and the thought remaining."

"The thought?" asked Butler.

"It matters not," said the shadows, "All that matters is you must send the girl away from here. The longer she is here, the greater Apophis' hold becomes, and the Midgard Universe and the Dar Universe become one and reality will shatter and mix, and the other serpents will slowly be drawn, and the beast will form."

Then, seven balls of light came from nowhere, each surrounded by.....by great beings. They were snake-like, and yet, beyond the confines of space and time. They slithered slowly through the void between voids, each one unique. They were not truly solid, but the two men could see them. They were all different, but all seemed to be lost, holding their universes like the Midgard Serpent held the universe of this Earth.

Then, they started moving together, one combining with another, then two, then three, their universes combining, and then, collapsing under a great paw, as the serpents became a great seven-headed dragon, like the one seen in revelations, roaring to the endless, empty void, the multiverse shattered in beginning to crack under its mass. Amos and Butler watched as the beast and everything, that of science, religion, cults and death, everything that man believed was permanent and impossible was shattered, reversed, burning without fire, drowning without water, pulled without air, and shook without earth. Days without light, darkness without blackness. Madness in the two men's heads drove them both to the ground and made them scream. Then it was gone, the shadows, the vision, the cold, all of it. They sat alone, in an empty room, with a crib, not knowing hours had passed while they had been up there, and it was midnight again, 2020, New Years.

Then, without warning, the room went dark again, and dread came over, then relief came in the form of Victoria, yelling in frustration, "Who the fuck cut the power?"

28

THEY FINALLY ARRIVED, AND THE town wasn't blocked, the barriers long since removed from the entering roads, the four driving in what looked like almost a ghost town. Shops, what few there were, were closed. The two restaurants were as well. Only, to Kamal and Abula's disappointment and to Walalwitz and Kempts' delight, the local bar was open, but they all couldn't mistake or miss the sound of a generator going. They also noticed save for the bar and their car's headlights and the occasional cars passing by, that there were no lights on anywhere, and the town was eerily quiet. They drove towards Belaphone Home, but were stopped by police barriers in the subdivision they pulled up in. Abulal, Kamal, Walalwitz, and Kempt were stopped by a large county deputy named Cavalin, who was about six foot six, wore glasses, and his hands the size of large birds. He looked down at the Arab Iman, the African Muslim, the Hungarian-Jewish rabbi, and the half white-half Korean priest with a mix of surprise and amusement, a joke forming in his mind.

"The President's nightmare," he muttered.

"Hello," said Abulal, his accent drawing Cavalin's attention, "We need to get through."

"Sorry sir," said Cavalin, "Only authorized personnel. We have a situation…."

"You don't understand sir," said Kamal stepping forward, putting his hand on Abulal's shoulder, "His son is in the house under siege."

Cavalin looked down at Abulal and said, "What's your son's name?"

"Amos," said Abulal in a trembling voice, adding the last name that Cavalin was forced to write down due to his inability to speak it.

"Wait in the car please."

The four men sat and waited for about ten minutes. Cavalin came up after and said, "You are free to go up to the inner barrier. A state policeman will meet you."

"Thank you," said Abulal.

They drove up, and saw one very large crowd, well actually, two. The outer barrier was made up of curious onlookers, counter-protesters, and police officers, all looking warm, and fed. The inner-circle was made up of three to four hundred protesters that, it was clear, haven't moved for almost two days. Their skin was red raw from the cold, and some looked like they were suffering dehydration or hunger, all but a fat, bespectacled, balling man in the middle. He was the only one who looked unfazed by the cold and snow and the slowly setting sun. Abulal saw the house and looked at it, meaning to jump out of the car, saying, "Iman…."

"No," said Kempt, pointing at the crowd, "You will stick out like a sore thumb in that crowd. I'll go with you Abula, make it look like we are friends."

Abula looked at Kamal, who nodded and said, "He will stick out less."

"Damn," said Walawitz, crossing his arms in a comical way and slumping back, "Knew I should have kept my Yakima at home. Catholics get all the fun, you shava."

Abulal and Kempt got out of the car, and both walked towards a man in a blue uniform, and captain bars on his shoulders, who looked down at the old black man before him, escorted by a far younger half Asian guy.

"You Abulal?" he asked.

"Yes, is my son ok?"

"Your son is safe," said the police captain with a small smile, "But the house has lost power. In fact, the whole town has lost power. They have a fireplace, so for now they are safe. We've been trying to disperse the crowd, but so far, nothing."

"Why not just start arresting them?" asked Kempt.

"We are trying to keep it as a last resort. It's hard to arrest over three hundred people, sir. Almost half the town is here, and the County Administrator is trying to keep it quiet, failing, but trying."

Abulal rubbed his forehead, "I need to call Amos. Is that alright? He needs to know we arrived."

"Excuse me," said a voice, and the men turned and Abulal's face went a shade darker in a blush. Liedy Dosa stood there, in a fur coat, long, dark hair tied in a bun, and God damn she looked fine.....stop Abulal.

"I'm sorry, are you Abulal? The one we have talked to on my channel?"

"Ye...yes," stammered Abulal, remembering the text. 'What's your son's name?' 'How old is he?' 'What does he do?' And so on.

Liedy turned to the officer and asked, "Mind if barrow Abulal for a while."

The officer shrugged, not caring.

She waved at the car carrying Kamal and Walawitz, who pulled up and Leidy, who said, "You can pull up behind me." She pointed to her van, and Kamal drove to the indicated spot when he was told, then five newcomers joined Liedy in the van. The news van/camper was warm, and Liedy showed them inside, where George sat in front of a laptop.

"Coffee," she asked, "tea?"

"Coffee," said Kempt and Walalwitz.

"Tea," said both Kamal and Abulal.

She nodded and flipped a switch on an electric stove with a coffee pot of water on it, "Only take a few moments."

"You mind if I make a phone call?" asked Abulal.

197

Leidy looked at the strange clothing of the Imam and the Rabbi for a moment of interest, but said, "No problem."

Abulal stepped outside and made a call.

Amos and Butler ran back downstairs, and saw Cathy and Victoria working at the fireplace quickly, while Katrina kept a small Masira close to her chest, her breast keeping the child warm.

"What happened?" asked Amos.

"The power went out," explained Victoria, "It happened all across Belaphone. We don't why, but it happened."

"We ok?" asked Butler.

"We have a gas stove in the basement," explained Cathy, "So we will still be able to cook, but without power, we have to stay in the living room for warmth."

"How much wood is here?"

"About two days' worth in the garage. We also have old papers and some old chairs in the attic and basement we can use, but once that's out…."

She didn't have to say more, all getting the implications.

Amos stood, "I'll get some wood."

"Need help?" asked Katrina, still lightly rocking a sleeping Masira.

"Nah," said Amos with a wink, but after getting a small smile, he added, "Will need help later though. If we need to burn furniture, we have to pick which ones will last use the longest."

Katrina nodded, rocking Masira, and Amos made a mental note to take over rocking duties when he got back. He missed his little…. well he missed holding her. He missed his father's first call, rushing to the garage, his pants pressing a button on the side of his phone, silencing the call.

Outside, after not getting a hold of Amos, Abulal, Kamal, Kempt, and Walalwitz had gone through the story of what was going on in that house, all they saw, all they knew, and all they suspected. The shadow men, the child found in the prison, Amos caring for her and trying to solve the mystery of where the girl came from. Liedy wrote it all down, her journalistic instincts helping her put the information into a detailed, though she knew, incomplete narrative, which, until such time as it was completed would not go on her channel. The story was going to have some tweaks, the elements that seemed supernatural were going to have to stay off until verified. Such stories of shadow men sound like they belonged more on Creepypasta or the tabloids and not serious journalism. That was until Kamal, the Iman, pulled up the video on his cell phone, and what she saw made her almost drop her pen and even George was speechless as he watched. While Liedy still had to be skeptical, she was less so when she saw that, and was presented the evidence by men of faith. These were men who, ironically, while believing in an ever-present God, didn't buy into supernatural stories that often as others did.

As she looked up, she saw a pained look on Abulal's face. It was a look that said, 'This hurt, and my son is in danger, and there is nothing I can do about it right now'. Liedy had an urge to reach out to him and tell him it would be ok. As a Dominican-American, she understood what it was like to feel helpless in this world sometimes, to feel trapped and isolated. Minority treatment was still a work in progress in America.

"So," she said, concluding her notes, for the sake of Abulal, "Amos is a social worker who works here in Belaphone, Michigan, and he the one trying to help find this girl's family, but ended up trapped by this preacher, who for some reason is hell bent on baptizing this baby because he believes she is part of some prophecy?"

"That seems to be short of it, yes," said Walawitz, "And as usual, the Jews have to save the day and not get credit for it."

There was a much-needed chuckle after Walawitz's statement, until....

"Hey, I saw something."

Leidy turned and joined her lover at the monitor.

"What is it?"

They had released several drones to keep an eye on the situation from above. The officers approved it as long as they were allowed to tap into the feed as well, Leon County not able to afford such drones themselves.

"I don't know, but it was at the side of the house."

Liedy and Kamal rewind the van feed, and saw a restless crowd surging a bit and officers stopping them. However, a man slipped passed in the chaos, heading to the side of the house.

Abulal grabbed the phone Kamal left on a seat and started dialing Amos as George and Liedy left the van to warn the officers.

It was that call that caused Amos to turn in time, maybe even save his life. He was stacking wood on the workbench, his head away from the side door, the room lighted by a flashlight he had found in the kitchen. He did not hear the lock being picked or the door softly opening. He did hear his jazzy ringtone from inside of his pocket and on instinct turned around, and saw the man slowly closing the door. He was large, with a beer belly, unshaven face, and blonde hair, but was surprisingly agile.

The two men were frozen in time for a moment, their eyes locking, but only for a moment. Then, a man charged Amos, yelling, "Fucking, Godless Nigger."

Amos was shocked for a hundredth of a second. While there were barely any African Americans in Belaphone, Amos had never experienced actual racial slurs in the town, as the population had mostly ignored him, and never openly insulted him. But his shock was replaced by instinct as a two-hundred-and-eighty-pound blonde guy was charging at him, with all the intent to kill him in his beady eyes. Amos dropped all but one piece of firewood from his arms and swung it at the man's head. He turned out of the way, but Amos did land a hard blow on his shoulder. Stumbling to his left, he hit the workbench hard, breath being blown out of him, and Amos went for another blow, but the man was ready this time, caught the wood in his right hand, twisted it out of Amos' grasp, and chucked it away.

The man swung at Amos, battering the side of his head, driving him against the wall. Amos, seeing stars, ducked another punch, and hit the man in his stomach. There was a growl, but the padding beneath the man's shirt gave Amos the instinctual impression that the man wasn't really fazed. Amos tried to move, but the man only smiled, and that made Amos nervous.

The man punched Amos again, hitting his ribs, driving the air out of his chest. Amos fell back, collapsing on the ground, as the man got on top of him and started to strangle him. Amos tried to push him away, but it did no good, as the man slowly crushed Amos' windpipe. Amos clawed at the man's hand, his fingernails digging into the man's skin, but not fazing him as he was crushing the life out of Amos.

There was a cracking sound, clicking, then the man screamed. He screamed like he felt the worst pain ever imaginable, like his very body was being crushed from the inside. Then, his dead weight landed on top of Amos, crushing him for a moment, until he was pulled off, and Butler stood there, along with two officers, one local, one County, tasers in hand, dragging the large man back outside, Butler yelling, "Make sure they put officers on all the doors."

Butler went to his friend, and helped Amos to his feet, letting the large black man use him for balance as they went back inside, the firewood left on the workbench.

29

ABULAL SAW THE MAN, DRAGGED by two officers, and he ran to the crowd trying to work his way past the barrier. The people wouldn't move when he yelled, "Out of my way, who is that! Amos, Amos!!"

A kind hand was on his shoulder, and Abulal turned and saw Kamal and he said, "It's not Amos."

"Where is he?" cried Abulal, "Where's my son?"

"Allah watches over him," said the Iman, embracing his friend, "I know he is safe."

Whether or not you believe in Allah, Yahweh or Durras, or the other names for the all mighty and he was looking out for Amos, the fact was when Butler walked in the Home with Amos, the only one on the earthly plain looking out for Amos was his friends and co-workers.

Amos' right eye was discolored, his cheek was swollen, and blood came out of his bottom lip. Upon seeing this, Katrina stood, handing the baby off to Victoria, who looked like she had never held a baby in her life, who handed the baby to Sam, who lost Masira to Cathy, a look of mistrust on her face. Katrina helped Butler get Amos upstairs, and laid him on the bed. She then went to the kitchen to boil water for a bath.

Two minutes later, Cathy was upstairs, a bag of ice in hand.

"Where's Masira?"

"Good old Butler's got her," said Cathy, "God, you got beaten down pretty good."

"Yeah," said Amos, smiling, and wincing at the same time, "You should see the other guy."

"Thought ISIS and Al-Qaeda were the exceptions to the nonviolent rule of Muslims. Guess I'll just start believing the news."

It took a moment for what she said to sink into Amos' battered skull, and then he looked up at her.

"How did you…....?"

"Amos, I did a background check on you when you were hired," explained Cathy with a smile, "Just didn't mention it to you. Your faith ain't my business. You had no record, just good recommendations from Detroit, a degree, and a good heart. That was all I cared about."

Amos nodded, "Alright, but why didn't you tell me you…."

"If you didn't want to talk about it, it wasn't my business, but let's just say, I'm glad you're ok. Did you recognize that guy who barged in?"

"No," said Amos, growling as he shifted slightly, "But I bet that he was part of that preacher's crazy Christian cult."

"Those boys and girls out there ain't Christian. My pastor, Obi, wouldn't stand for such nonsense. That what they are doing is unchristian. Hell, even Catholics would rarely go this far."

Amos shrugged then heard his phone from downstairs, not realizing it had fallen out of his pocket. Butler had grabbed it and put it on the kitchen table as he carried Amos out of the garage. Cathy smiled and said, "I'll get it for you."

As she left, Katrina came back and helped him sit up. Amos groaned as he did, a slight chill coming from the outside due to the lack of power, the cool air feeling good on Amos' sore body, but still moaning from the slight movement.

"Jesus that hurts," said Amos, his legs over the side of the bed. He looked up and noticed a shocked look on Katrina's face.

"Kat?"

"I never heard you use his name before," she said, slightly gasped, but with a small smile.

"What, Jesus, I'm not forbidden to use his name, hell, Muslims prefer to use his name in vain over Muhammad, peace be upon him. Did you know that he is in the Quran as well?"

She laughed at what she thought was a joke as Cathy brought up the still ringing cell and handed it to Amos. It was Kamal's number. Pressing the green icon, he brought the phone to his ear, and heard a string of French mix with Arabic going through the receiver. It was going a million miles per hour.

"Dad," said Amos loudly, over his father's voice, "Dad, I'm.... dad....I...Hey.....Dad......"

"Amos," said Abulal, Amos' voice finally getting to him.

"Dad, yeah it's me."

"Oh, thank God, Amos, what happened? I saw someone break-in."

"Got a little banged up but I'm ok........wait, you saw...dad, are you here?"

"Pulled up a little bit ago."

"Dad....."

"I told you, I was coming, take it and move on."

Amos rolled his eyes. "God Damnit Dad."

"Son, we are working on a way to get you and the child out of there to safety. Just....."

"Dad, there's nothing more that you can do here. And we are safe. The cops haven't...."

"Don't lie to me son, I saw the man they took out. You are not fine in there, and the cops are not doing shit about it."

"They're doing what they can dad," said Amos, both loving his dad was showing so much care and wishing that he would get off the phone already. He was saved when Victoria, Butler, and two officers brought up boiling pots of water, giving him an idea.

"Dad, sorry, got to go for a bit. Have to make sure the fire is still going. Got to keep this place warm."

Saying a string of words, and not all polite in Arabic and French, Abulal agreed and hung up. Amos was then helped to the bath by Katrina, who, after stripping him down, lowered him to the tub's bottom. The water was not overly hot, but it was comfortable, protecting him from the cold. He hoped Katrina saved some of the water for coffee. Still, it helped with his muscles and he was relaxed, for the time being.

30

LIEDY HAD ENOUGH TO GO on for one hell of a story. It wasn't the story of the century, but it was still a great one. Just one problem and that was Abulal. He was a worried father and publishing the story right now might do more harm than good, for Abulal. As if reading her mind, Kempt, who was the only one not sitting with Abulal, said, "Are you scared, my child, that telling the story now would harm that man?"

Liedy looked up. In the grand scheme of things, she wasn't a good Catholic. She did go every Sunday she could, confessed at least once a week said her rosaries. However, she had broken more rules of the Catholic Church than she could count. She looked at a picture of her daughter, that little bundle of joy, born of a union of love outside of marriage. Her reporting career had led her to a crazy life she would never trade for the world, but still, she wondered if she was near a line she shouldn't cross. She looked at Abulal. Would she cross that line? Not now, but, for the sake of the truth, and her livelihood, she would, but....but this was supposed to be a vacation, and a story was not in the plan when they came up here. Hell, she already missed New Years with her children, and they were safe at the cabin, having a backup generator after the power loss, confirmed after she called her son, but not with her. What was she doing, chasing stories, and not spending time with them?

Abulal looked over to Kamal and said, "I want to get in there."

"We can't risk it," said Kamal, not unkindly, "The place is surrounded. The cops wouldn't let us, and that crowd would push us back. They control the whole area."

Walawitz spoke up, "Not the back yard. There are people in the back, but not as many in the front, and they are all outside the fence."

Kempt looked over at him, squinting. He had known Walawitz for years, and when the rabbi got the glint in his eyes, you knew he had a crazy idea, for it was what Walalwitz did. Come up with crazy schemes that, on the whole, somehow worked. "What do you have in mind?"

Walawitz smiled, "Well, we going to be needing your car, Kamal."

Kamal looked over, nervous, and said, "I don't like this."

"Hey, the guys out there, they have what, maybe one God? Between all of us here, we got at least three. I say we got the odds in our favor. This thing you two can help with as well." Walalwitz looked at Liedy and George.

Liedy looked over at him, "I am so writing this."

Father Kempt looked at him, and said, "Well, if you go by my perspective, God has three aspects, the father, the son, and the wholly ghost, and there for…"

"Don't push it Father Kempt," said Walawitz, "Just follow my lead."

Several hours later, in fact, sundown on New Year's Day, Mackavoy looked over at and saw four strange men piling into a car. He saw them reverse out for their parking spot and begin to drive away. One wore a jersey from Notre Dame, another, a suit with a Yamaka, the third wore the clothing of an Imam, and the fourth, just in regular clothing.

Mackavoy decided to follow. He wasn't getting anywhere, and right now, he was nervous about the man who looked like an Arab Iman. Like many of this generation, he had a natural suspicion of those not white or Christian, though he hid it deep down. Giving command temporarily of the State Police Captain, Mackavoy got into his car, and drove behind turning down the street. When the other vehicle turned, Mackavoy pulled up at the corner, and saw more people at the back fence, and he noticed the vehicle he was following had stopped a little ways down the street, about a sixth of a mile from a group of people watching the back gate.

"They are scoping out the area," Mackavoy sensed, getting out, and walking forward. The crowd wasn't paying attention to him or the vehicle observing them. Threw the windows of the vehicle, he saw four people, illuminated by a house's outdoor fire pit and the setting sun. A white man with a Yamaka, an Asian man in a jersey, an Arab, and a black man were watching. He recognized the black man. Abulal, the father of Amos, one of the men inside the house, yes from the FBI report.

Mackavoy knocked on the window, and like a flock of birds, all four men's heads turned, and saw Mackavoy, holding up his badge. The rear driver side window rolled down, and the man in the Yakima looked at him. He had a thick beard, and other than his suite and Yakima it was amazing how much he looked like Santa Claus. Next to him, was the Asian man, in front the African and Arab. He also sensed a...a light....different from the shadow Serpent. It was comforting, almost, inviting, and it came from all the men.

"Uhhh," said Mackavoy, clearing his head, "You realize loitering is a crime, right?"

The Jew smiled and said, "Shalom, and we are not loitering, we are spying, you know, scoping?"

"That's also illegal," said Mackavoy, noticing how the other men were snickering in response to their friend's balls. The friend in fact reached out and taped Mackavoy's badge.

"I thought FBI agents were spies, but you can call us a new spy branch."

"What's that?"

"CMJU, Christians, Muslims, and Jews units. We cover all national crises."

"Putting yourself last," chuckled the Asian man, "That's a first."

"It's called being humbled," explained the Jew, "You Catholics should try it."

"Nah, we are still working on guilt and repentance."

"Hey," said Mackavoy, getting the feeling these people were performing this comedy act on purpose, and trying to get them back on topic, "This is a police matter, not one for the.....churches. You're not police."

Again, the Jew reached out, and tapped the badge with his accusing finger. "Neither are you."

Mackavoy looked at him stunned, and said, "Yes I am."

"Nah, you're a federal agent, which is different for a cop. Ergo, you are, in your own words, interfering in police matters. So, I guess we should arrest you."

Mackavoy was now annoyed, but then, he felt it, that sense of light, he felt that he should.....should help them instead of hinder. It went against everything he was trained for and yet, his instinct told him to help them. The instinct was powerful, and he could feel it pulling him in that direction, his mind, telling him to listen to what his instincts told him.

He looked straight into the Rabbi's eyes, and said, trying not to smile, "I am so tempted to have you arrested, but I am curious about your plan."

Walawitz was about to speak, then paused, looking at the man, and then, as if by intuition, he put his hand in his pocket, and pulled something out, opening his fist to reveal an object in his palm. It was a tile, like a coin, but on it was two hands, one black, one white, but where they intersected, the fingers turned grey. Mackavoy blinked, and for a long moment was silent, then, he pulled something out from under his shirt. It was a tile like Walawitz. Then Kempt and Arab men pulled the same tiles out of pockets as well. With Abulal looking on in wonder as Walawitz spoke.

"I see race, I know religion, I know hate, but we stand above them, and see the whole human race. All colors make grey, and grey is neutral. We create grey, through beauty and grace. I shake your hand, you shake mine, and together, we make beautiful Grey."

Mackavoy nodded, and said, "So, I ask again, what is the plan."

"Well, depends on Abulal up there," explained the Jew, and he had a wicked smile.

The Arab looked back and asked, nervously, "What have you got in your head?"

"Depends on if Abulal is willing to convert or not. Also, there are two reporters out front. If they are in, then we can proceed."

Abula looked nervous, but Kamal put a hand on Abula's hand and said, "Let's talk."

Deacon Drisdol was a shopkeeper on a corner in downtown Belaphone, selling old furniture, knick-knacks, and homeware that people found.....well.... as the middle age housewives would say, "Just so darn adorable." Deep down though, he hated every moment of his work but, through Anthony and his church did he see it only as a means of supporting his family, who were, at this time, astray. His wife had left him and joined another ministry in Mackinaw City, taking their two children with her, claiming abuse. Yes, he had disciplined them, but in the long run, a short hurt was worth it for a sinless existence, so said Anthony.

He was leading this group in prayer. Anthony wanted to ensure someone was there, both front and back yards, when those in the house saw the light and brought the infant, and so Drisdol prayed for it to happen as he stood behind the backyard fence. He turned and heard the sound of a car engine. He shrugged, not caring about it. He only cared about the house.

"He comes," yelled a voice, with an....African accent? "She has come, the child, oh Lord, for we have saved the child of Christ. Come forth, come forth, for she would soon be blessed. Come forth, come forth."

Drescol turned, and saw a red car going past, a man driving it, another out leaning the window, holding a bundle. Could it be? No, no it couldn't, they would know if the child was out of the house, but the buddle, it was shaped for a small baby. Oh God.

"After that car," yelled Drescol.

The small group ran after the car, Drescol himself leading, but the car stayed ahead. Drescol thought it was going rather slowly, as if......His head twisted around, and he nearly slid on the snow and ice, seeing three odd persons going over the back fence. Then there was a squealing sound and a chorus of screaming voices as the car turned one hundred and eighty degrees on the slick roads, and then barreled back down, letting loose a torrent of rags, many of which landed on shocked followers, including Drescol, who scattered to avoid the vehicle. Removing the cloth from his face, Drescol and the others started running back, realizing the ruse, the three odd gentlemen already climbing over the metal fence, and the red car pulling up, and two more men coming out the back of the vehicle. One black, one white, with a cell phone in his ear, running behind the other three already heading for the fence. The first three reached the sliding rear door, knocked desperately at it. The car sped off, back down the street, and Drescol charged in.

"Stop them," yelled Drescol, leading his followers back to the house. He then noticed the white man running up behind the first three pulling out a gun, and he realized that this man was a cop. Then he heard other sirens. Drescol ignored them, they just needed to reach the interlopers. They outnumbered them, five to one.

Drescol ran up the road, struggling on the slushy snow, hearing the desperate knocks as they drew closer and closer.

Butlers hear the knocking at the back-sliding door, as did the other officers. Pulling out his gun, he and Victoria took point, and saw..... saw a man with a beard and wearing a jacket and long white shirt, followed by a man who looked like a combination of a banker and Santa Claus in a Yakama, yelling, "It's always us they chase." A third man in a football jersey, Asian descent, had his back to the others and was waving his arms. In the light of the various pulling up cop cruisers headlights outside, Butler saw two more people running up the road. One with a gun, the other was.....

"That's Abulal," he said, shocked.

"Who?" asked Victoria.

"Amos' dad. I've never met him, but I've seen pictures. That's Amos' dad."

"They got company," said one of the officers, pointing at a party of people chasing them.

"Open the door!" yelled Butler running and fumbling at the door's lock and pulling it open against some light ice that had built up at the bottom.

The Kamal and Walalwitz tumble in, Kempt right behind them, and Abulal, halfway up the lawn. But Butler saw he was breathing heavily, and the man with the gun grabbed his arm, desperately helping him move faster as a crowd of people gave chase, vaulting over the fence.

"Let's go," yelled Butler, grabbing Victoria's arm, and running forward towards the two struggling men, the crazies only feet behind them, at least twenty. Butler and Victoria each took an arm of Abulal and half dragged, and half carried the man up the lawn. The man with the gun covered their rear. Kamal and Kempt worked at the door, trying to widen it to let the three threw at once, fighting against the ice, loud scraping noises echoing outside.

'We aren't going to make it,' thought Butler desperately, as they slipped and slid on the concrete of the back-yard patio, hands reaching desperately for them, the crazies so close, only a few feet away.

Two-gunshots rang out. Butler and Victoria didn't bother to turn, for whoever shot it allowed for the three to reach the steps and be pulled in by the two men at the door.

Mackavoy had been the one to fire. He was running behind Abulal, but the man started slowing. Mackavoy tried to keep him running from the crazies but then was helped by two people from inside the house. Mackavoy covered them, realizing that if not slowed, the crazies would get them. He turned, and fired two shots over their heads, causing them to pause and the two managed to get Abulal over the sliding door. Mackavoy turned, and started running, when something grabbed the back of his jacket, and the people at the sliding door, seeing this, turned back around, as another hand of the crazies latched on like a vice on Mackavoy's shoulder, as he felt a dark, coldness coming from them. Slowly, they dragged him back, some of the crazies getting in front of him, punching, beating, scratching, pulling, controlling.

Mackavoy was pulled to the ground, but as they started beating him, but then there were more shots, and the two that helped Abulal came out, firing at the crazies, just as two patrol cars emptied their officers, and moved in to help.

The confusion was enough for Mackavoy to get back up, the smell of blood in his nose and seeing it in his eyes, he blindly stumbled forward, when hands grabbed him again. Unable to see, he flailed for a moment, until a voice said, "We got you buddy."

He recognized Victoria's voice. Surrendering, he stumbled forward with them, nearly tripping as he stumbled up the stairs, and heard a slam and a lock. The house was cool in the kitchen, but they led him to the living room, where the fire warmed them. Then, Mackavoy heard Walalwitz say, "Well, that's social decay for you."

"They made it," said George, unable to believe the plan worked. He was the one who yelled from the car, Liedy drove, causing the distraction that let the five men slip past the crazies.

"Good," said Liedy, still sending her drone feed to the police, "Let's hope part two works as well."

31

ANTHONY RAN DOWN THE LAWN separating Belaphone home from its neighbors. He had heard the commotion and the shouting, and he and a few of his folk ran over and saw several policemen arresting the group left in the back. The street was dark, the power still out. It wasn't uncommon in Belaphone during the winter, as the driving snows could damage the power lines. But he wasn't concerned about that, for using his cell phone's flashlight feature, he went to the back of Belaphone where he had been told something was going on.

Drescol and twenty others were being dragged away in handcuffs while several of Anthony's people were scattering to the wind. They were running, running down the street, begging for their loved ones not to be arrested, as a mix of local, state, and county officers were arresting several of Anthony's people.

Anthony meant to run forward to help those being arrested, but dared not after a step or two, less he as well would be dragged off in manacles, seeing how merciless the group of officers were being.

"Lester," yelled a large woman, running past Anthony, Mrs. Celiani, as one of those being arrested, a teenage boy, who Anthony realized was her son, was being taken away. In fact, a few of his folk, dozens of them, were leaving their visual and going to family members, begging the police not to arrest their loved ones, tears freezing on their face as they so desperately begged, and in the end, it was for nothing, as the officer took the members of the flock away.

Mrs. Celiani began to walk past the police cruisers as they put her son in the car, and soon, followed by several men and women started walking away from Belaphone Home. Anthony huffed forward, reaching them.

"Mrs. Celiani, where are you…"

"I'm going to bail my boy out of jail," cried Mrs. Celiani, "I'll have to put my house up for collateral. My poor boy."

Anthony was stunned, so stunned that his feet seemed to freeze him in place.

"Wait," he called hoarsely, "You can't, God's work, it isn't…."

"Screw your work," yelled Mrs. Celiani, "My boy's been arrested. All these folks with me are going to have to beg to let our loved ones out of jail. Nobody was supposed to be hurt during this, Pastor Dean, instead, twenty loved ones are arrested for assaulting an officer of the law, and if God is good, they don't throw the book at them. We are leaving and that is final."

She walked up the road, her great bulk followed by several others. Anthony felt worried now. He looked over at his crowd, who, instead of being in silent prayer that those inside the house would see the light, were beginning to waiver in their faith, worried about what just happened, scared, several beginning to leave. How dare they. How dare they leave. Did not Jesus go to the cross, head held high for the benefit of mankind. What right did these insignificant creatures have in preventing God's work. Rejoining Tom and Hamish, Hamish bent his head in prayer, but Tom, desperate, whispered in Anthony's ear, "Anthony, this is going too far. We have to stop this before it gets worse, and…."

"We are doing God's work," snapped Anthony, "Nothing else matters. Jesus stood for us, and now we stand for…."

But he was sensing a lessening, as if the power that coiled around the flock had loosen, and less people were being affected by it.

"Jesus wouldn't want this," whispered Tom, desperate, "He was a man of peace, a teacher of the lord. You are causing a war. The power is out all over town, and you're still worried about this girl. Anthony, this has to stop."

"I think it's about time for another crusade," snapped Anthony, "We Christians have been told to be silent, and only caused Muslims and Hindus and some many other false religions to rise. It's time for us to walk the earth and cleanse it again. We will be a flood, purging the world of its sins."

Tom's eyes widened, Anthony looked like a mad man, and he said, "You're sounding like devils who walked the Earth before you. Hitler, Napoleon, so many others who walked with Lucifer, you sound more like them than a man of wholly virtue."

Hamish had stayed silent, but turning at the end of the exchange, he was seeing a glaring little man, poisoned by his work, he thought, 'I gotta get out of this.'

Mackavoy wasn't doing too good. He wasn't dying, but he was hurt. Blood covered his forehead, a shoulder may have been dislocated, and there was a disturbing clicking in his knees. Victoria was tending to him, using first aid, but he was bleeding badly. Kamal was helping as well. While having no medical training, he had taken several lifesaving classes and did work for Search and Rescue as a volunteer.

Amos was in the living room, Masira in his arms, mostly recovered from his own beating, checking his father, who looked shaken. Butler was on the phone, explaining who got into the house to the law enforcement outside, having his ear yelled off by both the state and local chiefs, not happy that the second FBI agent was trapped inside as well, while asking for medics to be sent in from Fair Creek.

"That was the dumbest thing you ever did, dad," snapped Amos to Abdual, as Mackavoy was being tended to.

"Not the dumbest," said Abdual, still breathless but recovering, "But one of the top ten. By the way, it's chilly in here."

Amos rolled his eyes. Katrina snickered.

"What the hell, dad."

Abdual shrugged, and said, "I needed to make sure you were safe."

Amos pulled out his cellphone, waving it in front of his father's face. "You really need to learn how to video chat." Then he turned to his Iman, and said, "And you, how did you go along with it?"

Kamal shrugged, and said, "Divine providence."

"Bull," said Butler, who came up from the kitchen with an ice pack, "But while you are here, what happened to the power?"

"Don't know," said Kamal, "It's out all over town. I don't know why, but it seems unnatural. The heavy snow makes sense, but wouldn't it only affect certain areas of the town?"

"The power is connected through Fair Creek," said Cathy, bustling around, bringing coffee to the new and unusually dressed group, "They handled it on their end. But it's still New Years, so it's going to take some time."

"We don't have time," said Victoria from the other room, her keen hearing shocking the lot of them.

"Wow, that lady has some ears," said Walawitz, under his breath, "Wish I had those."

Amos stood, and said, "Ok, seeing how we are still stuck here, why the hell did you guys force yourself in with no way out?"

"We have a way out," said Walawitz, "but, we just need to wait for the right moment."

"When is that?" yelled Amos, "When hell freezes over?"

"Amos," Abdual stood, flames glinting his eyes, "These men risk their lives to get here, and you show disrespect, how......"

Amos stood, handing Masira to Cathy, done listening to his father, went to the sliding back door, slammed it open, shaking the glass, went out it, and slammed it shut. He was angry. He was angry at his dad, angry at the people outside, and angry at himself. He winced when he sat on the snow-covered porch, his body still aching from his attack. The world seemed eerily dark, as the streetlights were not working due to the power outage, the very environment a reflection of the brooding anger inside of him. With dark emotion, dark thoughts also come. It has nothing to do about being of what race or religions you are. It comes from being human, and though many regret actions, many more regret their thoughts later in life. This was one that would haunt Amos for the rest of his days.

Amos looked out into the darkness, knowing that the people were out there, waiting for Masira like hounds. It would be so easy, so easy just to walk outside and give them the little girl. Amos adored her, but he wasn't her father. Outside his job as a social worker, he had no obligations to her. No one would blame him. The Serpent, well, fuck that thing, it had only been a dream, or he tried to make him believe that it was only a dream. He needed to protect Cathy and Katrina.....God, Katrina....from these people, who hour by hour were getting more restless as the teeth of the winter night closed around Belaphone. They needed to get the town back to normal, and it would be so easy......

"Amos," said a soft voice.

He turned, and saw her, Katrina, her dark hair could blend into the night so easily. Her mocha-colored body, the mix of black and native heritage, her blood caring the two histories of two people who suffered so much in America. The black slaves, and the native survivors of the near genocide of their people. Now again, they suffer, at the hands of white zealots. No, no, that wasn't fair. It was one man, one man who happened to be white who caused this.

"Are you ok?" she asked.

Amos bit his lip, then said, "Just worried. And thinking about Masira."

Katrina sat next to him, their jeaned legs touched.

"What are you thinking?"

"Things I shouldn't. Wondering if it's best to hand her over."

Katrina's eyes widened, "How can you even think that?"

"Kat, she was found in a locked Chapel in a prison, and all these supernatural things are happening around her. What if she is some kind of messiah and the reality is that we are doing more harm than good with her."

"What if she is?" she snapped, her voice cracking the darkness that was in Amos' head, showing a little light, "Are you telling me you think she would be better off in the hands of those bastards?"

"I don't know Kat," he said, "I'm just thinking."

"And thinking wrongly."

Both turned and saw Kamal, Walawitz, and Kempt all walking outside. Their outlines were lighted from the back via the fireplace glow that came from the living room, looking like men of another age, and an image of the magi, the three wise men who gave gifts to Jesus flitted into his mind. The Rabbi, the Imam and the Priest all looked down at Amos and Katrina.

"You overheard?" asked Katrina.

"More like eavesdropping," said Walawitz with a smile, "It's what men in faith do, we listen."

"Well, in that case," said Amos, "Tell me, what if she is some kind of messiah? What if Allah brought her here and has a purpose for her? What if this is the end of day?"

At this point, Amos knew he was rationalizing. The thing about rationalizing was that they were more comforting lies than hard as stone truths.

Kamal looked down at him, like an old teacher, letting his student finish his thoughts before the lesson.

"Because," he said, "it's not our duty as teachers of God to interfere with God's plan."

Kempt then spoke, "God tells his chosen ones what they must do. It's not up to the actions of others to influence his plans. And they try, and every time, they fail to move God."

"God lets his actions be known through his chosen ones," said Walawitz, "Not through actions of others who try to force his hands. Moses was told by God he would lead the Hebrews to freedom. Mohammad made God's profit on the mountain, where God spoke to him. And Jesus was told by God to die for the sins of mankind. Not the best idea for parenthood, but hey, I ain't one to judge."

"We as preachers, teach how to worship and love God," said Kamal, "And that is our duty. Anthony, he has twisted his teachings and thinks he is a sword. In reality, he is supposed to be a shepherd."

Kat then spoke.

"You three speak as if you're from the same religion."

"We are when you look past the surface," said Walawitz, "Through Abraham. The Jews and the Christians come from the line of Isaac, son of Sarah and Abraham."

Kamal spoke then, "And the Muslims are from the line of Abraham as well, through Ishmael, through Abraham and Sarah's slave, Hagar, who was also among the first to try and force God's plan. When Sarah gave birth to Isaac, Ishmael and Hagar were cast out. It was an evil thing that was done, but it was done."

"But," said Kempt, "Both Isaac and Ishmael, together, came to their father's funeral, not as rivals, but brothers. If more people saw this part of the story, there would be less conflict between our peoples."

"But what if she is a tool of God?" asked Amos.

"Then you are fulfilling God's will as well," said Kamal, "Do you think the Queen of Egypt knew that the boy coming down the river would lead the Hebrews out of Egypt and bring them to Israel. No, she saw a baby, a little boy, who needed her help. Those who help raise the chosen ones of God are the most blessed by him without knowing. For they act out of human kindness, which in many ways is more powerful than divine intervention."

"Like the Queen who raised Moses, God brought this child to you. You are her protector, Amos," said Kempt, "Are you going to turn your back on that divine gift?"

Amos' father then came out, the sliding door still opened, and went to his son, sat, and said, "I am proud of all you have done Amos. Please, don't turn your back on Masira. She needs you. She needs a normal life. Moses lived as a prince before he became the liberator of the Hebrews. Muhammad was a mercantile before the mountain. Jesus, most of his upbring was unknown because I believe God wanted him to have a normal life before his ultimate sacrifice. Will you deny a normal life to Masira?"

"Dad," Amos looked out from the darkness, but Katrina and Abdual put hands on him. He held back tears as he looked out into the night, the darkness deeper than even the Watchers' shadow.....

Suddenly, Amos stood, his eyes opened for the first time in a long time. A revelation hit his mind. It was so clear, so simple. He turned to Kamal and said, "You got a plan to get us out of here?"

"I do," said Kamal.

"Hey," whined Walawitz, "It was my plan."

"Talk to Butler, he can help. I need a few minutes upstairs."

Amos started taking off.

"Where are you going?" asked Katrina.

"To get reinforcements," yelled Amos over his shoulder as he ran past the others in the kitchen and living room.

32

AMOS GOT TO MASIRA'S ROOM a few seconds later. He closed the door behind him. It was dark, so he pulled out his cellphone, turned on the flashlight, and then a small light gave the room an orange glow. Hopefully, that would be enough. He looked at the walls and spoke.

"I know you can hear me. You want the girl gone, but I need you to come forth."

Silence.

"I need your help. You don't reveal yourselves, the girl won't go. I swear this."

More silence.

"And everything you have done up to this point will be undone, and you know it."

A flick. Amos saw it. Then another. The room got icier, colder even without the outside temperature affecting the room. Amos' teeth began to chatter. Before him, five Watchers revealed their humanoid forms on the wall, their empty eyes reflecting the wall behind them, giving them a demon-like quality.

"You threaten existence with your word," they said in their echoing voices, "The girl must go."

"Yeah," said Amos, "And you're going to help."

"We are not your servants; your existence means nothing in the balance of the void. We serve to keep the Serpents separate. You threaten to undo it. Why should we?"

"Because," said Amos, "You brought the girl to my world. I don't know the world she was taken from, or how she got here, but she is here now, and I protect her, as you do."

"We don't interfere in the lower planes."

"No, you do, now. You brought her here. You wouldn't have interfered if you didn't care. I don't know if your Angels, Demons, Jinn, or whatever. All I know is, as a servant of Allah, I have a duty to that girl, and you do as well. Help me, and she will be gone, and you never have to see me again."

"The humans won't understand."

"That's the point. They don't know who or what you are, or even if you exist. We can use that to get out of here. Please."

They stood motionless for a moment, then said, "What is your plan?"

Amos smiled, and then explained.

"I hope they're alright," said Liedy, watching the drone's camera through the van's monitor.

"They are fine," said George.

"You think Walawitz's plan will work?"

"They do their part, yeah."

"Honey."

George turned to her.

"Can you pray with me, for their safety?"

He smiled, "I can't remember the last time we prayed."

"It was after Violet's birth."

He smiled and joined his lover in prayer.

An hour later, the door opened, and Leidy saw Amos. The tall, muscled black man with a beard, holding a bundle.

Liedy and George knew it was time. She pulled out her cell phone and dial. A man with a deep voice answered on the third ring.

"Hello, Pastor Gerald here."

Liedy took a deep breath and said, "Pastor, we need to talk."

Amos stepped outside, holding a bundle in his arms. Butler had communicated with the cops on the outside. They knew to keep the crowd back and to not interfere. They did what was asked of them, though they didn't like what was going on so far.

The crowd of worshippers had shrunk from four hundred to one hundred over the past few hours. Some were arrested, others left to help their loved ones, and still others just left because of the power outage. And there he stood at the front of this freezing crowd. Anthony, his belly, glasses, and balding head looked almost non-threatening, even as he was eyed with fear by Tom and Hamish. What Amos didn't know that minutes before, the three had almost broken.

"This is insane, Anthony," yelled Tom.

"This is God's work," yelled Anthony, not seeing the cops looking for that breaking point to arrest the ring leaders.

"This isn't God's work," yelled Hamish, "We've been out here for almost three days, Anthony, it's now a new year in fact. This must stop. People are getting frostbite out here Anthony."

"We suffer for the glory of the Kingdom of Heaven."

"Anthony," yelled Tom, "Be reason….."

But then the door opened, and the large black man came out with the buddle, and Anthony rejoiced. "You see, it is God's will that we have the child."

He worked his way forward so Amos could see him, the street lighted by dozens of head lights from the police vehicles.

"Give the girl to me so she can fulfill God's promise!"

Amos spoke, and his voice was strong, stronger than Anthony, and he said, "You will all leave. I'm taking the girl somewhere safe. Away from you. She will have a normal life."

Anthony was shocked, and even Tom and Hamish were looking at this man in awe. They were impressed by the power behind the words. Anthony was shocked for another reason. This fucking nigger had just defied him. No, not just him. He saw something around him, something grey, that grey snake again, with blue eyes, there, but like a heat shimmer. Again, he blinked, and it was gone, and the black man stood steady before him.

"You dare defy God?"

"I protect this child by the will of Allah," snarled Amos, "You are not wholly man, you're just a man, Anthony. Let us pass. This girl doesn't need you. She needs a real home."

"Her home is my church!" screamed Anthony, "She is meant to save it."

"Go away Anthony," yelled Amos, "I'm warning you."

"You will be smited by God if you don't hand her over."

"She doesn't belong to you," he yelled, "Allah gave us all free will."

Anthony's jaw dropped, finally hearing Amos' God name over his anger. "You're a dirty Muslim, a God damn Sand Nigger. You dare defile her with your dirty, unclean hands."

"I am Muslim, and I'm proud of it. I am also this girl's protector. I am Amos Diouf, I am a Senegalese Muslim American. I value my faith, and I value the freedom to practice it. And I value Masira's freedom, and I won't let you take that away from her."

Anthony bark a laugh, "You dare say you stand for freedom? 911, the middle east wars, that was Muslim doing."

"As the Crusades, World One and Two, Colonialism, the deaths of millions are in your faith's hands. But it's time to move past and look to the future. Be a man Anthony, and step aside. Let Masira have her own life. She deserves it."

"Don't call her that dirty word, Sand Nigger!"

Amos took a step forward, his feet crunching on the snow, and said, "This is your last chance."

"No!" yelled Anthony, "God choose me."

He screamed the last into the night.

"Very well."

Amos closed his eyes and started speaking in Arabic. He said, "Allah, protect this child."

Suddenly, in the lights of the cars, the shadows appeared, glowing on the house. It was the watchers, more than a hundred, and they appeared on the houses, the cards, the street, everywhere. The crowd of people, the police, and even Anthony stared in shock at the vision before them. In English, Amos declared, "Be true, angels of God, protect this child."

The Watchers moved like lighting and Anthony's crowd began to run, even Anthony turned, fearing for his life. The cops did as well, trying to catch those who ran. The shadows zig and zagged across the street. One went to a power line, slid up it, and hit the transformer. For a moment, all Belaphone was alight but then the transformers exploded, one after the other, sparks flying, and the crowd screamed even more. They trampled over each other; children being left behind by scared parents as they ran. Amos smelled smoke and saw several lines catching on fire. They soon melted, landing on to houses that were set ablaze, turning the homes into infernos, fire rushing, as if ready to engulf Belaphone in a fiery hell.

"No," yelled Amos, holding Masira to his chest as the baby started to scream, "No, don't hurt them."

A hand grabbed his shoulder. It was Butler.

"Amos, we got to go, now!"

"But the people….." yelled Amos.

"Nothing we can do, go."

Katrina came out, and Amos followed in a daze as Liedy pulled up in her van, and George came out of the back, holding the door open.

"Get in!" he yelled.

Amos and Masira got in, then Katrina, then Butler. Victoria, Sam, and Mackavoy followed next, then followed by Kamal, Walawitz, Abdual, and Kempt, piling in the back. The Deputies and local cops went to control the chaos. Amos handed Masira to Katrina as they got to the van, then turned and saw Cathy coming out.

"Come on," yelled Amos

"I'm staying."

"Cathy…."

"Amos, get Masira out of here. Go."

There was a gunshot, Cathy collapsed, a bullet blowing off the back of her head, blood pumping out of it.

"Cathy!"

Amos heard more gunshots, and saw Anthony with a slain state policeman's gun, turning away from Cathy, aiming at the van.

"No," Amos yelled, jumping out. In a blind bull charge, he tackled Anthony who had just pulled the trigger. The bullet went wild, hitting a burning house as the two fell to the ground. Amos slapped the gun out of a shocked Anthony's hand, and it skittered to the ground. He then started to punch Anthony as the chaos grew around them, and the cops and civilians who had guns tried to fire a shot at the shadow creatures moving in the streets, unharmed by the weapons.

"Murderer," screamed Amos, his fist connecting to the coward before him, who was rolled up in a ball, his two friends long having abandoned him due to the chaos. Then a hand was on Amos' shoulder. It was Katrina who held him back, tears coming out of his eyes. Amos saw her fear and sadness, but she gestured to the car where Butler held Masira. He then looked down at the cowering man and saw not an evil thing, but a misguided man, scared and afraid.

"That was for Cathy, you son of a bitch," were the last words he ever spoke to Anthony as he and Katrina went back to the van.

They jumped in, and Amos took back Masira as Butler yelled, "George, shut the door", and yelled to Liedy, "Drive."

Liedy put the van in drive and drove out, people scattering to get out of the way. More shots were fired, and one shattered the passage side mirror, close to where Walawitz sat.

"Holy shit!" yelled Walawitz, but they managed to get out of the subdivision. For a few of them, it would be the last time they ever saw Belaphone again.

Anthony stared at the fleeing van in shock as he struggled to his feet. His cheek and areas of his chest were bruised, his left eye felt puffy, and his jaw had felt dislocated. He had failed. He had failed God. He failed his church. He was just a failure. Everything he held true, now shattered. The shadow creatures were gone, but the nigger had managed to summon them, invoking God's power. How?

Then he felt it. A horrible, hissing, rattling in his head. It said, "You had failed." Anthony felt him leave his body again. He flew up into the nothing void again and beheld the Serpent. The shadowy, cloud form Cobra that had fuel his nightmares. It stared at him and Anthony noticed it's red eyes, and felt almost like they were burning him, and then he flew forward, and the Cobra's mouth opened, vast enough to swallow billions of suns. Then it closed around him, and Anthony saw nothing but darkness. Burning darkness, and slowly, he felt himself disappearing into the dark, not just himself, but his mind. It felt like everything he was being erased, disappearing into the creature.

"No," he screamed as his memories left him, feeling his damnation come, "Please, no."

And then, the last memories of Anthony disappeared into oblivion.

"I think he had a stroke," said Officer Dean, a young black kid with Belaphone PD. The State trooper put a hand on Anthony's cirrhotic artery and felt nothing.

"Well," he said, "Saves the taxpayers money."

They drove ten miles outside Belaphone, until they reached the official line between Belaphone and Fair Creek. There, a larger cargo van was waiting, and a black man came out. He had a mustache, wore a nice suit, and had a white woman with him, wearing a nice dress and a fancy raincoat.

When Liedy got the van pulled over, the two outside walked forward, and George opened the camper van's door. Amos got out, as did Katrina, as well as Walawitz, Kamal, and Kempt. Obi came forward and embraced the last three.

"Good to see you Obi," said Walawitz.

"Yeah," said Kamal, "Let's hope this nightmare will soon end."

Obi nodded and said, "Sorry you went through that. Leidy told me everything. Got out here as quick as I could. Be happy I was covering in Dodger Ville."

Amos held Masira in his arms, tears still going down his and Katrina's faces. Obi asked, "Why do you cry?"

"Lost a friend," said Amos, sadly, "Cathy."

"She was a Godly woman," said Mrs. Gerald, her alabaster face showing true compassion, "She will be missed from this world."

"You knew her?" asked Katrina, looking up, wiping her eyes.

"Of course," said Obi, "Several of my flock fostered children from her."

Sam stared stupidly, Kamal holding his shoulder. Sam looked shaken and spooked, looking down at his shoes. Kamal said, "Sam will need to go with you, Amos. He has nowhere to go."

"We will take him in," said Mrs. Gerald, "We'll contact people when this is done. Tonight, he can stay with us. Hey Sam, I'm Ashely."

He looked up at Ashley and said, "I want my mom."

She hugged him.

"I'm messed up," he said, "Cathy helped me, she was the only true mom I had, and I didn't realize it."

"I got you, sugar," Ashley said.

"You better go," said Butler, as he, Victoria, and Mackavoy came out of the car, Mackavoy still wincing, as Abdual joined his son and Katrina.

"You're not coming?" asked Katrina.

"We need to help Belaphone," said Victoria, "I don't know how you did that, but that town is going to be damaged and people are going to be hurt."

"Me and Kempt are going back too," said Walawitz, "They will need help, and I need to get the car back."

Kamal embraced his two friends. "Be careful my friend. And don't scratch my car."

"You got it," said Kempt.

Amos gave the sleeping Masira to Katrina as he embraced the Priest and Rabbi.

"Thank you."

"Take care Amos," they both said, as they loaded back in the van. Liedy came out next, and Abdual blushed.

"You guys be safe," she said, "And I hope we meet again."

"Same," said Katrina, holding Masira.

"Amos," said Liedy. She came up, and gave him a peck on the cheek, "You're a hero."

Then she turned to Abdual and kissed him on both cheeks. Abdual blushed and said, "Oh, there is a dream come true."

Liedy smiled. She turned, got in the car, started it, and started the car.

Mackavoy stepped forward and said, "We'll keep you off the radar. Give you time to hide. Give me updates."

"Thanks," said Amos, "I don't even know who you are, but you helped us."

"That's my job." The two shook hands.

He turned and got in with Victoria. Butler hugged Katrina, kissed Masira on the forehead, and patted her head. Then he turned to Amos and said, "I'll miss you, my old friend."

"You be safe."

"I will."

The two embraced, holding for a moment, then, he got in the van. Liedy started it and drove back to Belaphone.

"Shall we go?" asked Obi, "We will stop in Fair Creek for gas, but after, we should be good."

"Where are we going?" asked Amos, taking back Masira.

"Hardhome. Got a friend who is a pilot there. He will fly you to Smith Island, off the coast of Boston. You will be safe there."

Amos, Abdual, Katrina, Kamal, and Masira loaded up, and the Preacher began to drive. As they did, Kamal handed something to Amos, and said, "You will need this."

It was a tile. On it were two hands, one black, one white, and they met in the middle, the finger forming a grey pattern.

"What is it?" asked Amos.

"A key."

"I'll explain later," said Abdual, "But, these are good people."

Amos was confused but too tired to complain. He looked down at the baby, and she looked up at him. He tickled her under her chin. He tried not to think about Cathy's body. God, he should have grabbed her body, but there wasn't time. Then a thought.

"Cathy's body is still there," he said to Obi, "Can you make sure she is taken care of after you help us?"

"I will."

They drove for about half an hour, and passengers were beginning to nod off when there was a sudden stop. Amos jerked, and looked around, as well as Katrina who was resting on his shoulder, and they looked around. Obi got out of the car. Amos looked at his phone, realizing it was the second of January 2020. 12 am to be precise. Then he saw it. The road was cut. It was gone. In its place, earth at least three feet down, nothing but earth. Amos gave Masira to Katrina, and got out of the van, along with Kamal and Obi, Abdual was still sleeping. The three gazed into the hole. It stretched for miles. The trees, the road, everything was gone.

"This is the road to Fair Creek," said Obi, in horrified wonder, "What happened?"

Amos' anger boiled and he cried to the sky. "What did you do?! What did you bastards do?!"

Kamal grabbed his arm, but Amos' legs gave way. He began to cry. What did he unleash? What did the Watchers do?

"They did nothing," said a calm voice, "They weren't even here."

The three men turned, and saw a man in a suit, Arab features, dreadlocks, and a thick beard. Amos stood, ready to fight, his body as tight as a drum.

"If you're looking for Fair Creek, I'm afraid you missed it. It's gone."

Amos opened his mouth but before he could ask, the man said, "This has nothing to do with the Watchers."

"How do you know?" asked Kamal.

"It's something more powerful than they in this universe. However, it matters little to you what happened to Fair Creek. Your best hope for salvation is in Hardhome."

Amos then noticed the gas can in the man's hand, and he put it on the ground, saying, "This will get you to Hardhome. After that, I'm afraid you're on your own."

Obi spoke then, "Who are you?"

The man smiled, and said, "That is a deeper question than you know. Just someone needed here. You are needed somewhere else."

Kamal went forward, grabbed the can, and went for the gas tank in the back of the van. The man came up to Amos, and said, "You are a great man, Amos, and you will protect the child well. I foresee that she will have great happiness."

"How do you know my name?"

"That matters not. All that matters is that you get out of the UP. Go, and be blessed. Find a new life, and new love."

Kamal came back. "We are good."

"Go," said the man, "I will help Fair Creek. Don't worry, everything is going to be alright."

Amos turned with Kamal and Obi and went back to the car. As Obi turned the car around, Amos watched the man in wonder, feeling a great power from him. It was a power he had no words for, but he believed the man. He never learned who he was, but he believed him.

Then he turned to Katrina, who was still holding Masira, and he smiled, and went in for a kiss. Katrina reciprocated it. It would be a hard road for them at first, but with love and patients, the three would manage to make a home for themselves. They would get to Hardhome and fly out of the UP and get to this fable Smith Island.

Watching the van turn to a side road, a bear came up to the mystery man. It was a spirit bear, and when it reached the man, the man smiled and said, "So, it begins."

(As you predicted,) said a voice in his head.

The man turned, still smiled, "Shall we get to work, Watu?"

(We shall, old friend.)

The two, man and bear turned to the hole before them, and began to explore what used to be Fair Creek, and the mystery behind its disappearance. But that is a story for another time.

As the night wore on, Masira, for the first time in days, slept the whole way through. From that night on, she would feel no cold, and see no more moving shadows, and she would have two great, loving parents. What's more, she would have a great future, something that all children should have. She had just started her true little destiny.

*****THE END*****